UNSEEN MOTIVES

Joan Hall

PrimaCasa Press, Lower Burrell, PA15068
PrimaCasa Press is an imprint of AIW Press, LLC.
https://aiwpress.com

ISBN-13: 978-1-944938-23-9

This book is a work of fiction. Any similarity to real persons, living or dead is entirely coincidental and not intended by the author.

Unseen Motives

To John, my husband, my encourager, my best friend.

Prologue

Driscoll Lake, Texas
September 13, 1991

Stephanie Harris stood on the sidelines with the rest of the marching band and scanned the crowd at the high school home opener. Her parents would be there, along with a sizable number of the town's ten thousand residents.

Her stomach flopped. If she missed a step or turned the wrong way, the whole town would see.

She recalled her father's words at breakfast that morning. "Don't worry, honey. You'll do fine. You've had years of practice."

"But not with the high school band. Maybe I can't do this. What if I mess up?"

"Haven't I always said you could do or be anything you want?"

"Yes, but—"

"No buts about it. Go out there tonight and do what I know you can do. Your mom and I will be there watching."

Knowing her father was in the stands cheering for her boosted her confidence. The visiting band finished their performance. When the drum major called the Panther

Band to attention and they took the field, any reservations Stephanie felt dissipated.

The marching routine was a bit more complicated than the ones Stephanie was accustomed to in Junior High, but she kept in step. At one point, when she was at the head of the row, she executed the turn with military-like precision. The applause from the home crowd told her the others followed in her steps.

The band finished their routine to a standing ovation and marched off the field. When the drum major gave the fall out command, Stephanie breathed a sigh of relief.

Christine Starnes, Stephanie's best friend, came up to her. "We did it! Let's take our instruments back to our seats and then get something to eat. We have the entire third quarter for our break."

"Good idea. I've been so nervous about marching, that I was afraid of getting sick. I think I could eat now."

They left the bleachers and walked toward the concession stand along with most of the other band members. After they had taken a few steps, Stephanie stopped. A cold chill crept down her body, and she shivered.

"What's wrong?" Christine asked.

"Nothing," she said. "Felt a chill."

"In this heat?"

"Yeah. Weird. I'm okay now."

Brian Nichols, who played drums, called out to her as he walked by. "Great job Stephanie." He smiled and winked.

"Thanks," she said.

Brian was a troublemaker, responsible for several pranks, the least of which was when he climbed the city's water tower and spray-painted graffiti on the tank.

Although no one could prove it, many thought he was responsible for starting a fire at an old abandoned house on the outskirts of town. He and some of other boys would often hang out there to drink beer.

"I think he likes you." Christine lowered her voice so as not to be overheard.

"Brian? He's a rebel."

"Yeah. That's what makes him cool."

Stephanie rolled her eyes. She wasn't interested in Brian Nichols. She only had eyes for one boy—the quarterback of the football team, Matt Bradford. Not that he ever noticed her. She was just another freshman to him. It wouldn't do her any good if he did show interest. Her parents wouldn't allow her to date until she was sixteen.

When they neared the concession stand, Stephanie looked toward the bleachers. Her mother sat next to Christine's parents, but she didn't see her father. It was unusual for him not to be at home games. But he hadn't been acting like himself the past few days. Maybe it was because of the long hours he worked. Since the company's CEO, Phillip Denton, disappeared a few weeks earlier, Robert Harris spent most of his time at the office.

But he told me he'd be at the game.

Stephanie ordered a hot dog and a Coke. She looked for her father at the concession stand but was unable to find him. She and Christine mingled with other students.

A siren wailed in the distance. When the sound drew nearer, she saw the police chief hurry from the stadium to his squad car. An ambulance passed and turned in the direction of the factory. Chief Rivers pulled out of the parking lot and followed.

When the quarter ended, Stephanie and Christine went back the bleachers with other band members. The fourth quarter was almost over when an announcement came over the PA system. "Kathryn Harris please report to the ticket office."

Stephanie frowned. Why would someone page Mom? She looked at Christine.

Christine shrugged in answer to the unspoken question.

The game ended in a victory for the Driscoll Lake Panthers. In tradition, the band members and cheerleaders went onto the field to congratulate the home team. Caught up in the excitement, Stephanie forgot about the call for her mother.

Several of the cheerleaders and band members who dated football players walked arm-in-arm with them off the field. Stephanie looked around for number eleven, wondering if he had a girl to walk with him. She saw him near the sideline, with his helmet in hand, walking alone toward the locker room.

Someone called out to him. "Hey, Bradford. Great game."

He turned to see where the voice came from, and his eyes met Stephanie's. He smiled. "How's it going?"

She felt her pulse quicken and her face grow warm. "Uh. I— I'm okay."

Another player ran up and slapped Matt on the back. "Come on man. Coach is waiting for us." They left the field together.

Stephanie watched him walk away. He noticed her, and all she could do was act like a tongue-tied, silly kid. When Christine called out, she jumped in surprise.

"What's up? You look all starry eyed. Let's get out of here before Kyle Lawrence finds me. I don't want to see him."

"What's wrong with Kyle?" Stephanie asked as they made their way toward the stadium entrance.

"He's okay, but I wish he'd learn to stand up to his overbearing father."

They walked toward the main gate. Upon reaching the ticket office, they saw the school counselor leading Rachel Jackson from the stadium. Rachel was crying. Her stepfather was Phillip Denton, the missing CEO of Cameron Manufacturing.

"I wonder what's wrong with her," Christine said. "Maybe they found Mr. Denton's body."

"She wouldn't cry over him. I don't think she even likes the man."

"Yeah, you're probably right."

When they reached the front gate, Stephanie was surprised to see her father's cousin Carol standing beside Christine's mother. Something was wrong. Carol rarely left the house. When she did, she avoided crowded places.

"Your mother had to leave," Carol said. "I need to tell you something. Let's go to my car."

Mrs. Starnes looked at Christine. "We'd better go with them, honey."

They reached Carol's car, and she turned and put her hands on Stephanie's shoulders. "There's not a good way to say this. I hate to be the one to tell you, but your father and Madelyn Denton are dead."

"Dead? How?"

"It happened at the factory. Apparently, someone killed them."

"No." Stephanie shook her head. "No, you're wrong. It can't be. Daddy is alive. It's a mistake."

Even as she spoke the words, she remembered seeing Rachel Jackson a few minutes earlier. Madelyn's death would explain the reason for Rachel's tears.

Stephanie turned toward Christine, who was looking at her mother. Mrs. Starnes nodded her head, and Christine turned to face Stephanie, tears in her eyes.

"No. Nnnnnoooo!" Stephanie pounded her fists on the car. "Not my father. Please, please not my father."

Chapter One

September 11, 2011

Stephanie Harris took a deep breath and exhaled slowly as the plane lifted from the runway. It was too late to turn back. For the first time in twenty years, she was returning to her childhood home.

The past few days had been a whirlwind. First, the regretful interview in which Stephanie unintentionally declared her father's innocence on live television. Next came the unexpected phone call from her great aunt's neighbor Nell Bradford, Aunt Helen's deathbed request that Stephanie return to Driscoll Lake, and her surprising agreement.

Had she taken the time to consider the consequences, she would have refused. She had no fond memories of Driscoll Lake. In fact, they were quite the opposite—hurt, contempt, betrayal.

Stephanie relaxed and stretched her legs. In the last minute scramble to find a flight, first class had been her only option. She had to admit a more comfortable seat and extra legroom were nice. She brought her iPad and earbuds. She'd had her share of chatty passengers to deal with over the years, and today she had no interest in engaging in idle conversation.

This time she was in luck. The middle-aged woman who sat next to her only smiled and offered a brief greeting as she sat down. Now that the plane was in the air, the woman pulled a book from an attaché case, opened it, and began to read.

Stephanie glanced at the cover and recognized her latest novel, *Forgotten Memory*. She slipped on the earbuds, tapped the music app on her iPad, and selected a favorite playlist.

She soon dozed off but woke up when the plane hit an area of mild turbulence. A flight attendant walked down the aisle with a beverage cart. Stephanie asked for water and mumbled a polite thank you when the attendant handed her the cup.

The woman next to her ordered a cola. She closed the book and laid it upside down in her lap. She looked at Stephanie's photo on the back cover, then turned to Stephanie and smiled.

"I thought I recognized you when we got on the plane, but I realize privacy is important. I didn't want to disturb you."

"Thanks." Stephanie smiled. "Hope you're enjoying the book."

"It's your best one so far, and I've read them all."

"Thank you. It was my favorite one to write, yet in many ways the hardest."

"I can understand." The woman spoke in a low voice. "I saw your interview with Jennifer Moore on *Between the Pages*."

Stephanie lowered her eyes. She might as well get used to it. People everywhere would be asking about her past and her father's crime. "Yes, well. I should have left some things unsaid."

"I know what it's like to be in an awkward situation. My ex-husband committed a horrendous crime. All the evidence pointed toward him. Even so, I believed in his innocence for a long time, choosing to believe the courts had convicted the wrong man."

Stephanie felt an instant sense of affinity with this woman. "I believe my father was guilty. Can't imagine why I said otherwise."

"Maybe deep down you think he was innocent."

"I wish I could." Stephanie glanced out the window and took a sip of water. "It's hard to argue with autopsy reports and a suicide note."

"I'm sorry. I haven't introduced myself. My name is Deborah Morgan. I'm a clinical psychologist."

Stephanie shifted in her seat. "I see."

"Don't worry. I'm not here to analyze you. Just wanted to let you know I've been in a similar situation and understand what it's like. Please, call me Deborah." Her smile was genuine.

"Thank you."

"At any rate, I thought the reporter was way out of line in insinuating you were hiding something about your father."

"I knew Jennifer Moore was ruthless, but she did catch me off guard."

They sat in silence much of the rest of the flight. Stephanie jotted some ideas for her current manuscript. Her laptop was in the overhead bin, but she didn't have the inclination to pull it out. She had promised her editor the first draft in October, so she planned to write while in Driscoll Lake. She'd purchased an open-end ticket, unsure of how long it would take her to see to Aunt Helen's affairs.

It was possible Stephanie wouldn't have to do anything. She had reconnected with her great aunt only a few years earlier, and they had taken several trips together. However, even though she was the only living relative, it didn't mean Aunt Helen had named Stephanie as her heir. Not that it mattered. The money wasn't important. Stephanie was grateful for the few years they had together.

When the captain announced the plane would be landing shortly, Stephanie turned to Deborah. "Are you stopping in Dallas?"

"No, I'll continue to Orlando. I'm going there for a conference. And you?"

"Getting off at Dallas, and then driving to my old hometown." She shook her head. "A family member passed away. I can't believe I'm going back. Only a few days ago, I vowed I would never return."

**

Matt Bradford stirred restlessly in the recliner and stared at his parent's fifty-five-inch television. The high definition picture was almost life-like, but he found it difficult to muster up any enthusiasm for the game. He had no interest in watching a bunch of overpaid men pushing and shoving one another in the quest of taking a ball across a goal line. Matt was beginning to think football was a stupid pastime.

That hadn't always been true. He once loved the game, especially during his days as a player. He still remembered the excitement of those Friday nights in high school. The adrenaline rush. The cheering crowds and marching band. The thrill of victory.

He'd looked forward to spending the afternoon watching the game with his dad. Since Dan Bradford's retirement, Matt's parents spent much of their time on the road in their RV, having returned from an extended trip to the Grand Canyon a few days earlier.

Matt's day started out fine. After an early morning run, he attended the services at Driscoll Lake Community Church. He rarely attended, but today was the annual program to honor the first responders of the community. As police chief of Driscoll Lake, he could ill-afford not to go. Although the town had grown considerably over the past decade, it was still small enough to have plenty of gossips, and he wanted to maintain a good rapport with the community.

After the service, the church hosted a potluck lunch. His mood turned sour when Judge Curtis Lawrence took it upon himself to give a speech about the city's police force and firefighters being like family.

It would have been a good speech, had it been true. The Judge's statement about how fortunate the town was to have "some of their own" to serve the community was a farce.

Curtis Lawrence was a fine one to talk about family. His attitude toward his own son was despicable. Before lunch, Matt heard him bashing Kyle over his recent story in the local newspaper.

If that wasn't enough, he'd overheard the town gossip, Madge Sinclair, talking with one of Driscoll Lake's newer residents. He felt certain she'd waited until he was within earshot to speak.

"Judge Lawrence just acted polite. He opposed Matt's appointment as police chief. I think it had something to do with an accident involving Matt's wife. I overheard his mother tell someone he blamed himself for her death. There are rumors—"

"I don't think this is the place for that kind of talk," the other woman said. "In fact, I despise gossip." She left, leaving Madge opened mouth.

It took every ounce of restraint for Matt not to tell Madge off on the spot. If Kyle Lawrence hadn't stopped him, he would have probably done so.

"Leave it alone. Madge isn't worth it." Kyle looked across the room where The Judge sat talking with the mayor. "Neither is my father."

Kyle saved him from what would have been an embarrassing situation. He had a few choice words for Madge—none of them complimentary, and certainly not appropriate to say in church. The fact that Madge spoke the truth was what angered him most. Tara would be alive today if not for him.

Hypocrites. Driscoll Lake had plenty of them. Too many people had hidden agendas. After listening to Madge and Judge Lawrence, Matt wanted to be alone. But he'd promised his dad he would stop by to watch the game. When he tried to back out, his mother pleaded with him.

"Please come. We're only in town for a couple of weeks. We wanted to see you today."

"Yes, son," his father said. "We don't see you that often when we're home."

Dan was right. Since Tara's death, Matt avoided most social contact—including his parents. He sensed they needed him today, especially his mother. She was upset over the death of her next-door neighbor, Helen McKenzie. Nell Bradford had ridden in the ambulance with her and remained at the hospital until the end.

Helen and her late husband George already lived at Lakeview Estates when Dan and Nell Bradford decided to purchase a lakeside lot. After George had died, Nell took it upon herself to look after her aging neighbor. Matt knew Helen's death would leave a void in his mother's life.

It was almost ironic that Helen died nearly twenty years of the date of her nephew, Robert Harris. The scandal that arose following his suicide shook the citizens of Driscoll Lake and affected many lives, including some of Matt's friends and classmates.

The crime had been instrumental in his decision to study criminal justice and enter law enforcement. Kyle Lawrence's demeanor changed. He abandoned his plans to follow his father in the legal profession and decided to study journalism. Even Brian Nichols straightened up his life. He had been well on his way to juvenile detention or worse.

The scandal affected Rachel Jackson and Stephanie Harris more than anyone. Both left Driscoll Lake shortly after that. Rachel went to live with her father. Stephanie moved away with her mother.

Rachel recently returned to the area to take a position at the hospital in Brewster, and now Stephanie was coming back for the first time in twenty years. According to his mother, Helen's dying wish was for Stephanie to be here for the funeral. Matt wondered why she hadn't visited before Helen's death. What good would it do for her to come back now? Maybe Stephanie had an agenda.

A cheer from the home crowd turned Matt's attention back to the television screen.

"Way to go! That was some move," Dan said.

"Uh. Yeah. Sure." Matt had no idea what happened.

"Exciting game?" Nell walked into the room from the kitchen where she had been busy for the last half hour.

"It is now," Dan said. "Do you have everything ready for Stephanie?"

"Yes. I should check the thermostat at Helen's place. The house didn't seem cool to me when I was there earlier. And I want to make sure Whiskers is okay. Stephanie will be here soon."

"Where's the key?" Matt asked. "I'll go."

Nell reached in her pocket. "I thought I had it here. Must be in my purse. Just use the one Helen kept hidden."

"She had a hidden key? That's a bad idea."

"I know, but she wouldn't listen. Kept it underneath a flowerpot near the front door."

Matt got up from the chair. "After I check the house, I'm going home."

"I hoped you would stay for dinner."

"No, thanks. I'm not very hungry."

"It's only a light meal. Please reconsider. You've hardly stopped by since we've been home."

Matt rubbed his forehead. "Okay, but I can't stay long."

***

Matt lifted the flowerpot and picked up the key beneath. He shook his head. It wasn't even a heavy pot. He could never understand why some people went to such great lengths to protect their property only to be careless enough to leave a key hidden. A doormat or flowerpot would be the first place someone would look.

He started to insert the key in the lock but discovered the door slightly opened. There weren't any signs of forced entry, but Matt entered the house cautiously. Helen's cat Whiskers was asleep on the back of the sofa.

Matt checked all the rooms and other doors. Everything appeared to be in place. Satisfied, he checked the thermostat and left by way of the front door, making certain to lock it behind him. He pocketed the key. No sense in leaving it where someone could easily find it.

He assumed his mother must have left the door unlocked when she was here earlier. Normally, she wasn't so careless. He considered telling her but changed his mind. She was already troubled about Helen's death—no point in making her more upset.

***

Stephanie had forgotten how hot Texas summers could be. When she stepped out of the terminal and made her way to the rental car, her silk designer pants and matching jacket clung to her body.

No one dressed up for traveling these days. She had been foolish to do so when she would have been more comfortable in jeans and a simple cotton shirt. Stephanie remembered her mom always said, "Dress for success. Dress for confidence. The right clothes make all the difference in how you feel and how you portray yourself."

Today she needed all the confidence she could muster. More than once, she'd considered backing out of the trip. While waiting to board the plane in Denver, she'd been tempted to walk away from the airport. If she hadn't already checked her luggage, she would have probably done so. But to not board a flight—especially on the anniversary of the September 11 tragedy—would have sent up red flags everywhere.

Why the sudden need to feel confident? She was a well-known author. Before that, she had a lucrative career with a popular travel magazine. By the world's standards, she was successful.

She hated to admit it, but her choice of attire was more a case of trying to impress the people of Driscoll Lake. She wanted them to know Stephanie Harris had succeeded in the world despite   of the way they acted after her father died.

Even the Louis Vuitton handbag she carried spoke of money. It had been a gift from her publisher after her fifth book went on the bestseller list. She rarely used it, but at the last minute pulled it from her closet.

Stephanie placed her luggage in the trunk of the rental, got into the car, and turned the air-conditioner to high. She hoped the cold air would ease her anxiety and dry the dampness of her blouse.

The Sunday afternoon traffic was light, and soon she left the tall skyscrapers of Dallas behind. Traffic thinned along the rural highway. When she reached the exit for Driscoll Lake, she moistened her lips and tried to ignore the flutter in her stomach. She questioned why her aunt had requested her to come. Why was it so important after all these years?

Stephanie realized some people in Driscoll Lake would second-guess her reasons for returning. The fact that she hadn't visited while Helen was still alive would be a source of gossip for many. However, she couldn't concern herself with what others thought.

She was surprised at how much the town had grown since she was last here. Twenty years earlier, there were only a few small businesses. Now there were hotels, several well-known restaurants, and shopping centers. The home-owned grocery store that once stood on the corner of Main Street was now an antiques store. A larger grocery chain had built a supermarket two blocks away, and numerous subdivisions surrounded the town. It was obvious the area had recovered from the loss of the factory—at least economically.

Helen lived in a gated community called Lakeview Estates. Twenty years ago, it was a place for vacationers and weekend visitors. Stephanie recalled several family outings when Uncle George and Aunt Helen first bought their lot and built a small cabin. They had cookouts and enjoyed swimming and boating on the lake.

Residential homes now stood where weekend cabins once dotted the shoreline. Nell had told her to turn east onto Lakeside Drive. "It's about a quarter of a mile. Our house is a two-story brick next door to Helen's place."

She almost didn't recognize the house. The once rustic cabin was now a charming cottage with a carport and manicured lawn. The flowerbeds contained a variety of roses. The small deck that overlooked the lake was now a larger screened in porch.

Stephanie parked in the driveway and glanced in the rearview mirror. Nell and Dan were the first of several people she hadn't seen in twenty years. She wasn't nervous about seeing them, but she had plenty of apprehension about meeting up with a few others.

"Okay, Stephanie. Whatever happens, it's time to face the music."

She got out of the car, walked next door to the Bradford house, and rang the doorbell. A dark-colored extended cab pickup sat in the circular driveway. She guessed they had visitors, so she planned to stay only long enough to retrieve the house keys.

When the door opened, she expected to see either Nell or Dan. Instead, a man in his mid-thirties answered the door. He had dark brown hair, a tanned complexion, and a scar just above his chin. Stephanie took note of his athletic build—indicative of someone who spent a lot of time in the gym. The man's eyes took in her appearance.

His firm set jaw and crossed arms gave her the impression she had annoyed him by ringing the doorbell. For a minute, she wondered if she was at the right house. However, upon closer look, she recognized the deep blue eyes of Matthew Bradford.

"Matt? Matt Bradford?"

His eyes narrowed. "Stephanie Harris. So, the famous author has finally decided to grace Driscoll Lake with her presence."

Chapter Two

Matt's attitude caught Stephanie off guard. She thought he would be more welcoming. If everyone else acted the same way, the sooner she tended to Helen's business and left town the better. She squared her shoulders and looked him in the eye.

"I never expected to come back. If it's any consolation I don't plan to stay long."

He shrugged. "Makes no difference to me."

She opened her mouth to reply but was interrupted when Nell came into the foyer.

"Stephanie! It's so good to see you." She brushed past Matt and wrapped her arms around Stephanie in a warm embrace.

Although she was twenty years older, Stephanie would have recognized Nell anywhere. Her complexion was still smooth, and she wore minimal make-up. Her ash blonde hair had only a tiny amount of gray.

"I'm happy to see *you*, Mrs. Bradford," Stephanie said, hoping Matt would catch the emphasis. He acted indifferently, and Nell didn't seem to sense any tension.

"Oh honey, you can call me Nell. No need for formalities. I'm sure you remember our son, Matt."

"Of course. How could I forget?" She hoped the sugary smile she sent in his direction succeeded in irritating him.

Matt met her gaze but remained silent.

Stephanie cleared her throat. "Well, I only stopped by to get the keys. I'd best be on my way."

"Won't you stay for supper? It's only sandwiches and potato salad, but you must be tired after the trip. Matt's staying, and I hoped you would join us."

Stephanie was tempted to decline the invitation. She'd like to get her things from the car and settle in for the evening. However, she was hungry—and a bit curious to see how Matt would react.

"Thank you. I'd be delighted to stay." She glanced in Matt's direction, but he was hard to read.

"Wonderful. It will give us time to catch up." Nell turned toward her son. "Matt, would you mind telling your father it's time to eat?"

He nodded, turned, and walked into the den.

***

Despite Nell's attempts to keep the dinner conversation light, Stephanie felt tension in the air. Matt hardly spoke and kept his head down through most of the meal. He apparently felt some animosity toward her. She couldn't imagine why—they hadn't seen one another since high school.

She wasn't about to give him the satisfaction of knowing his attitude upset her. When Nell approached the subject of Stephanie's career choice, she eagerly answered her questions.

"What made you decide to become a writer?"

"It's something I always wanted to do. Dad's cousin Carol encouraged me toward a career in journalism. She always took the time to read my stories. Like her, I wanted to travel the world."

"I suppose working for the travel magazine was exciting," Dan said.

"It was. Thanks to that job, I was able to visit many places I wouldn't have on my own. But my real desire was to write fiction."

"I'm surprised someone as lovely and attractive as you isn't married."

"Nell, you shouldn't pry," Dan said.

Nell's face flushed. "I apologize. That was rude of me."

"It's okay," Stephanie said. "I was married once, but it didn't work out."

Matt jerked his head and looked at Stephanie.

Nell cleared her throat. "I'm sorry. Let's have dessert." She stood up and hurried from the table.

Stephanie found herself growing weary after eating the cookies and raspberry sherbet. The long trip and restless night had begun to take its toll.

"Thanks for the delicious meal." Stephanie stifled a yawn.

"I'm afraid we've kept you too long," Nell said. "You must be exhausted. I'll walk next door with you."

Stephanie smiled. "Thanks, I am rather tired."

Dan and Matt stood while Stephanie and Nell rose from the table.

"Thanks for your hospitality," Stephanie directed her words to Dan.

"It's good to see you again," he replied before leaving the room.

"I'll get the key," Nell said and walked into the kitchen, leaving Matt and Stephanie in the sunroom.

Nell called out from the kitchen. "Matt went over earlier to check on things. Everything was okay—including Whiskers."

"Whiskers? Who's Whiskers?"

"Helen's cat," Matt said.

"Oh, okay. I didn't know she owned a cat."

"You don't like animals? Guess you've changed in more ways than one. Don't worry. Whiskers is well behaved. He won't tear your designer clothes."

Stephanie didn't miss the smirk on his face. She smiled. "Oh, I love animals. They're kinder and more understanding than most people I know. It's just that Aunt Helen never mentioned owning a cat. You can rest assured Whiskers and I will get along fine."

***

Nell helped Stephanie take her luggage from the car and into Helen's house. When they opened the front door, the cool air was a welcome relief. Even the few minutes spent unloading the car made Stephanie feel hot and dirty. She looked forward to a shower and a relaxing evening.

"Is the temperature okay?" Nell asked as they sat her luggage in the foyer.

"It's fine. Thanks for having Matt check it earlier."

"Helen never kept the house very cool—she was cold most of the time. I think she's the only person who didn't mind our heat wave." Nell turned away, but Stephanie saw tears in her eyes.

Stephanie placed her hand on Nell's arm. "It's okay to cry. I'll miss her too. We were just getting to know one another better. I regret not staying in contact with her over the years."

Nell flashed an appreciative glance toward her. "Thank you for understanding. Both she and your Uncle George were special to us." She cleared her throat. "Sorry for rambling. I know you want to rest. I made up the guest room. Helen's bedroom is the larger one with a view of the lake, but I wasn't sure."

"The guest room is fine."

"Come along, then, and I'll show you around the house. I took the liberty of stocking the refrigerator this afternoon."

"Thanks, but you shouldn't have gone to any trouble. I'll be glad to pay you back."

"Nonsense! Consider it a welcome gift."

A black and white cat made his way into the foyer. "Oh, what a beautiful cat. This must be Whiskers."

"The one and only. Helen said he had the longest whiskers of any cat she'd ever known—hence the name."

"You do have some long whiskers. Stephanie bent down to scratch behind his ears. He rewarded her with a gentle purr as he brushed against her legs.

She was impressed at how the house had changed from the simple weekend cottage she remembered as a child. She loved the open floor plan of the den and kitchen area. If she had plans to remain in Driscoll Lake, she could envision herself living in this cottage. "It looks so different than what I remember."

"Many people encouraged George to tear the old place down and start new, but he maintained it was structurally sound."

"I love the look. The builder did a great job."

"Helen had some remodeling done a couple of years back. Brian Nichols did it. He also built our house."

"Brian Nichols? Dorothy's son?"

"The same. He's one of the best."

"When I left here, I was sure he'd end up in juvenile detention or maybe even prison."

"He came close to the detention center a few times, but he straightened out his life shortly after you left town. He owns a construction company and seems to be doing quite well. Too bad some people haven't given him the benefit of the doubt."

"Oh?"

"You know how some people can be—especially in small towns. They don't easily forget and forgive."

"Yes, I do. All too well. Maybe I shouldn't have come back."

"Oh honey, I didn't mean you. No matter what happened twenty years ago, you weren't responsible. I should have kept my mouth shut. I'd better get out of here and let you get some rest. You have a big day tomorrow."

"Miles Parker asked me to phone once I got into town. I'll call his office first thing in the morning."

"Helen always said Miles was the only person she trusted to be her attorney."

After Nell left, Stephanie placed her luggage in the guest room closet, took a quick shower, and slipped into a t-shirt and shorts. The shower revived her. She grabbed a bottle of water from the refrigerator and took her laptop into the den.

She could get in some writing time. It was far too early to go to bed. She placed the bottle of water on a coaster, sat down on the sofa, and opened the computer. Whiskers hopped beside her, and she scratched behind his ears before turning her attention to her manuscript. He curled up next to her and quickly fell asleep.

Almost an hour passed—the room quiet and still except for the soft click of the computer keyboard. When the phone rang, it startled both Stephanie and the cat. He jumped off the couch, his eyes wide and ears pricked, then sat down on the floor, still as a statue with his tail curled around his legs.

Stephanie walked into the kitchen to answer the phone. Nell's number appeared on the caller ID. "Hello."

"I hate to bother you, but I forgot to ask if you'd like me to go with you tomorrow when you make the funeral arrangements."

"That's kind of you. If possible, I'd like to meet with Miles first. Would you like to meet me at the funeral home later in the morning?"

"I can do that."

"I'll let you know the time."

"I'll be ready. And please, don't hesitate to call if you need anything."

When Stephanie hung up the phone, she saw a folded piece of paper on the counter. Curious, she opened it. The calligraphy style printing was precise and neat.

She gasped as she read the words.

Be careful. Things aren't always how they appear, and some people aren't what they seem.

***

Three days had passed since Pat Turner returned from her Mediterranean cruise, but she still suffered some effects of jet lag. She enjoyed spending time with her sister, but Pat was a homebody at heart. She was ready to get back to her job as editor of the *Driscoll Lake Reporter.*

She hoped Kyle Lawrence had been able to handle things in her absence. He was a good journalist but lacked self-confidence. It was the main reason he'd never been able to secure a job with a larger newspaper. He had the talent to succeed, but his lack of assertiveness kept him from obtaining a more lucrative position with a major publication.

Kyle maintained he was content to live in Driscoll Lake with his wife Christine and their daughter. Pat felt fortunate to have him on staff. Not only was he a talented writer, but he also had excellent organizational skills. He was responsible for organizing the newspaper's back issues into on-line archives.

Pat believed the reason for his low self-esteem was because of his father. Curtis Lawrence had little regard for his son's career choice. The man was a tyrant who loved power and prestige. He looked at members of the press with disdain unless he could use them to further his political career. "The Judge," as most people called him, portrayed himself as having strong family values but hardly acknowledged his own family.

After a light dinner, Pat poured a glass of iced tea and took it outside to her patio. She usually stayed away from caffeine in the evenings but needed something to help her stay awake for a few hours. A large stack of mail had accumulated during the three weeks she was away. She'd put off sorting it long enough.

If there was any consolation to the intense heat, the lower humidity levels made the early mornings and evenings bearable.

Her next-door neighbor had done a good job of keeping her azaleas and roses watered. She'd given up on her lawn weeks earlier, but her flower gardens were a source of pride. Helen McKenzie had planted some of the roses before she moved from this house to the lake.

Pat smiled when she thought of Helen. She was a good-natured and caring person who possessed a quiet inner strength. Numerous tragedies had befallen her family, yet she remained steadfast. Pat was saddened to learn of her death.

She took a sip of tea and looked at the stack of mail, trying to decide what to open first. She separated the sales ads and junk mail and scanned the envelopes before reaching for the latest edition of the *Driscoll Lake Reporter*.

The front-page headline, "Twenty Year Mystery Still Unsolved," by Kyle Lawrence caught her off guard. The photos of Phillip Denton, Madelyn Denton, and Robert Harris accompanied the article.

She had to read the story.

Twenty years ago, a scandal with all the makings of big city crime hit the small town of Driscoll Lake. A missing person. Murder. Suicide. Embezzlement of company funds. It began when Phillip Denton, President, and CEO of Cameron Manufacturing, disappeared without a trace. It ended when Driscoll Lake's major employer closed its doors. But did it end? There are still unanswered questions.

What happened to the money? Although Robert Harris was the prime suspect, the money trail grew cold. Officials investigated his family but found no evidence they had knowledge of his alleged crime.

There was also the incident with Phillip Denton. Although presumed dead, authorities never located his body.

Pat read the remainder of the article with interest. She was both surprised and pleased that Kyle had taken the initiative to write the article. He usually stayed away from controversial stories. If only the timing had been different. The paper published each Wednesday. Helen was a subscriber. Pat hoped she hadn't seen the story before her death and allowed it to upset her.

She could hardly blame Kyle. No one knew Helen would die so close to the twentieth anniversary of the biggest scandal to hit Driscoll Lake—one in which her nephew was a key player.

Pat knew responsible journalists were obligated to report the news—both good and bad. As editor of the local newspaper, she always tried to be unbiased and objective even on the most controversial stories. There were times when she had to report things that she would have preferred not to. Such was the case twenty years earlier with the Harris murder-suicide.

Like many people who had known Robert Harris, she didn't want to believe he was guilty of the crimes alleged against him. She'd often wondered what happened to Phillip Denton and if anyone would ever find his body.

Pat found the article intriguing and well written. She would commend Kyle for the story, but she wondered how others felt about it. Madelyn's daughter Rachel had returned to Driscoll Lake.

If Stephanie Harris came for Helen's funeral, she might see the article. Coming back for the first time in twenty years would be awkward enough. Having to relive memories involving her father would only things more difficult.

By nine o'clock, the light had grown dim, and Pat returned inside. Her body hadn't fully adjusted to the time change. She dressed for bed but wanted to stay awake for a while.

A copy of *Forgotten Memory* was on her nightstand. Picking it up, she immersed herself in the pages of the book. It was almost midnight when her eyelids grew heavy. Closing the book, she turned out the lights and soon fell asleep.

Sometime later, she awoke with a start, sat up in bed, and looked at the bedside clock. She had slept almost four hours. A wave of unease enveloped her. A nagging feeling tugged at her memory.

Pinpointing the source of her apprehension was difficult. Something in the book? A recent encounter? The newspaper article? Her mind wandered in a dozen different directions.

Pat was still awake when the first pale light of dawn appeared, wishing she could remember what set off the alarm bell in her head. She glanced at the book on her nightstand. *Forgotten Memory*. What was in the recesses of her mind that caused her anxiety and why couldn't she remember?

Chapter Three

Unnerved after finding the note, Stephanie had found it difficult to concentrate on her manuscript. How long had it been on the kitchen counter? Did someone leave it for Helen before she died, or was the message intended for Stephanie? What did the writer mean about people and things not being as they seemed?

Stephanie had written about mysterious warnings, hidden clues, and strange phone calls. Those things were all part of writing suspense and mystery novels. Being the receiver of such a note, if indeed she was the intended recipient, was another matter.

She considered calling Nell and Dan but decided against it. She didn't want to act like a coward. Helen didn't have an alarm system, so Stephanie made certain to lock all the doors and windows and secure the dead bolt.

Even though it was after midnight when she finally fell asleep, she was wide awake at six-thirty. Plenty of time for exercise. A run around the lake would get her adrenaline pumping and clear her mind. She had several items on her agenda today, none of which she looked forward to doing.

She fed Whiskers, put on her running clothes, and did a few warm-up stretches before leaving the house. The road was smooth—perfect for running. Few cars were about this time of day. Several residents were already outside doing yard work, no doubt trying to finish their chores before the temperatures became too hot. Some of them smiled and waved as she passed.

Stephanie ran to the north end of the lake and paused briefly before crossing the dam, trying to determine how far she had run. Her daily goal was at least two miles.

She considered driving the route later in order to measure the distance. Silly. She won't be in Driscoll Lake long enough for it to matter. Stephanie shook it off and continued her run.

The road curved on the other side of the dam. Stephanie rounded the corner and saw Matt Bradford jogging toward her. Considering the way he acted the evening before, she was tempted to ignore him but didn't want to give him the satisfaction of thinking he'd upset her.

"Good morning. I see you also enjoy an early morning run."

"Every chance I get. Any problems last night?" he asked.

"Problems? Should there have been?"

"Just checking. "

"Both Whiskers and I are fine. Anyway, I used to live here, remember?"

"Yeah, well, that was a long time ago. Things are different now."

"Don't worry about me. I can take care of myself." She resumed her run, not giving Matt time to reply.

***

Stephanie returned from her morning run, placed a call to Miles Parker, and arranged for a ten o'clock appointment. She stared at her phone, knowing it was time to make another call. Her mother wouldn't be pleased she was in Driscoll Lake but would want to know about Aunt Helen.

After her father's death, Stephanie and her mom moved away from Driscoll Lake. Because her father's death was ruled a suicide, his insurance policies didn't pay off. And like all of Cameron's employees, there was no money left in his retirement account. Kathryn Harris had to work to support them.

Stephanie's grades enabled her to receive a full college scholarship. Shortly after she began her freshman year, her mom remarried. David Armstrong was a decent man who did his best to make Stephanie feel part of the family, but it was hard for her to think of him as a stepfather—or his sons as her stepbrothers.

Stephanie took a deep breath and pressed the speed dial button. "Hi, Mom."

"Honey, how are you? I'm glad you called. David and I are planning a trip to the Florida Keys in a couple of weeks. We hope you'll join us. Steven and Tim will be there with their families. Should be a delightful time. We can shop and—"

"Come up for air, Mom."

"Sorry, hon. Just hoped we could have the entire family together."

"I can't think about taking a trip right now. I'm afraid I have bad news. Aunt Helen passed away."

"Oh, I'm so sorry. I know you had become close these past few years."

"Yeah. Her death came as a surprise. Guess she didn't want me to know she'd been sick."

"I'm sure you'll send flowers, so if you'll order a larger arrangement, and include my name on the card, I'll send you the money."

"I'm in Driscoll Lake."

There was a moment of silence.

"Mom?"

"Tell me I didn't hear you correctly."

"You heard right."

"What in heaven's name made you decide to return to that place?"

"It was Aunt Helen's dying request."

"Why? What's the point now that she's gone? Honey, I tried so hard to protect you after your father's—"

"I know you did, but I'm not a teenager anymore. Besides, I only plan to stay long enough for the funeral and to take care of her business. There's nothing left for me here."

"I'm glad to hear you say that. You know how I feel."

"Yes, but this isn't about you or me. It's about paying my respects to the last relative on Dad's side of the family. I loved Aunt Helen. I regret that I waited so many years to spend time with her."

"Are you saying that I'm to blame for that?"

Stephanie rolled her eyes. "I'm not blaming you. You did what you thought was best for me. I made my own choices after I grew up."

"I still don't understand why—"

"Mom, I have to cut this conversation short. I have several errands this morning. Call my cell phone if you need me."

"I know I won't be able to change your mind. But I love you and don't want to see you hurt. Being in Driscoll Lake could bring up too many memories. People may start asking questions again."

"I can take care of myself. I'll call you later."

Stephanie hung up the phone. Her mother seemed to have forgotten about the many years they lived here when her father was alive. Happy. Content. A family. Why was it so hard for her to remember the good times? Stephanie hated to admit the fact her mother always chose to dwell on the negative things.

***

Kyle Lawrence whistled as he walked along the sidewalk leading to the offices of the *Driscoll Lake Reporter*, hoping to arrive before the receptionist, Madge Sinclair. He was in good spirits after his visit to the coffee shop and didn't want the town's well-known gossip to ruin his day.

She'd been in fine form at the church luncheon yesterday. Whenever Madge found someone who would listen to her diatribe, she would gloat about it for days.

He didn't want to deal with her this morning. However, she was already at her desk and on the phone when he walked in the building. Kyle hurried into his office without acknowledging her and closed the door.

His recent article had stirred up a lot of conversation. While it was true some people weren't happy about it, most people he encountered had positive things to say. When he stopped at the coffee shop this morning, several people commented on the story.

A longtime resident complimented him. Another person told him they had always been intrigued by the case.

Even a newcomer to Driscoll Lake commented. "I didn't know something like that happened here. Your article makes me wonder if there is someone still around who knows more about the case than they will admit."

Kyle's father wasn't pleased. "You must be desperate for a story. Don't you know better than to drag up old memories? The town doesn't need that kind of negative publicity."

The Judge's reaction wasn't surprising. Kyle had long since given up trying to please him. Still, it would be nice if his father would say something positive about his work at least once.

Over the years, Kyle had kept up with the story of Robert Harris and the disappearance of Phillip Denton. He frequently searched the Internet for any new developments on the Denton case and familiarized himself with the archived stories published in the area newspapers.

Two weeks ago, he received a phone call from an anonymous source stating he had information. Kyle agreed to a meeting.

"I'd like you to do a story about the incident. The only stipulation I have is that you don't use my name. Some of the things I'm going to tell you must remain confidential."

"The twentieth anniversary is coming up. Approach the article with that in mind. Maybe it will generate new interest or someone will read it and come forward with new information."

A knock sounded at his door, and Pat Turner came into his office. "Good morning, Kyle. Wanted to thank you for taking care of everything while I was away."

"No problem. Welcome back. Hope you had a good vacation."

"I enjoyed the time with my sister but now I'm ready to get back to work. I read your article about the Harris-Denton case. You did a good job, but I'm curious as to why you chose to write about it."

"I overheard someone talking, and since the twentieth anniversary is coming up, I thought it was a good idea. Is there a problem?"

"The timing couldn't have been worse with Helen McKenzie's death. I'm sure it was upsetting for her to read about her nephew."

"*If* she read the story."

"Stephanie or her mother could come for the funeral. How do you think this would make them feel?"

"Do you think Stephanie would come back after all these years? And Driscoll Lake is the last place I'd expect to see Kathryn Harris." Kyle chose not to admit he'd overheard Nell Bradford tell someone that Stephanie had planned to come.

Pat sighed. "You're probably right. I'm just upset over Helen's death. Well, what's done is done." She left the room and closed the door behind her.

Kyle sighed. He hated not telling Pat everything, but he'd made a promise, and he intended to keep it.

Later that morning Madge stuck her head in Kyle's door to announce the newspaper had already picked up five new subscriptions. "They said it's because of the article. One person said he'd be interested in knowing more. People are asking questions."

It was Kyle's turn to smile. He may not be able to please his father, but he knew the article had achieved exactly what he intended.

***

Miles Parker's office was located on the corner of Main Street and Hudson Avenue. Stephanie slowed the car and pulled into the parking lot. She found an empty parking spot, got out of the car, and looked around.

Some sights were familiar—the newspaper office across the street, Willard's Drug Store, First State Bank. Others were new such as the sandwich shop on the opposite corner. The Parker Law Firm was still in the same location, but the building exterior looked as if it had recently received a new facelift.

Like the rest of the town, the legal business was apparently growing. The sign now read Parker and Davis. Miles Parker had taken on a partner.

The young woman seated at the receptionist desk smiled when Stephanie entered the building. "Good morning. How can I help you today?"

"I'm Stephanie Harris. I have an appointment with Mr. Parker."

"So you're Stephanie!"

"Yes. I am. Is there a problem?" Stephanie straightened her shoulders.

The woman's crestfallen expression made Stephanie wish she could retract her question.

"I'm sorry. I didn't mean to sound rude. It's just. Well, I've read all your books, and I'm excited to meet you in person. I've never met a famous author before."

"Thank you, but I'm just an ordinary person who happens to write novels." Stephanie was relieved to know the woman's reaction wasn't because of her father's crime. She looked at the nameplate on the desk. "Heather?"

"Yes. Heather Stevens. Mr. Parker is expecting you. He's with another client now, but shouldn't be long."

"No problem. I am a little early."

"Would you care for a cup of coffee or some bottled water?"

"No, thanks." Stephanie sat in a chair where she could watch as people entered or left the office. It came as second nature to take every available opportunity to observe people and places.

Miles had also remodeled the interior of the building. It smelled of fresh paint and new carpet. The furnishings were tasteful, but not overly expensive.

A few minutes passed when an interior door opened. Stephanie looked up to see a man dressed in jeans, t-shirt, and work boots standing in the doorway. He appeared to be in his mid-thirties, with a lean silhouette and strong muscular arms. Stephanie guessed from his tan he spent a lot of time outdoors.

"I appreciate your help in expediting this matter," he said to the person inside the office. "I'm anxious to get started on the project as soon as possible."

"I'm glad everything worked out for you."

Stephanie recognized the voice of Miles Parker. Not wanting to eavesdrop, she turned her attention back to the magazine she'd been reading, but not before noticing the young receptionist. Heather got up from her desk and stood beside a ficus tree close to Miles Parker's door.

She made a pretense of tending the plant, but it wasn't hard to figure out she was trying to listen to the conversation. Stephanie didn't see a single dead leaf. She wondered why Heather was so interested in the conversation.

Heather caught Stephanie's eye, blushed, and walked back to her desk.

"I appreciate your support." The man closed the door and turned to leave. He looked at Stephanie, nodded, and then stopped.

"Stephanie?"

"Brian Nichols?" Brian's mother Dorothy had been her father's secretary.

"It's me." He walked toward her and extended his hand. "I'm sorry for your loss. Mrs. McKenzie was a kind person. She'll be missed."

"Thank you." Stephanie swallowed. "I heard you still lived in Driscoll Lake. I confess I didn't think you'd be around."

"Don't tell me you're another one who expected me to end up in prison."

He smiled as he spoke, but she couldn't determine whether or not he was serious. "No, not that. You often talked about moving away."

"I surprised a lot of people by staying."

"Count me as one of them. I thought your biggest ambition was to become a rock star."

"Yeah, but I grew up. I own a construction company. But you're the one who's made a name for yourself. Every time you write a new novel, it's the talk of the town."

"I'm sure it is. What do people say about the daughter of the man who nearly destroyed this place? That it's not fair because I'm successful and the rest of Driscoll Lake suffered because of my father. His crime affected your family as well."

"Stephanie, people have moved on with their lives. The town is thriving. New families have moved in. Many of them don't know what happened, nor do they care."

"That may be true, but the sooner I can finish my business and leave here, the better. I never intended to come back."

"You're not planning to stay?"

"No longer than necessary. After the funeral, I'll tie up a few loose ends and be on the first available flight to Denver."

"I can't say I blame you. Some folks were pretty rough on you back then."

"Yeah, well, I've tried hard to forget, but it isn't easy."

"I guess not."

"How is your mother?" Stephanie had always been fond of Dorothy Nichols. Her life hadn't been easy with an alcoholic husband and rebellious son. When the scandal with Stephanie's father happened, Dorothy had been one of his staunchest supporters.

"Mom has a few health problems, but doing as well as can be expected. She's in an assisted living facility."

"She was always kind to me. Even after..." Stephanie looked away as she fought the lump in her throat. She couldn't afford to let her guard down. Showing the slightest amount of weakness to anyone here wasn't an option.

Brian nodded. "Mom was very fond of you. She spoke of you often after you moved away. Always said it couldn't have been easy for you to deal with."

"It wasn't." The door to Miles Parker's office opened and Stephanie stood up. "Guess I'd better run. Mr. Parker is expecting me, and I'm sure you're busy. Maybe I'll see you around before I go."

"I'd like that." Brian smiled and turned to leave.

"Brian."

"Yes?"

"Thanks for the words of encouragement."

Chapter Four

From his office window, Kyle watched Stephanie get out of the car and walk into Miles Parker's office. Years had passed since they had last seen one another, but he would have recognized her anywhere. She looked exactly as she did on the cover of her latest book.

She walked with her head held high—her steps purposeful and intentional. It seemed as if she defied anyone to question her motives or to mention her father. Kyle didn't blame her. People had been less than kind to her in those days. Many people treated her as if she was responsible for her father's actions.

"What's so interesting?" Pat asked.

He turned to look at her. "Stephanie Harris is in town. I just saw her go into Miles Parker's office."

"Stephanie's here? Are you sure?"

"Positive."

"Then there's a chance she'll read your story. At the least, someone will call her attention to it."

"Maybe. Who knows?"

"Speaking of the article, Madge told me about the new subscribers. I'm glad."

"Guess I did something right."

"I overreacted earlier. You did a good job. And you're right. People are still interested."

"Thanks."

"Some people probably won't be pleased, but that's the nature of journalism."

"If Stephanie reads the story, she may even have some questions of her own."

"You may be right. I admit I've often wondered if we knew everything about what happened that night." Pat turned and left the room.

Kyle turned away from the window. Stephanie would read the article. He'd find some way to make certain of it.

***

Miles Parker was one of the few people in Driscoll Lake Stephanie felt she could trust. When the scandal broke concerning her father, he was quick to lend support to her family.

Stephanie remembered him as a kind man who always looked out for others. She figured he must be in his seventies now.

When she walked into his office, he crossed the room to meet her and extended his hand. "My, my. The last time I saw you, you were still wearing braces. You've turned into a beautiful young woman—and quite successful too. Robert would be proud of you."

"Thank you, Mr. Parker. I hope he would be."

"You have my deepest sympathy for your loss. Helen was a fine woman and an upstanding member of the community."

"I'll certainly miss her."

"Please, have a seat." He pointed to a chair and then walked around to sit behind his desk.

"She spoke about you often the past few years. I think she thought of you as the granddaughter she never had."

Stephanie blinked back tears. "I regret not spending more time with her."

"Don't think about what might have been. Focus on the time you had together. Everyone has regrets."

"I guess you're right."

"I'm sure you have a lot of things to take care of, so I'll make this brief. I'll schedule a formal reading of the will. Helen left everything to you. Her affairs were in good order. She had no outstanding debts and made wise investments."

"I see."

"Do you plan on staying in town a while?"

Stephanie shook her head. "Only as long as necessary."

"Since you were the only heir, there's little chance of anyone contesting the will. I'll do my best to expedite the probate process."

"If I'm required to return for the hearing, I can arrange that."

"We can discuss the details later. Helen's body is at Crawford's Funeral Home. They're in a new building on Vine Street."

"I plan to go there next. I don't know what type of service Aunt Helen wanted. Nell Bradford offered to help. She's meeting me there."

"Knowing Helen, she probably had everything arranged in advance. George Crawford will go over all the details with you."

"I appreciate your help with everything." Stephanie started to rise.

"Before you go, there's one more thing." He reached into his desk drawer and drew out a plain white envelope.

"Helen gave me this a few weeks ago. She asked that I give it to you after her death."

Stephanie took the envelope from Miles. "After her death? Why then?"

"She didn't say. I don't know what's in the letter, except she assured me it wasn't a handwritten will. You're welcome to read it now, but you may want to wait until you have some privacy."

"Thanks, but I would rather be alone when I read it."

"Don't hesitate to call me if you need any advice—legal or otherwise."

"I'll be sure to do that. Thanks for taking the time to see me on such short notice."

Stephanie placed the envelope in her purse and turned to leave, but stopped when she got to the door. Miles Parker was an honest man who would maintain confidentiality.

"Mr. Parker, can I ask you something?"

"Yes, of course."

"Tell me about Matt Bradford. I saw him last night and again this morning. He seems hardened. Almost hostile. I got the distinct impression that he doesn't want me here."

"Matt? Can't imagine why he'd think that. You probably just caught him on a bad day. You do know he's our police chief."

"No. I didn't know."

"Driscoll Lake isn't like it once was. His job can be stressful."

"That could explain some of it."

"Matt's a good person, Stephanie. Don't be fooled by first impressions."

"Guess you can't expect someone to be the same person they were twenty years earlier. I appreciate your thoughts."

She considered mentioning the note she'd found the night before, but decided against it. Except for Dan and Nell, who else had known that she planned to stay at Helen's house? Driscoll Lake had grown, but it was still a small town. Word travels fast.

One thing was sure. Matt knew she was here—and he had been in the house only hours before she arrived.

***

Stephanie smoothed a non-existent wrinkle from her skirt, paused, and took a deep breath before entering Crawford's Funeral Home. She'd never had to assist in planning a funeral before and didn't look forward to it.

Although she and her aunt vacationed together several times over the past few years, she had no idea as to Helen's wishes. She hoped Miles Parker's assumption about Helen pre-planning her service was correct.

Stephanie's initial impression of George Crawford didn't help matters. He was a small, scrawny man who wore wire-rimmed eyeglasses too large for his face. He fidgeted with his tie and cleared his throat when she walked into his office. It would have been difficult for a bystander to determine who was more nervous—Stephanie or the funeral director. She was grateful Nell had already arrived.

Any misgivings she had soon dissipated when the funeral director stood up and held out his hand. His handshake was gentle, yet firm—not like a limp dishrag—a characteristic she despised.

"Ms. Harris," he said, "you have my deepest condolences for your loss."

"Thank you, Mr. Crawford. I have no idea what my aunt wanted, so I appreciate any advice." Stephanie tucked a strand of hair behind her ear.

His smile was warm and genuine. "Let's sit down, shall we?" He waited until Stephanie and Nell took their seats before walking behind his desk and sitting in his chair. "Mrs. McKenzie was a wise woman. She did what I wish more people would do in making pre-arrangements. Takes the burden off you and guarantees she'll have exactly what she wanted."

Stephanie pressed a hand to her stomach. "That's a relief."

"She did this shortly after your uncle passed away, but about a month ago she gave me a detailed list. Everything from the pall bearers to the music she wanted. The only thing left to do is to decide the day and time."

"That does make things easier. I certainly want to follow Aunt Helen's wishes."

"I took the liberty of contacting Mrs. McKenzie's pastor. He said the church is available any day this week."

"You mean Driscoll Lake Community Church? Why there?"

"That's what Mrs. McKenzie wanted."

"Why not hold the service here in the chapel? It's large enough, isn't it?"

"Yes of course, but—"

"Then it's settled. The funeral will be here. I refuse to have the service at the church."

"Is there a particular reason?" George Crawford began to fidget with his tie again.

"My parents attended there. When my father— Let's just say folks weren't kind to us. I'm sure some of those people are still around, and I have no desire to see them."

Nell put her arm around Stephanie's shoulder. "I realize it be might difficult for you, but it's what Helen wanted. You did say you wanted to honor her wishes."

Stephanie rubbed her forehead and sighed. "Okay. You're right. The church it is."

George Crawford appeared relieved. "It's settled then. What about Wednesday? We have a time available at ten."

"That's fine."

"What about the visitation service?"

"Visitation?"

"Mrs. McKenzie didn't specify anything, but most families have a visitation. It gives those who aren't able to attend the funeral a chance to pay their respects to the family."

"Absolutely not!" Stephanie was adamant. "I'm won't stand around for others to come by in a feeble attempt to offer condolences. Too many people in this town disowned Mom and me twenty years ago."

Nell reached and patted Stephanie's hand. "Honey, not everyone felt that way."

"I'm sorry, Nell. If people want to come to the funeral to remember Aunt Helen, that's fine. But I won't be a spectacle or source of gossip for them. It's a little late to make up for the way they acted."

***

After finalizing the funeral arrangements, Stephanie and Nell decided to have lunch at a small teashop in town. The relaxed atmosphere helped calm her nerves. It was mid-afternoon before she arrived back at the lake.

She changed into comfortable clothes and settled on the sofa with Helen's letter. Perhaps it would explain her reasons for wanting Stephanie to come home.

Aunt Helen's home, she reminded herself. She'd ceased thinking of Driscoll Lake in those terms long ago.

She opened the envelope and began to read.

August 15, 2011

Dear Stephanie:

I'm writing this having recently returned from our vacation. The Hawaiian Islands were beautiful. I can't believe I waited so many years to visit them. George often wanted to go—sadly, we never took the time.

Words can't describe how much our trips have meant to me. I'm grateful for having seen such beautiful sights but most important has been the time I've been able to spend with you. I'll always treasure the memories.

I understand your reasons for not returning to Driscoll Lake. The things that happened were difficult for all of us to bear, but especially for a fourteen-year-old whose whole life was ahead of her. Your mother did what she thought was best for you by moving away. She thought it was the only way for the healing process to begin.

I know people can be cruel. People said things in haste. The events surrounding your father's death affected many lives— their jobs, retirements, their homes. I'm not justifying the way some of them treated you, but often people lash out at innocent victims when they are trying to make sense of a situation.

In the years that followed, wounds healed. The town recovered. Everyone went on with their lives. Some of the same people who blamed your father were the very ones who often asked about you. They stood by George and me when we lost Carol and later were there to support me when my beloved George died.

Miles will go over the contents of my will, but I'm leaving you everything. Even though you are my only remaining heir, there is no one else I'd rather have my small estate. The house on the lake has been a place of healing for me, but you are not obligated to keep it. Do with it as you think best.

I had hoped to live long enough to see your father's name cleared. Although I accepted his guilt, I often questioned whether the original investigation was thorough. Deep down I never gave up hope some new evidence would turn up to exonerate him. I guess that will never happen.

When you read this letter, I will be gone. I don't feel my time on earth is much longer. I've lived a good life and I'm ready for the next chapter.

Maybe you'll come back to Driscoll Lake someday. I understand you would probably never want to live here, but please don't harbor any bitterness or anger in your heart.

You have been like a ray of sunshine in my life these past few years.

All my love, Aunt Helen

Stephanie's eyes filled with tears, and she put the letter aside. She walked to the windows overlooking the lake and then into Helen's bedroom. Photographs of Uncle George, Carol, and Aunt Helen sat on the dresser. Another photo taken of Helen and Stephanie from their trip to Alaska two years earlier sat beside it. Stephanie picked it up.

"I'm going to miss her. We had such fun together." She sat the photo back on the dresser and turned to leave the room when another one hanging beside the door caught her eye.

She and her parents had taken a vacation to the Grand Canyon about a year before her father's death. Stephanie remembered the occasion. It was near sunset, and they stood on the rim of the canyon. Another visitor offered to take the picture. They had been so happy that day.

Everything changed on a September night. Her father's actions tore the once happy family apart. People who had once heralded Robert Harris pointed accusatory fingers at her mother. "Surely you had knowledge of what he was doing."

"Oh, Daddy." A lump caught in her throat. "I wish I could believe you were innocent. Why did you have to destroy our lives?"

She walked back into the den, flipped through the stack of mail, and came to a copy of the hometown newspaper. The front-page headline surprised her. "Twenty Year Mystery Unsolved." Kyle Lawrence had written the article. She opened the paper and began to read.

...Twenty years later, many questions remain. Where is the missing money? What happened to Phillip Denton? If he's dead, as the police assume, where is his body? When Robert Harris died that September night, did the secret die with him? Or is there someone alive who knows more than he or she is willing to admit?

Stephanie threw the paper on the coffee table. Was Kyle insinuating her father also killed Phillip Denton? Authorities never considered him a suspect in Phillip's disappearance. Or, did Kyle believe her father had an accomplice?

The article gave her another reason to take care of Aunt Helen's business and leave town as soon as possible.

It also made her realize something. She had been hiding. She could have visited years ago. By staying away, she gave the gossips more ammunition.

Yes, her father was guilty, and many people treated both Stephanie and her mother with contempt. But they had survived. She'd show this town she was strong—beginning tomorrow night. Her decision made, she picked up the phone and punched in the number for Crawford's Funeral Home.

"Mr. Crawford? This is Stephanie Harris. I've changed my mind about the visitation."

"I'm glad to hear you say that, Ms. Harris. I don't think you'll be sorry. Many people will want to pay their respects. Tomorrow night from 7:00 to 9:00?"

"That will be all right."

"Good. I'll post the obituary online and send a notice to the newspaper."

"Thank you. I'll see you tomorrow evening." She hung up the phone.

No more running. She would face every cruel person who had mistreated her. This time, she wouldn't back down.

Chapter Five

Stephanie awoke long before daylight, having fought a losing battle for sleep. Reading the letter left her even more perplexed. Only three weeks before her death, Aunt Helen wrote she understood why Stephanie had never returned to Driscoll Lake. Yet moments before her death, she requested Stephanie's presence. What happened to make her change her mind?

At five o'clock, resigned she wasn't going back to sleep, she got out of bed. It was too early for a run, so she dressed and went outside to the screened-in porch. It was quiet and peaceful this time of day. A gentle breeze blew across the lake. The trill from crickets and other night insects began to fade as daylight approached. A mockingbird called from nearby. She could understand why her aunt loved it here.

She made a mental note of things she needed to do and decided she would need to stay at least through the upcoming weekend. She needed time to meet with Miles Parker concerning the will. Someone would have to sort through Helen's personal belongings, and Stephanie couldn't imagine leaving that task to someone else.

There was also a matter of the house. There was no reason to keep it, but for some reason, she couldn't think about selling it right away. The cottage was her last physical tie to Driscoll Lake. Still, she couldn't envision living there or keeping the house as a rental property.

She also thought of the newspaper article. What purpose did Kyle Lawrence have for drudging up a twenty-year-old story? He had been one of her biggest supporters in school. When others turned away, he stood up for her.

"It's not Stephanie's fault," he had said, "no matter what her father did or did not do."

Forgotten Memory. Her thoughts went back to the television interview from a few days earlier. So much had happened since then it seemed like a lifetime.

Maybe the reporter had been right. Perhaps she had chosen to forget some things. Stephanie tried to recall her father's disposition in the days leading up to his death. He had seemed preoccupied. If he had been innocent, why did he take his life? Her memories of that time had lain dormant for a long time.

Stephanie couldn't deny it was a clear case of murder-suicide—no matter what she said on Jennifer's show.

The missing company funds were another matter. Yes, her father authorized the initial transfer to the overseas account, but what happened after that? The money trail went cold. Many people believed he was guilty, but no matter what they said, she couldn't imagine her father as a thief. Then again, she'd never imagined him as a murderer.

When the first rays of morning light appeared, Stephanie went back inside the house to get ready for her run. She pocketed the house key, double-checked the locks, and headed out. She ran in the opposite direction from the previous day, not wanting to encounter Matt again.

When she returned an hour later, Matt's pickup was in his parents' driveway. The sun was above the horizon, and the forecast called for another hot day. She was hungry after her run, so she peered into the refrigerator. Nell had stocked it well—she had all the ingredients for an omelet, but she wanted a smoothie.

"No reason why I can't go into town." Driscoll Lake was sure to have a coffee shop. She decided to take her laptop and do some writing.

After a quick shower, she dressed in jeans and a light-colored shirt, pulled her hair into a low ponytail, and applied minimal makeup.

Before leaving, she went into the kitchen to feed Whiskers. She stopped when she noticed the calendar pinned to the back of the pantry door. September 13, 2011. Today was the twentieth anniversary of her father's death.

**

Stephanie located a coffee shop a few blocks from Main Street. She ordered a strawberry banana smoothie and a bagel with cream cheese, then found a corner booth facing the door

She pulled her laptop from the carrying case, and opened the writing software program. Coffee shops were not only good places to write, but also to watch people.

Brian Nichols had told her many new families had moved to Driscoll Lake, a fact made evident by the number of new subdivisions and businesses. Even so, she expected to see a few people she knew from the past. But she was surprised at the number of individuals who came into the coffee shop that she didn't recognize.

She had just spread cream cheese over the second half of her bagel when Kyle Lawrence walked in. He had married her best friend, Christine Starnes. At least, Christine used to be her friend. That changed after her father died. Like many of the others in school, Christine turned away when the accusations against her father came out.

Kyle nodded and went to the counter to place his order. After paying, he walked to the booth where she sat.

"Stephanie. Nice to see you again. I mean— I'm sorry it's not under more pleasant circumstances."

"You don't have to apologize, Kyle. I understand. Do you have time to sit down?"

"For a minute, thanks."

"People don't have to treat me like they're walking on eggshells. I'm tough. I've dealt with a lot worse."

"Yes, you have. Some aren't sure how to act after the way many of them treated you."

"Well, I moved on. I survived. What happened twenty years ago doesn't really matter."

"I don't know if you saw the newspaper story."

"I did." Stephanie took a sip of her smoothie and sat the cup down harder than she intended.

"I wouldn't blame you if you were upset. I wrote the story because it was the twentieth anniversary of the event."

"Yes, I was upset at first, but I've worked in journalism. I understand how it works. Everyone loves a mystery."

"A lot of people still have questions. The story stirred up interest. The newspaper picked up several new subscribers, but that wasn't my purpose in writing the article."

"I understand. No matter how I feel, it's news."

"Some people regret the way they treated you."

"Oh?"

"I'm talking about Christine."

"Yeah, well it's a little late now." Stephanie took a bite of her bagel.

"She wants to see you."

"That won't be possible. I'll be busy the entire time I'm here. Besides, I didn't come for a social visit."

"Do you plan to stay for a while?"

"For a few days. Not sure when I'm leaving."

He stood up. "I need to get to the office. I'm sure you have things to do."

"I plan to sit here and write for a while. This is my one free day."

"Stephanie, think about what I said. Christine is sorry."

"I may see you around before I leave." She didn't intend to see Christine Lawrence. Broken bonds aren't always easy to mend.

***

Stephanie was surprised to look up from her laptop and discover over two hours had passed. She made good progress on the manuscript and lost track of time. If all writing sessions were like this one, she'd have the first draft completed ahead of schedule.

She packed away her laptop and ordered a Chai iced tea to go. When she got in the car, she turned on the radio. Van Morrison's "Wild Night" came from the speakers. The song brought back memories of riding in the car with her father with the radio playing loud. He would tap his fingers to the beat of the music and sing off-key. The thought made her smile.

Stephanie put the car in reverse, cranked up the volume, and started singing. Like her father, she had no musical talent, but she shared his enjoyment of classic rock. Her mother's musical interest was a bit more refined. When she was in the car, they rarely played the radio. Neither Stephanie nor her father cared to listen to Mozart.

A wave of nostalgia swept over her, and she decided to take a drive around town. Some places looked familiar, such as her old neighborhood. She slowed to take a closer look at the house where she once lived.

It was nice to see the yard still maintained. The live oak trees her father planted when they first moved to the house had grown tall.

She drove past the school and the football stadium. The last time she'd attended a football game was the night her father died. She stopped short of driving by the old factory, although she caught a glimpse of the rusting metal building from a distance and was surprised to see it still standing.

When she drove back through town, she spotted Rosa's Taqueria. Rosa's had once been her favorite place to eat. She and her father went there often, and Rosa's guacamole was the best Stephanie had ever eaten. In all her years of travel, she had yet to find any as tasty.

She glanced at the dashboard clock. It was almost noon. Her mouth watered at the thought of eating of one of Rosa's burritos. The parking lot was crowded, so she pulled up to the drive-through window and ordered a deluxe burrito and guacamole.

The temperature had already reached triple digits by the time she returned to the lake. Although this year was unusually hot and dry, she wondered how she'd ever survived the long hot Texas summers. It was time to kick off her shoes and relax in the air-conditioned coolness.

She grabbed her purse, laptop, and food and hurried to the front door. After she inserted the key in the lock, she noticed a folded piece of paper jammed beneath the door.

She sat her purse and food on a table before retrieving it. It was another note written in the same calligraphy-style writing as the one she found two nights ago.

Hope you took my first message seriously. Some people don't want you back in town.

Stephanie felt a sudden chill. This time there was no question someone intended the message for her. She was certain the note wasn't there when she left the house this morning, or she would have seen it on the way out.

"Maybe Nell saw someone." She reached for her cell phone to make the call but stopped. Matt's pickup was in Nell's driveway when she left the house this morning. He was in the house on Sunday. He had the opportunity to leave both notes.

But why? What did he care if she stayed? It was true he hadn't acted as if he were glad to see her on Sunday evening, but the following morning, he seemed a little more like the person she once knew. Something wasn't right.

Stephanie put the phone down without calling. If she couldn't trust Matt Bradford, could she trust anyone?

***

Carlos Gonzales rarely read the *Driscoll Lake Reporter*. Instead, he preferred the daily paper from Brewster or the *Dallas Morning News*. He remembered the days when the local paper read more like a gossip column. Carlos realized things had changed, but it was hard for him to imagine it being a reliable source of news.

However, when he and his wife Maria moved to Driscoll Lake, she insisted upon a subscription. "How else will I keep up with current events? If I don't know about the local activities and clubs, I'll never get to know anyone or become involved."

Carlos merely smiled. Maria had an outgoing personality and never had trouble making new friends. He suspected her desire to read the local paper was to get an idea of what small town life was all about. She had always lived a big city, but both of them wanted to live in a small town after retirement.

After thirty years as a homicide detective with the San Diego Police Department, they decided to move to his hometown of Driscoll Lake. Although both of his parents were still active and able to care for themselves, he wanted to be close to them during their remaining years.

Carlos expected to take life easy and enjoy the benefits of retirement. He had always wanted to learn the game of golf but never could afford the time while in San Diego. His father grew a large vegetable garden each year, so he decided it would be good to have one of his own.

However, he soon discovered retirement was not all he thought it would be. He was unable to keep the garden watered due to the drought and water rationing. The plants withered and died.

The mild San Diego climate made it difficult for him to adjust to the heat of the Texas summer, so he spent very little time on the golf course. At any rate, he decided he didn't like the game.

After a few months of boredom, he spoke to Matt Bradford about working for the Driscoll Lake Police. He would have volunteered his services to have something to do. The timing was right—Matt had a position available.

"It won't be what you were accustomed to in San Diego, but Driscoll Lake has grown," Matt said. "Crime has increased, and we need someone with experience."

In three months, he investigated several burglaries, a couple of drug possessions, and a few domestic disturbances. Driscoll Lake didn't have a high rate of violent crimes. The last homicide occurred five years earlier. But the job was what he wanted after spending so many years investigating brutal murders.

It was Tuesday morning before he had a chance to read the front-page story about Robert Harris. Maria had saved the newspaper, thinking it might be of interest to him. She was right.

His parents had written him about the murder-suicide involving Robert Harris and Madelyn Denton along with the disappearance of Madelyn's husband Phillip. A few people thought Harris might be involved with Phillip's disappearance, but police hadn't considered him a suspect.

However, authorities never located Denton's car or his body. A subsequent investigation led to the discovery of missing company money.

Carlos found it hard to believe the Robert Harris he knew was capable committing such a crime. He'd known Robert from their school days. They played football together in junior high and high school.

After he read the article, he laid the newspaper on the kitchen table. His investigator's mind began to churn. How deep did they go with the investigation? What about forensic evidence? Did they question Robert's family and co-workers?

Maria walked into the room. She looked at the newspaper—the front-page article still visible. "Interesting story, huh?"

"You read it?"

"Yes. I didn't know something like that happened here."

"Fortunately, crimes of this magnitude don't often happen in Driscoll Lake."

"Did you know the people involved?"

"I knew both Robert Harris and Madelyn Denton. We were all in school together. Dad wrote to me about the incident when it happened."

"Did you know the other man?"

"Phillip Denton?" Carlos shook his head. "No. He didn't grow up here. Dad said he was a highly decorated Vietnam War vet. Apparently did a lot of things to support the community."

"What do you think?"

"I find it hard to believe Robert Harris would kill anyone or steal money."

"Maybe he didn't do it."

"The evidence seemed clear cut—at least on the surface. I knew the police chief from those days. I wonder if he gave the case the attention it deserved."

"Was he honest?"

"Yes, but he tended to be lazy. In his defense, he wouldn't have had the experience to work a case like that one. He could have called in an outside investigation team to assist, but with a suicide note and admission of guilt, he probably considered it open and shut."

"But you aren't so sure?"

"Based on my knowledge of Robert, no, I'm not. But, then again, I didn't see the evidence."

"Do they still have the case file?"

"Yes, the information would still be available. Technically, until Phillip Denton's body is found, his case is still unsolved—although that wouldn't be in Driscoll Lake's jurisdiction since he disappeared in Fort Worth."

"Why don't you take a look at the file?"

"I might—if I get a chance."

"Humph. You're not that busy. Besides, you have that look on your face."

Carlos reached for Maria's hand. "You know me too well. Maybe I will review the file—if for no other reason than to satisfy my own curiosity."

Chapter Six

Christine Lawrence looked forward to her afternoon break. Much of Driscoll Lake was abuzz with the news of Stephanie's arrival in town. Nobody spoke of her accomplishment as a bestselling author but rather the recent newspaper article about her father.

People inundated Christine with questions throughout the day.

"Didn't you attend school with Stephanie Harris?"

"Why did your husband write that article?"

"I heard you were best friends with Stephanie. Were you surprised to learn about her dad?"

Christine hoped to find the teacher's lounge vacant. She liked to use her off period to prepare lesson plans or grade papers, but today she needed an escape.

She and Stephanie had been best friends. Christine was present when Stephanie learned of her father's death. She remembered thinking how she would have felt if she had been in Stephanie's place.

Christine stood by her side for the next few days, offering to listen, supporting her as best friends do. When people began to accuse Stephanie's mother of having knowledge of the missing money, kids in school began to turn against Stephanie. Christine allowed peer pressure to interfere with their friendship.

In the years that followed, Christine regretted her actions, but never had an opportunity to apologize. She wanted to see Stephanie and ask forgiveness. Kyle said she hadn't acted interested in meeting, but Christine wasn't going to give up easy. Their friendship might not ever be like it once was, but she could at least try to apologize.

Her hope of having a quiet break vanished when she saw two grade teachers in the lounge. She found a table as far away from them as possible, pulled a book from her purse, and began to read. However, she couldn't help but overhear their conversation and found it difficult to concentrate. They sounded like a couple of chattering magpies.

"Did you hear Stephanie Harris is in town?"

"I always wondered why she stayed away all those years. Why did she wait until her aunt died to come back?"

"It's my guess she thinks Helen McKenzie planned to leave her some money. I mean, what else could it be? Stephanie never bothered to visit her when she was alive. Did you happen to see Stephanie's interview a few days ago?"

"No, why?"

"She had the audacity to say her father was innocent."

"You're kidding me!"

"Can you believe the timing of that newspaper article? I wonder if Helen read it before she died. Do you think that could have contributed to her heart attack?"

Christine rolled her eyes and reached into her purse for her iPod and ear buds—hoping the music would help drown the conversation. It didn't work.

After a few minutes, one of them called out. "Hey, Christine."

Christine did her best to ignore her, but Nadine was persistent. "Christine. I asked you a question."

She removed the earplugs and asked, "What did you say?" She'd heard Nadine's words but tried to feign indifference.

"I asked if you and Stephanie Harris were once friends."

"Yes, we were." She placed the device back in her ear, hoping to deter further questions.

"I heard a lot of people turned against Stephanie after the news came about her father stealing money."

Christine didn't bother to answer.

"Why did your husband write that article?"

Christine slammed her book closed and stood up. "Because he's a *reporter*, Nadine." She gathered her things and hurried from the room. Fifteen minutes remained on her break period, and she didn't want to waste the last of it listening to their gossip.

Nor did she care to answer any more questions about Kyle. He'd always had a rather strange fascination with the Harris-Denton case—almost to the degree some people did with the Kennedy assassination. He kept files of newspaper clippings, made copious notes, and was eager to discuss the case with anyone who was interested.

Although she never questioned his reasons, she often thought his interest was more like an obsession. She'd always wondered why but never dared to ask him. Sometimes she wondered if she really wanted to know.

***

Stephanie almost regretted her decision to have a visitation service. Finding the second note troubled her. Anyone could be the person responsible for the messages.

It could be someone with a long-standing grievance against her father.

She considered the possibility someone might think she had knowledge of the money. The notes could be someone's idea of a joke. Stephanie hoped that was the case.

She was grateful Nell and Dan offered to drive her to the funeral home and stay for the entire visitation. Even though she had some misgivings about Matt, she didn't doubt their sincerity. They looked after Helen for several years, and her aunt had never spoken any negative words about either of them.

"Doing okay?" Nell turned to look at Stephanie in the back seat.

"I'm all right." Stephanie twisted her watch. "Why do you ask?"

"You seem a little nervous."

"Guess I am. Some people may not want to see me tonight. Maybe they'll try to run me out of town." Her half-hearted attempt at a joke fell short.

"Why would you think that?"

"Because of my father."

"Nonsense. If someone mistreats you, they'll have to answer to me."

"Nell's right," Dan said. "Why would you think anyone would hold a grudge against you?"

"I—" Someone didn't want her around. She started to mention the notes but changed her mind. There wasn't any reason to involve Nell and Dan. "Guess I'm being silly."

Dan slowed the car as he neared the funeral home. Stephanie was surprised to see several cars already in the parking lot.

"Is there another visitation tonight?"

"Not that I'm aware of," Nell said.

"I'm sure they're here for Helen." Dan pulled the car beneath the canopy. "I'll drop you ladies at the door and find a place to park."

Stephanie opened the car door and took a deep breath. It was time to face the music. She straightened her shoulders and walked inside with Nell.

Several people had already gathered. Stephanie didn't know some of them but recognized a few—the local bank president and his wife, Pat Turner, Miles Parker.

Stephanie had forgotten how life in a small town could be. She smiled when she overheard the conversation of two older women who stood close to the guest register and lamented about never seeing one another unless someone died.

Other people sat on a sofa and chairs in the lounge area, visiting, talking, and reminiscing about "old times." It brought back memories of her childhood. Back then, she was happy to live in a town where everybody knew everybody, neighbors cared for one another, and violent crime was virtually non-existent. All that changed when her father died.

Despite her earlier misgivings, everyone acted cordially. No one mentioned her father and their words of condolences seemed sincere. A few people even inquired about her mother.

Several of Aunt Helen's long-time friends came. Some of them told amusing anecdotes, and others shared their favorite memories. One woman told of how she and Helen had been friends for more than sixty years.

"We met in high school," she said. "Although we lived far apart for much of our lives, our friendship never wavered. Helen stood by me through thick and thin."

The crowd had thinned considerably when a young woman walked through the front door. Stephanie guessed they were about the same age. She had shoulder length strawberry blonde hair, wore slacks, a short-sleeved print blouse, and sandals. As she came nearer, Stephanie recognized the china blue eyes and dimpled chin. It was Christine Lawrence.

Of all the people who turned against her years ago, Christine's betrayal hurt the worst. Kyle had said Christine was sorry, but forgiveness wouldn't be easy. The wound was too deep and too painful even after all these years.

When Christine's eyes met hers, she stopped as if hesitant to come closer. The ball was in Stephanie's court. It would be rude not to acknowledge her. At least Christine had made an effort to come.

Stephanie nodded, and Christine walked to her.

"I'm sorry for your loss."

"Thank you."

Christine cleared her throat. "Mrs. McKenzie was a great lady."

"Yes, she was." Stephanie managed a polite smile but kept her hands clasped behind her back.

"Well, I just wanted to pay my respects. Guess I'll be going now." She turned to walk away.

Stephanie thought she detected a hint of sadness in Christine's eyes. Was it due to her curt responses? Maybe it was hearing the words of Helen's longtime friend, but she couldn't allow Christine to walk away. No matter what happened years ago, the friendship they once shared should count for something. "Christine, wait. Thank you for coming."

Christine turned back, and there was no mistaking the tears in her eyes. "There's something else I need to say. It probably won't make any difference, but I'm sorry for the way I treated you years ago."

"We were young. Emotions were high."

"I was wrong. If you never speak to me again, I wouldn't blame you. I don't deserve forgiveness, but I am sorry for what I did."

"I forgive you." Stephanie was amazed at how easy the words came. A great weight lifted from her shoulders and she pulled Christine into a warm embrace. "You were caught in the middle. I should have realized that. I might have acted the same way, given the situation."

"Thank you." Tears trickled down her cheeks. "It means a lot to hear you say that."

Stephanie reached for a box of tissues sitting on a nearby table and handed one to Christine. "We've all said and done things only to regret them later."

Christine wiped another tear. "I know I have. This isn't the time or place, but I would like to talk some more. Can we get together sometime while you're in town?"

"I'd like that very much."

Christine smiled. "Thank you. Can I reach you at your aunt's number?"

"Yes."

"I'll call you soon."

Stephanie put her arms around her friend. "I look forward to it."

***

Dan insisted on seeing Stephanie to her door when they returned home that evening.

"It's not necessary," Stephanie said. "I can walk next door."

"No, I'm going to make certain you're safe inside. We've had a few burglaries in the area and some cases of criminal mischief. I tried to convince Helen to install a security system, but she didn't think there was a need."

"Criminal mischief?"

"It's most likely kids. Old Mr. Langdon on the next street had a few nasty notes left in his mailbox. He'd called the police on some kids who threw a loud party."

"Oh really?"

"Another woman who lives across the lake reported someone snooping about her place. She said they knocked on her door, but ran away before she could answer. I figure it's kids playing pranks, but one can never be too careful."

Maybe that explained the reason for the notes. Someone knew Helen passed away and heard Stephanie would be in town. It could be someone who knew about the types of books she wrote and decided to have a little fun at her expense.

When she entered the house, she looked to see if more notes were lying around. It was a relief to find everything as she had left it.

Whiskers greeted her by rubbing against her legs and purring loudly.

"Well, Whiskers. I think the notes were in bad taste, but it's good to know someone probably meant them as a joke."

She reasoned that someone slipped both beneath the front door. Matt probably found the first one when he came to check the house the day she arrived and placed it on the kitchen counter.

Stephanie went to bed that night with a lighter heart. No one seemed to care she was back in Driscoll Lake. What happened with her father was in the past, and she intended to leave it there.

Chapter Seven

Mourners filled the sanctuary of Driscoll Lake Community Church for Helen's funeral. Stephanie felt uncomfortable walking into the church for the first time since her father died.

It was a new building and a different pastor, but she recognized many of the people who attended there twenty years ago. It was hard to forget some of the words they had said. She was glad for the support from Nell and Dan.

She looked at the pew where the pallbearers sat. Helen had selected each of them, including Matt. He sat next to the center aisle and looked at her when she entered the church. She nodded her head in acknowledgment.

The pastor seemed to be a kind person. Nell said he moved to the area a few years earlier. If he knew about the scandal with Stephanie's father, he didn't mention it when they met the evening before.

Stephanie glanced around as the soloist began to sing. Flowers and potted plants filled the altar and surrounded the casket. If the number of people in attendance was an indication of their affection toward Helen, she had many friends.

When the song ended, the pastor stood up and walked to the pulpit. "We are gathered here today to honor the life of a much-loved member of our community. Helen Marie McKenzie was born on April 8, 1934. She departed this life on September 10, 2011.

"She endured many hardships and tragedies in her life, but her faith remained strong. Only two weeks ago, we spoke of her daughter, Carol."

Stephanie listed as the minister continued. Per Helen's wishes, several people stood up to tell their special memories. Some stories were sad, others funny, but all of them left no doubt as to how people loved and cared for her.

One person spoke of Helen offering comfort and understanding when she lost her daughter. "She understood like no one else could. She'd been through the same thing."

Another young woman shared how Helen's dedication to teaching younger women was instrumental in helping her refrain from making a wrong decision. A young college-age girl told how Helen had encouraged her to pursue a degree in veterinary medicine. Many others had discouraged her because of the odds of being accepted to an accredited school were high.

Tears came to Stephanie's eyes when Nell stood up and told how Helen talked of the wonderful times she had with Stephanie and their many travel adventures. She would miss those trips and wondered whether she would ever feel the same about traveling again.

After Nell had spoken, the soloist sang "Amazing Grace," and the pastor closed in prayer. When people filed past Stephanie for the final viewing, she recognized several of them, including Kyle Lawrence and Brian Nichols.

One of the last people to walk forward was a young woman, mid-thirties, with auburn hair pulled back at the nape of her neck. She carried herself with an air of sophistication and professionalism.

Stephanie hadn't seen her at the visitation but assumed she attended the same church or perhaps lived in the neighborhood. She paused briefly at the casket, took a tissue from her purse, and dabbed her eyes. When she turned to walk away, Stephanie caught her profile. Even though twenty years had passed, there was no mistake. It was Rachel Jackson—daughter of Madelyn Denton—the woman Stephanie's father murdered.

***

Matt Bradford tried to stay focused on the minister's words but found it difficult to concentrate. His thoughts were on Stephanie.

When she entered the church, he couldn't help but notice what an attractive woman she'd become. She wore a simple black dress that swirled around her long, shapely legs. Her long dark brown hair fell loosely around her shoulders.

She walked with an air of confidence. But had it not been for his parents, Stephanie would have been alone in the family section. Helen often said Kathryn Harris had an intense dislike of Driscoll Lake since the incident with her husband. Still, Matt thought she could have put aside her feelings and come to support her daughter.

He caught a flicker of sadness in Stephanie's eyes at the mention of her father's name, but she smiled when the minister told an amusing story. It was hard to discern the look on her face when she saw Rachel Jackson.

The burial service was brief. When Dan Bradford escorted Stephanie to the gravesite, she had to walk beside her father's grave. Matt noticed she never wavered or looked at the headstone. He wondered how she felt about the man whose actions tore her life apart.

When the service was over, Matt placed his boutonniere on the coffin and joined the other pallbearers in offering condolences to Stephanie.

"I'm sorry," he said. The words seemed shallow—a cursory offering of sympathy.

"Thank you." She whispered the words but quickly averted her eyes.

He'd been unfair to her. Caught up in his own selfish thoughts, he didn't stop to consider how she might feel. Who was he to question her motives? In judging her, he was no different from Curtis Lawrence or Madge Sinclair.

Stephanie was only fourteen years old and had no choice than to leave Driscoll Lake with her mother. As an adult, she could have chosen to return, but given the way many people treated her, he couldn't blame her for staying away. How would he have felt if it seemed like the whole town turned against him and his parents? He probably wouldn't have come back either.

He'd acted like a jerk toward her the day she arrived. His half-hearted attempt at making conversation the following morning didn't constitute an apology. Stephanie's arrival had stirred up long dormant emotions within him. Someday he might tell her the truth, but for now, he needed to apologize. He hoped she would listen.

***

Wednesday was unusually quiet at police headquarters. The telephone hardly rang all morning. Except for a few traffic violations and a minor accident, the patrol officers were bored for lack of anything to do. Carlos Gonzales guessed it had something to do with the hot weather—people stayed inside and therefore kept out of trouble.

Matt phoned him at noon. "Anything going on?"

"No. Everything's under control."

"I just left Helen McKenzie's funeral. I think I'll take the rest of the day off."

"Glad to hear that. You work too much."

"What else is there to do?"

"You know the answer. Relax and get some rest. I know where to reach you if needed."

"Okay, I'll see you tomorrow."

Carlos decided the afternoon would be a good time to look at the files on the deaths of Robert Harris and Madelyn Denton. After a quick lunch, he rose from his desk and went into the archive room. Old cases were arranged alphabetically and by date.

It didn't take him long to locate both files. He was surprised to find them rather thin. He had expected them to be larger. Carlos took both to his office, closed the door, and began to read.

He first opened the file on Robert Harris. A janitor found the bodies when the cleaning crew came in that evening. Robert was slumped over his desk. Madelyn Denton's body lay on the floor near the office door.

The janitor stated he immediately called the police. Except for the cleaning crew, no one else was in the building or the adjacent factory. The plant had closed for weekend maintenance after the last of the day shift workers left at four. That afternoon, Robert had told his secretary he would be working late and would lock up the office.

A typed suicide note with Robert's signature was in the file. According to the report, police found it on Robert's desk. The note was brief, apologizing to his wife and declaring his love for her and their daughter.

Carlos read the autopsy report next. Harris died from a single gunshot wound to the head from a 32-caliber handgun. The point of entry was the right temple. The autopsy report concluded the wound was self-inflicted.

The murder weapon matched the serial number of a gun belonging to Robert Harris. Kathryn Harris confirmed Robert bought the gun several months earlier after a rash of break-ins at area businesses in Driscoll Lake and surrounding areas. She told investigators after a businessman was shot and killed in Brewster, he said he felt safer with the gun.

The file on Madelyn Denton was even thinner. She died from a gunshot to the chest, fired from the same gun. The point of entry was near the heart. According to the autopsy report, she died instantly. Investigators concluded Robert killed Madelyn and then turned the gun on himself.

Carlos turned back to the Harris file. On the surface, the evidence appeared cut and dry. Robert Harris was guilty. Powder marks on his hand indicated he fired the weapon. However, Carlos thought the investigation seemed shoddy at best.

Other than Kathryn's statement about the gun, there were no notes in the file to indicate the police interviewed fellow employees or family members. Questions remained unanswered. Had Robert Harris been despondent? Did anyone else see him in the building after his secretary left? Why was Madelyn Denton at the office that evening?

He shook his head. Although he found nothing that warranted reopening the case, Carlos couldn't shake the feeling there was a smoking gun somewhere. Something didn't add up.

After Robert and Madelyn died, an outside consulting firm audited the company's financial records and discovered several million dollars of company funds missing, including the employee retirement fund.

Once again, Robert Harris appeared guilty. Carlos's father told him some people in town speculated his wife Kathryn had knowledge of the embezzlement scheme, but it was only hearsay. No one found evidence of her involvement.

The FBI handled the embezzlement case. Carlos knew some of the agents in the Brewster office. He considered calling one of them, but he had no reason to at this point. There wasn't any new evidence to report.

He then turned his attention to finding information regarding Phillip Denton. His last known whereabouts was in Fort Worth. Rather than contacting the Fort Worth police, Carlos decided to search the Internet for information. He found several newspaper articles.

Denton disappeared after returning from a business trip a few weeks before Madelyn and Robert died. He boarded a plane in Los Angeles and arrived at DFW at 10:30 p.m. At approximately 10:50, he phoned his wife from the airport to say his plane arrived late and that he expected to be home around 2:00 a.m.

He never made it home. He used his credit card to purchase fuel at a convenience store near the airport. A surveillance camera showed him alone inside the store at approximately 11:30. The attendant reported seeing Denton talking to another man outside, but wasn't sure if they left together. He wasn't even able to give a description and stated, "It appeared to be only a casual conversation."

It was the last time anyone saw Phillip Denton alive. A few days later, a rancher northwest of Fort Worth found bloody clothing, a bloodstained briefcase, and a wallet containing Denton's driver's license. The wallet was empty of cash, and Denton's wife stated he often carried large sums of money. His credit cards were still inside. DNA tests later determined the blood was Denton's, but an extensive search yielded no other evidence. Police never located his car or a body.

Carlos shook his head. His instincts told him there was more to this case than what was on the surface. He couldn't shake the feeling there was something important he wasn't seeing.

Chapter Eight

Stephanie opened the refrigerator and pulled out a bottle of water. Several friends and neighbors had brought casserole dishes, vegetables, and desserts. There was no way she'd ever be able to eat all the food.

She reached for her cell phone and called Nell's number. "Would you and Dan like to come for dinner? I have enough food for a small army."

"Oh, that sounds lovely," Nell said, "but I had already invited Matt for dinner."

Stephanie bit her lower lip. "That's okay. He's welcome too." She didn't exactly look forward to seeing him after the way he'd acted Sunday evening, but today he had been cordial. The last thing she wanted was to hurt Nell's feelings by not including him. She and Dan had gone out of their way to help her through an otherwise difficult time.

"I'm sure he'd be glad to join us."

"Then I'll see you at six. And please dress casually."

Stephanie took the bottled water into the den. She kicked off her sling-back pumps, sat down on the sofa, and propped her feet on the coffee table. The mid-day heat was excruciating. She'd spent less than a half-hour outdoors but felt wiped out. Mid-September was too late for triple digit temperatures—even in Texas. A refreshing shower was in order, but for now, she needed some time to relax.

Whiskers jumped on the sofa and nudged her arm with his head. Recognizing the gesture as a sign of affection, she reached and scratched him behind the ears. He rewarded her with a loud purr before jumping off the sofa and strolling to the kitchen. In a few seconds, she heard a crunching sound as he nibbled on his food.

She sighed. Now that the funeral was over, it was time to get down to business. Tomorrow she could begin to sort through Helen's personal things. She would probably want to keep a few items, but she had no use for the clothes and furniture.

Whiskers presented another dilemma. Stephanie didn't know of anyone who might want him. Nell seemed fond of the cat, but it wouldn't be feasible for her to own a pet. She and Dan spent too much time away from home. Even if it meant taking him back to Denver, Stephanie refused to relinquish him to an animal shelter.

Stephanie took a sip of water and reached for her laptop. She opened the writing software program and spent most of the afternoon working on her manuscript.

At five, she took a quick shower and then went into the kitchen to prepare for dinner. She set four places at the table, turned the on the oven to heat a dish of lasagna, and began assembling a salad.

The doorbell rang at a quarter to six. When she opened the door, Matt stood outside. He was dressed in denim shorts, sandals, and a blue t-shirt that brought out the color of his eyes. His hair was damp as if he had recently showered. Damn, but he looked good.

"Matt, how are you?"

"I'm okay. I know I'm early, but I wanted to talk to you. Can I come in?"

"Of course." Stephanie led the way to the den. "Please have a seat. Would you like something to drink?"

"No, thanks. I'm all right."

He sat in a chair near the windows and Stephanie sat opposite him on the sofa.

Matt leaned forward, his elbows resting on his knees, and his hands clasped. "I want to apologize for the way I've acted. I haven't treated you right."

Her lips parted, and she quietly exhaled. Matt's words were a relief, but she remained silent. She was curious as to what he would say next.

"There's no excuse for the way I acted. I had a lot on my mind the day you arrived, but I shouldn't have taken it out on you."

A slow smile crept across her face. "I wasn't exactly cordial, either. I was tired from the trip. Not to mention being hot in those clothes and wishing I chosen something more comfortable to wear.

"Oh yeah?"

"I'm much more comfortable in a pair of jeans than I am in Prada."

Matt laughed. "Sounds like my kind of girl."

Stephanie raised her eyebrows.

Matt's face colored. "I mean—I hope you'll forgive me."

"Of course, I do. To be honest, I was surprised at the way you acted. You weren't the Matt Bradford I remembered."

"Well, if you stick around, I'll—" He stopped at the sound of the buzzer on the oven.

Stephanie got up from the sofa. "Sorry. I need to check the lasagna."

In the kitchen, she pondered Matt's words. My kind of girl. If you stick around? What had he been about to say? And why was the thought of getting to know him better so appealing?

***

Rachel Jackson exited the hospital and walked slowly toward the parking garage. It had been a long and frustrating afternoon. Six new admissions—two patients critical. She had to deal with a belligerent patient who frequently refused to follow orders and insisted upon an early discharge. Rachel knew his history. He would be back in a few days.

Later, a forty-four- year-old construction worker and father of four arrived at the emergency room in full cardiac arrest. He didn't survive. The hardest part of her day came when she had to tell a sixty-two-year-old grandmother her condition was terminal. Although trained to deal with this type of circumstance, she found it the hardest part of her job.

The patient and her husband had recently retired and looked forward to spending time with their eight grandchildren. They'd counted on having at least fifteen or twenty years left. She had ninety days at best. Sixty-two was not old—not much older than Rachel's mother would have been.

Rachel often wondered what life would have been like had her mother lived. She found it difficult to imagine Madelyn at age sixty. In Rachel's mind, she would always be forty.

The twentieth anniversary of the murder had been painful. Today, after attending Helen McKenzie's funeral, old memories flooded back. There were times when she wondered if moving back to this area had been a wise decision. Today was one of them.

She unlocked her SUV and climbed inside. She didn't want to go home to an empty house, so she drove to a favorite Mexican restaurant. She hated the thought of being alone tonight. A crowded restaurant was the next best thing to having family or friends around.

The hostess seated her near a window. After she placed her order, she thought about Helen. Rachel didn't often attend the funerals of her patients, but she'd come to have a special affection for her.

She had been Helen's attending physician several times over the past few months. They never talked about the past except Helen said she would understand if Rachel would rather not have her as a patient.

Once Rachel assured her the past wouldn't matter, they eased into a comfortable doctor-patient relationship. Helen never mentioned her nephew again until the day she died. Something had her upset.

She kept mumbling words about Robert Harris being innocent. She seemed almost desperate to make someone listen to her words. Rachel replayed the scene in her mind.

Helen was short of breath, and her words were difficult to understand. "Robert... didn't kill... He's... innocent. Journal."

"Mrs. McKenzie, don't try to talk now. You need to rest. You'll feel much better after we get some of the fluid off your lungs."

"No... have to... tell you. Rachel, you need to... know..." She struggled to breathe, her voice barely above a whisper. "I think he's... alive..."

Rachel patted her hand. "Mrs. McKenzie, you need to remain calm."

"No. Please tell... Stephanie... to look..."

A monitor indicated Helen's heart rate had increased. She seemed to make her words clear.

"Please. You need rest now. I'll come back later when you're feeling better. I promise we'll talk then."

She never had the chance. The next time she entered the room was with a code team when Helen was in full cardiac arrest.

Why was she so distressed? Rachel assumed she was trying to convince her Robert Harris wasn't the killer.

She puzzled over Helen's words, "He's alive." Did she believe her nephew wasn't dead? She didn't take any drugs that would cause hallucinations and she'd never shown signs of dementia.

The server returned with her food, interrupting her thoughts. She ate her meal in silence and lingered longer than necessary, dreading going home alone to a big, empty house.

***

Stephanie slept late on Thursday, having stayed up past midnight. She was tired from all the activities of the past few days and decided to take the entire day to rest. Sorting through Aunt Helen's things could wait another day.

The atmosphere at dinner the evening before was much different from the day she arrived. Matt joined in the conversation and seemed much more relaxed.

When dinner was over, Stephanie said, "Why don't we have dessert on the screened in porch?" There's a nice breeze from the lake. I can brew some coffee."

"I'll help." Nell followed Stephanie into the kitchen, while Matt and his father went outside.

"Thanks for coming to dinner," Stephanie said. "I really didn't want to spend the evening alone."

"I enjoyed it very much." Nell looked outside where the men sat talking. "I haven't seen Matt this relaxed in some time. Not since his wife died."

"He was married?"

"Yes. Tara died in a car accident a few years ago. Matt had a hard time dealing with her death."

"I see." Matt hadn't mentioned the fact he'd been married. Then again, until this afternoon they had barely been on speaking terms. There was no reason for either of them to talk about their private lives.

Stephanie remained awake long after everyone went home. Her mind was on her aunt, and couldn't help but think she'd let her down. Why was it so important for Stephanie to come to her funeral?

She thought of the letter. Although Aunt Helen said she didn't blame Stephanie for not returning, between the lines Stephanie saw a lonely woman. A woman without any family members left who did her best to be content with surrounding herself with friends.

Stephanie realized she shouldn't have listened to her mother all those years. Even today, Stephanie could sense animosity and bitterness in her. So far, everyone here had been kind—coming back was nothing like she expected.

Driscoll Lake had never been her mother's home. Kathryn had no ties to the community. Even in the best of circumstances, she would have eventually found a way to return to Atlanta.

Stephanie had family here. There hadn't been any reason for her not to visit. She could have come when Carol died. Her mother should have told her about Uncle George's death. Aunt Helen was all alone with no family to comfort her.

In the early evening, Stephanie poured a glass of iced tea and went outside to sit on the porch. A mockingbird called from a nearby tree. Its sweet song belied its aggressive behavior. Stephanie had often seen them attack larger birds as well as animals and even humans. Mockingbirds weren't afraid to face their giants.

Stephanie rose from her chair and walked to the edge of the porch to look at the lake. The back yard was as lovely as the front one. San Augustine grass covered the yard as it sloped away from the house. A white gazebo stood near the shoreline, surrounded by a variety of rose bushes.

She opened the screen door and walked down the path toward the dock. She stood for a few minutes looking over the lake. Even though she had spent most of her adult life away from Driscoll Lake, she felt more at home here than any place she had lived.

"Stephanie, would you like to join me?"

She looked up to see Nell Bradford sitting on her deck.

"I'd like that."

She walked the short distance to Nell's house and sat in a lounge chair.

"I love to come out here in the early mornings and late in the evening," Nell said.

"It's so peaceful. We used to spend time here when I was younger. I never imagined it ever being more than a place for weekend cabins. I can see why people choose to live here."

"George and Helen are responsible for us purchasing our lot. They were good neighbors. I sure will miss her." Nell brushed back a tear.

"Nell." Stephanie paused and looked toward the lake where a heron waded near the shore. "Did Aunt Helen ever talk about me visiting her? I mean before she asked for me that last day."

"Not except to say she understood why you wouldn't want to come. Why do you ask?"

"She left a letter with Miles Parker and instructed him not to give it to me until after her death. She said she understood my reasons for not coming back here. She also said she had hoped to live long enough to see my father proven innocent."

"I see. She didn't talk about your father often. She told me once it had been hard to accept his guilt. The day she died was the first time I heard her mention the possibility of him being innocent."

Stephanie turned to look at Nell. "She said that?"

"Yes. Her breathing was labored and she struggled to talk, but she mentioned Carol and something about a journal. That's when she said Robert was innocent and asked for you to come."

"That's it? She didn't say why she changed her mind?"

"No. I'm sorry."

"Something must have happened between the time she wrote the letter and her death."

"Maybe she just was expressing her hope of his innocence."

"Could be. It just seems strange to me."

"What do you think?"

"I believe he was guilty—even though I said otherwise on that TV show." Stephanie shook her head. "Deep down I've often wished some new evidence would surface that could prove his innocence. Mom and I had a lot of unanswered questions. I wish I knew the entire story—even if the truth hurts."

Nell reached out and patted Stephanie's hand. "Both Dan and I found it hard to believe your father was capable of murder."

"I've decided to stay in Driscoll Lake a while longer. I'm more than halfway through with another novel and can write as easily here as in Denver. I need to sort through Aunt Helen's things and decide what to do with the house. Once the court probates her will, I'll talk to a real estate agency about putting the house on the market."

"Don't rush into anything. Before you decide, make sure it's what you want. Lakefront lots sell fast here. I would hate to see you make a quick decision and then regret it."

"I can't imagine ever returning to here to live, but I won't make any hasty decisions. A week ago, I never dreamed of coming back, but for some reason, I don't want to leave right away."

"I'm glad to hear you say that. It won't be as lonely having you next door for a while."

Stephanie returned to Helen's house, feeling good about her decision. It made sense to stay a while rather than necessitate making return trips to finalize the estate. When she walked into the house, Whiskers met her at the door. His loud meow left little doubt he was hungry.

"Whiskers, it looks like I'm going to be here a while longer. What do you think of that?"

He rubbed against her legs. When she bent down to pet him, he reached out his paw.

She laughed. "Guess that's my answer. If Whiskers approves, I must be doing the right thing."

Chapter Nine

The early morning air was a bit cooler as Stephanie stepped outside to begin her run. Now that she planned to stay for a while, she could track the distance and maybe even find a few alternate routes.

She did a few stretches before starting out. As she had done the first day, she turned left out of the driveway and followed Lakeside Drive. A construction crew was already busy at the house across the street.

She passed another jogger. The young woman smiled and nodded her head, ear buds in place. Although Stephanie would sometimes listen to her iPod while running, she preferred to hear the sounds of nature—especially in the early morning.

When she neared the north end of the lake, she saw Matt jogging toward her. Her pulse quickened.

She slowed her pace and watched as he approached—taking note of his muscular arms and legs. He looked more like an athlete than a police officer. Then again, Matt had always been athletic—even in high school.

Upon reaching Stephanie, he stopped. "Hey. I had hoped to see you out this morning. I've missed you the past couple of days."

"I didn't do much of anything yesterday, but it's time to get back to my routine. If I go several days without running, I tend to get lazy."

"What's your game plan? It's a little more than two miles around the lake."

"I wondered about that."

"I usually run the distance."

"My goal is two miles each day."

"Let's run together. I can change course. You've already run almost a mile."

"As long as you don't go off and leave me. I'm not sure I can keep up with someone as tall as you."

Matt looked at her. His gaze lingered for a moment on her legs. "I think you can keep up."

They ran for another half-hour, stopping on the opposite side of the lake from Helen's house.

"Thirsty?" Matt asked.

"Yeah. Now that I plan to be here a while, I need to get used to the heat."

"You've changed your mind about staying?"

"It doesn't make sense to go back to Denver only to have to return later. One advantage of being a writer is that I can do it from anywhere."

"I'm glad you decided to stay. My house is only a couple of hundred yards further. We can stop there for water."

"Sounds like a great idea. Foolish of me not to bring any. Next time, I'll be more prepared."

Matt turned off Lakeside Drive and onto a street leading away from the lake. The area had fewer houses, and the lots were larger than those on the lake. They ran up a slight incline before he stopped. "This is it."

Stephanie looked at the wooded lot. Matt had left it in a more natural state, which somehow appealed to her more than a manicured lawn. A long, curved driveway led to a two-story log cabin. "Wow," Stephanie said. "It's gorgeous."

"You like the rustic look?

"Yes. My dream is to own a log house someday—preferably beside a lake or near the mountains.

"You won't find any mountains here, but come inside. I'll give you the grand tour."

The lot behind Matt's house sloped away toward a creek. The back yard had more trees, which allowed for privacy. The cabin had lots of windows, a wrap-around covered porch, and a hot tub in back. The detached garage allowed unobstructed views from all sides. They entered through a side door.

Stephanie loved the natural interior and open floor plan. "Nice. I like it."

"Thanks," Matt said. "It's not fancy, but its home." He reached into the refrigerator, pulled out two bottles of water, and handed one to Stephanie.

She walked toward the front windows. The living room had a corner fireplace with a fieldstone hearth. Stephanie could envision sitting by the fire on a cold winter evening.

Stairs led to an upstairs bedroom with an open sitting area on the opposite end. Stephanie thought it would be a perfect writing spot. It had plenty of room for a desk, along with space that could be used for reading.

She turned and saw Matt watching her. "Penny for your thoughts."

"I, uh. Gathering ideas. Like I said, I'd like to own a cabin someday."

"A three-bedroom house is bigger than what I need, but I lived in a small apartment far too long. Several people have expressed a desire to buy it, but I can't bring myself to sell."

"I don't blame you." Stephanie took a sip of water. "I guess I should go. I have an appointment later this morning and need to run some errands. You probably want to get ready for work."

"I'm taking the day off. People tell me I work too much."

"Do you?"

Matt grinned. "Maybe. Carlos can handle anything that comes up. He'll call if he needs me.

"Who is Carlos?"

"A new detective I recently hired. He worked as a homicide investigator for thirty years in San Diego. Used to live here and moved back to be close to his parents. Said he was bored and came to me about working part time. I'm lucky to have him."

He picked up a key from the kitchen counter. "I intended to bring this to you the other day. It's a spare key to Helen's house. She kept it under a flowerpot. I used it to get in the house the day you arrived and forgot to give it back."

Stephanie frowned. "Oh. Okay."

"It's not a good idea to hide keys, but apparently Mom couldn't convince Helen otherwise."

"Sometimes I think she was too trusting." Stephanie glanced at the clock. "Guess I should be going."

"I'll drive you home. I have some business in Brewster, but I'll be back for the football game tonight. Would you like to go with me?"

"No, thanks. I appreciate the offer, but I don't think I could handle it. I haven't been to a football game since the night my father died."

***

Rachel Jackson welcomed her day off. She intended to sleep in—weary after being on call all week. However, she was wide-awake at 6:00 a.m. After fighting a losing battle to return to sleep, she got out of bed, dressed, and made her way downstairs to the kitchen.

She reached into the cabinet for her favorite coffee mug, placed it on the Keurig, and selected a morning blend. Less than a minute later, she had a steaming cup of coffee in her hand.

Rachel went outside to the patio. Most days she enjoyed a few laps in the pool before leaving for the hospital, but for now, she was content to sit quietly and absorb the early morning sounds.

She couldn't pinpoint what it was that had caused her to feel so melancholy. Maybe it was thinking about her mother's death, the newspaper article, or Helen McKenzie's dying words. It could be a combination of all those things, although she suspected it was due to seeing Stephanie. It brought back too many memories of how others had treated her. Rachel had done nothing to stop their cruel behavior.

She admired Stephanie for coming back home. It may have taken her twenty years, but she was here. It didn't matter what people had said in the past or what some might say today. That took courage.

Rachel realized she had been unwilling to let go of the past. After her mother's death, she went to live with her father in Austin. The trust fund her grandfather Cameron had set up for her took care of her college education and medical school. As sole heir, she inherited the family home as well as the property where the old factory once stood.

The trust administrator arranged for caregivers to live in and maintain the house. When Rachel turned twenty-five and came into full control of the trust, she was reluctant to sell any of the Cameron properties. The first Cameron ancestor to move to Texas had homesteaded the land. Her great-grandfather, Lucas Cameron, built the house for his new bride.

When she returned to the area to take a staff position at the hospital in Brewster, she decided to move back into the family home. After living in it for several months, she realized the house was too big. Too lonely. Too empty.

Maybe it was time to make a change. The real estate market was booming in Driscoll Lake. She felt sure she'd have no trouble selling the house and surrounding property.

As a single woman with no immediate prospects of marriage and a family, she didn't need a large home. The horse stables were vacant and unused—she hadn't ridden for many years. She considered leasing the stables and surrounding pastures but didn't want people around on a consistent basis. Rachel valued her privacy.

Her decision to sell the factory had been easy. The building had sat vacant since the plant closed. Many people thought of it as an eyesore. When Brian Nichols expressed interest in the property, she jumped at the idea. An out of state firm, C. R. Investments, also inquired about purchasing the factory.

It wasn't the first time they asked. Shortly after Rachel began medical school, a real estate agent representing them contacted her. She was too busy to think about making a decision and refused to sell.

They inquired a second time after she entered residency. They were persistent. Earlier in the summer, they made a third offer. The price was well above the market value but included the stipulation she would include the mineral rights in the sale. She didn't know the people or know what they intended to do with the property. Brian's offer was much less, but more in line with the current market value. He wasn't interested in the mineral rights, but wanted to restore the buildings.

"I don't care what's below the ground," he said. "I care what's above it. With the right renovations, it would make a nice place for a restaurant and specialty stores. The buildings have a long history in Driscoll Lake, so I would be careful to preserve the historical aspects."

Rachel liked the idea of someone local owning the place, although she stood to make more money by selling it to C. R. Investments. Brian had worked hard to establish his business and build up trust with the community. Lord knew he got a bad rap because of his drunken father and his past escapades, but he was a far different person than the teenage would-be juvenile delinquent she'd known years ago.

Retaining the mineral rights was a smart move, should she ever need more cash. Rachel shook her head. Money wasn't a problem. A wave of sadness swept over her. "I'm a trust fund girl and a doctor. And all alone with no one to spend my money on."

She looked toward the empty stables. I probably should sell this property. This would be a perfect place for someone to train or breed horses. Not to mention it would be an ideal home for someone with children. It doesn't look like I'll ever have any of my own.

The temperature was already starting to climb, so she went into the house and changed into her swimsuit. Then hurried back outside and dove into the pool.

The water was warm but nonetheless refreshing. Rachel swam the length of the pool twice and then turned on her back to float. Her melancholy mood brightened, and she felt she could face the day with a lighter heart. After a half hour, she climbed out of the pool and toweled off. She looked toward the house. A smaller home in a gated community would serve her better. Lakeview Estates was a beautiful area—she was certain to find something suited to her needs.

But she was hesitant. The house and land were the last of the original Cameron properties. She didn't want to make any rash decisions only to regret them later. "Maybe someday I'll decide to sell. But not today."

***

It was after eight when Matt dropped Stephanie at her house. While she unlocked the door, the telephone rang, and she hurried inside to answer it.

"Ms. Harris, this is Heather Stevens from Parker and Davis."

"How can I help you?"

"An urgent matter came up, and Mr. Parker won't be able to meet with you today. He understands you may not be in town much longer, but said he could discuss matters by phone if necessary. Otherwise, it will be next week before he can see you."

"Next week is fine. I've decided to stay here a while longer."

"I guess Mr. Parker misunderstood. He was under the impression you planned to leave right away."

"That was my original plan, but I changed my mind."

"I see. He's available on Monday afternoon at two. Will that work for you?"

"That's fine. Thanks for calling."

Stephanie hung up the phone and hurried to shower and change clothes. Now that she didn't have to drive into town, she had some time for writing. She made a strawberry smoothie and fed Whiskers before taking her laptop to the breakfast nook.

She placed her fingers on the keyboard and stared at the blank page. The words didn't flow. After a while, she gave up and closed the laptop.

Helen's letter was on the small desk in the den. Stephanie picked it up and read through it again.

I had hoped to live long enough to see your father's name cleared. Although I accepted his guilt, I often questioned whether the original investigation was thorough. Deep down I never gave up hope some new evidence would turn up to exonerate him. I guess that will never happen.

What made her suddenly think he was innocent?

Whiskers rubbed his head against Stephanie's leg and hopped on her lap.

"I wish you could talk. Maybe you could tell me something." She thought back to her conversation with Nell the evening before.

"Wait a minute!" She spoke the words so loud that Whiskers jumped down from her lap. He looked indignant that she dared to disturb him. "Nell said something about a journal."

Stephanie dialed Nell's number and hardly gave her time to say hello. "Tell me again what Aunt Helen said about a journal?"

"She said it belonged to Carol. Helen was short of breath and talked in broken sentences, but she acted like it was important for you to find it."

"Did she ever mention this before?"

"No, that was the first and only time."

"She didn't say anything to me on our last trip. We talked about Carol, so I think she would have mentioned it. The journal must have something in it that caused her to change her mind about Dad."

"Then she must have read it recently. Dan and I were out of town for a few weeks. We didn't return home until the day before she died."

"There has to be a connection. Carol was living in Driscoll Lake at the time Dad died. Maybe she knew something."

"If that was the case, don't you think she would have told someone?"

"Yes, I do, but I'm still going to look. I'll talk to you later."

Stephanie hung up the phone and looked around the room. Helen had several bookshelves, all of them full, but Stephanie doubted she would put the journal there.

She opened the lap drawer of the desk. A legal pad was on top with some notes in Helen's handwriting. Stephanie pulled it out and began to read.

Robert died September 13. Carol saw someone at the lake. Saw same man a few years later. Carol thought she could prove Robert's innocence? Need to call Lisa Duncan. Asked if Carol talked to her.

"Lisa Duncan? Wonder who she is." Stephanie continued to read. At the bottom of the page, Helen wrote in bold letters. *Should have read her journals a long time ago. Answer may be in one of them.*

"The journal has to be here somewhere." Stephanie looked through the drawer again. Toward the back, beneath a stack of papers, she found a leather-bound book with the word journal inscribed on the front. She opened it to the first page, dated January 1, 1996.

The year Carol died.

Chapter Ten

Stephanie took the journal to the sofa and opened it to the first page. The first entries contained stories about Carol's arrival in South America. She skimmed the first few pages.

January 1

New Year. New beginnings. It's taken me several years and a lot of therapy, but I feel I'm finally over the PTSD. Arrived in South America on Saturday. Can't wait to look around. Excited about starting a new job tomorrow.

January 5

I like my new roommate. Her name is Lisa Duncan. She's outgoing and fun-loving but takes her job seriously. She'll show me the ropes here.

That answered the question about Lisa Duncan's identity. Stephanie wondered if Helen had spoken with her recently. She scanned the remaining pages for any reference to her father.

June 1

It's been over five years since the accident took Jeff's life. A part of me died also. The PTSD nearly destroyed me. Years of counseling have helped. I've had a few setbacks along the way, but I feel as if a dark cloud has finally lifted.

Carol was on assignment in Kuwait during the Persian Gulf War when a land mine exploded killing her fiancé and three others. She witnessed the accident. When doctors diagnosed her with Post-Traumatic Stress Disorder, she spent several weeks in a hospital before returning to Driscoll Lake during the summer of 1991.

Stephanie recalled how Carol kept to herself the first few weeks. She often stayed at the lake house and refused to see anyone except for family. There were times when she seemed to zone out, but by the end of summer, she started to open up.

June 5

I love my job here in South America. No more covering wars for me. The people here are friendly. Many of them live in poverty, but they are happy. I think we could learn something from them.

June 15

I saw a man today—one that reminded me of the man at the lake. His face is different, but he's about the same age and height as the man I saw the night of Bob's death. I never told anyone, because I was afraid people would think I was crazy.

June 16

I saw him again. We made brief eye contact, but I don't believe he knows me. There's something about him—I'm certain it's the man from the lake. Why is he here? I wish Lisa was around, but she left yesterday on an assignment. I can tell her everything. She'll understand.

June 17

I'm not imagining things. Today is the third time I've seen him. People thought he was dead, but he's alive. There's no other explanation. He's the person I saw at the lake—I'm sure of it now. I should have said something, but people would have thought I was having flashbacks or worse—hallucinations. Back then, I questioned my sanity. Things might be different today if I had talked.

June 20

A man asked about me at the office while I was out. He didn't give his name—said he was an old friend and wanted to surprise me. He asked them for my address, but they refused to give out personal information.

I asked the receptionist to describe him. It's the man I've been seeing. Why is he asking about me? How does he even know who I am? I should probably go to the police, but I have to leave early in the morning for Costa Rica. I wish I could talk with Lisa. I'm frightened, but everything should be okay until I get back. Lisa will advise me on what to do.

The rest of the journal was blank. Stephanie did a quick mental calculation. She had finished her first year of college and had gone home for the summer when Carol died. They had been to dinner to celebrate her mother's birthday when they got the call informing them of Carol's death. It was June 21.

Stephanie picked up the legal pad. *Plane crash may not have been an accident. I believe someone killed Carol.*

She furrowed her brow. What had Aunt Helen meant? Did she think someone sabotage the plane? Stephanie didn't know much about the accident, but perhaps she could learn more through an Internet search. She opened her computer. It didn't take long to get some hits about the crash. She clicked on a link to the initial news story.

The chartered plane left the airport route to Costa Rica with five people aboard, including the pilot. It lost power shortly after takeoff and crashed in the nearby hills. She read other stories about the investigation. After several months, investigators determined the cause of the accident to be mechanical failure. The charter company had several previous citations due to maintenance issues.

Stephanie knew the FBI traced the stolen money to South America before they lost track of it. Carol was in South America. Was there a connection between the missing money and the person she saw?

The crash probably was an accident, but Carol was afraid of something. Who was the man she saw? Stephanie looked back at Helen's notes. *Need to call Carlos Gonzales. Doubt the initial investigation was thorough. Maybe he can find something they missed.*

Carlos Gonzales was the detective Matt mentioned earlier. Without giving the matter a second thought, Stephanie picked up her phone, dialed the police station, and asked to speak to him.

***

Stephanie hesitated outside Carlos Gonzales's door. The thoughts of a dying woman and a few journal entries didn't warrant opening a twenty-year-old case. Now that she'd had time to think it over, her call to him was a bit impulsive. However, he had agreed to see her, so she might as well go through with the meeting.

He stood and extended his hand when she entered his office. She guessed him to be about the same age as her father.

"Thank you for agreeing to see me on such short notice. This won't take long."

"That's quite all right. By the way, I'm sorry for your loss. Mrs. McKenzie was a wonderful person."

"Thank you. It's because of my aunt that I'm here."

Carlos raised his eyebrows. "Oh?"

"I don't know if you are aware of what happened twenty years ago with my father. He committed suicide after murdering Madelyn Denton, the owner of Cameron Manufacturing."

"I did know. I grew up in Driscoll Lake but lived away at the time. My father told me about the incident."

"Aunt Helen left a letter for me with her attorney. Most of it was personal, but she also referenced my father. Said she had hoped to live long enough to see him proved innocent. She wrote it three weeks before her death." Stephanie paused and looked to him for affirmation.

"Go on."

"The day she died, Aunt Helen told Nell Bradford she believed my father was innocent. According to Nell, Aunt Helen always said she had a hard time accepting his guilt. Something happened to make her change her mind.

"I see. Have any idea what?"

"She said something about a journal belonging to her daughter, Carol. I found it today. Before I read it, I believed my father was guilty. Now, I'm starting to have doubts. At the least, I have questions."

"Why is that?"

"Carol lived in South America when she wrote the journal. Were you aware that's the last place the FBI tracked the missing money?"

"Yes, I was."

"She saw a man there a few days before she died. Became convinced she'd seen him at the lake around the time of Dad's death. She didn't give a name, but she was afraid of this man. I think there's a connection to my father and maybe even the missing money."

"I see." Carlos took a legal pad from his desk. "Please continue."

Stephanie told him about the contents of the journal. "I realize it's not much, but this person frightened Carol.

Aunt Helen even wrote that she feared the plane crash wasn't an accident."

He shook his head. "It's interesting, but still not much to go on. Do you know for sure Carol was talking about your father? She could have been referring to someone else named Bob."

"Yes, I'm sure. Carol always called him Bob. As for the lake, she had to have been talking about here. She often stayed at the lake house around the time of Dad's death."

Carlos leaned back in his chair and crossed his arms. "I'll be honest. I knew both your father and your cousin Carol. I found it hard to believe he was capable of murder. I read Kyle Lawrence's article a few days ago, so I decided to look at the old case file. From what I read, the evidence supports a murder-suicide. You realize your father left a note."

"Yes, we were told he confessed."

"Without something more concrete, there isn't enough evidence to reopen the case. I'm sorry."

"I was afraid of that, but I understand. Thank you for your time." Stephanie considered mentioning the warning notes she'd found, but decided against it.

"You're welcome."

Stephanie stood and walked to the door. She placed her hand on the knob, but stopped and turned around. "Mr. Gonzales, can I ask you one more thing?"

"Of course."

"Do you think the police did a thorough investigation? My aunt insinuated that might not have been the case."

He hesitated before answering. "I might have done things a bit differently, but I didn't see any blatant mistakes. The FBI investigated the stolen money, so I have no jurisdiction there. Fort Worth police handled the missing person's report on Phillip Denton. I'd like to help you. The Robert Harris I once knew wouldn't have committed the crimes alleged against him."

"Thank you for saying that. I appreciate your time."

"Wish I could have been more help."

***

Stephanie decided to stop at Rosa's Taqueria for lunch after she left the police station. She'd thrown away the burrito and guacamole she purchased on Tuesday. After she had found the note, she had no appetite. She would eat inside the restaurant today. No sense in taking a risk going home to another message and waste another burrito.

The place was full with the mid-day lunch crowd. Unless someone left soon, she'd have to make the order to go. She could take it to a nearby park, but the weather was too hot to enjoy the outdoors.

Out of options, she decided to settle for fast food today. When she turned to leave, she heard someone called her name.

"Stephanie, care to join me?"

She hadn't noticed Brian Nichols sitting at a small table near the back.

She smiled. "Yes, I will. Thanks." She placed her order at the counter before taking the seat opposite him.

"I hear you might be staying for a while."

"Word still gets around fast here. It seems as if I can't do anything without the entire town knowing."

"Sorry. I talked to Matt this morning. He told me."

"A little longer than I originally anticipated. It will save me having to make a return trip. I have everything I need to continue work on my current manuscript, so I don't have to rush back to Denver. I can work from anywhere."

"One of the perks of being a writer."

"There are a few." She smiled. "So tell me, what made an aspiring rock star decide to go into the construction business?"

"I grew up. I knew I had a better chance of becoming a building contractor than succeeding in the music world. My dad may have been a drunk, but he taught me how to swing a hammer the right way when I was very young. He wasn't always a failure, although most people made him out to be one. I still hear talk."

"We all say things we don't mean. I've been reminded of that recently."

"Yeah. People said some nasty things about you. I've also said plenty of stuff that hurt others."

"I say it's time to put the past behind us."

Brian smiled and raised his soft drink in a toast. "To the future."

Stephanie lifted her glass of iced tea. "Yes. To the future."

"I thought about you many times over the years."

"You did?"

"I wondered how you adjusted and what your life was like after losing your father."

"Our circumstances were different, but I think you probably understand better than most people."

"I was angry with my dad for a long time. I hated him for drinking and despised him because of the way Mother had to work to support our family."

"She never seemed to let things get her down."

"When my father died, I hated him even more for leaving us too soon. It took a long time for me to forgive him. I never considered the fact he needed help for his alcoholism."

"I've also been angry at my father. I tried to focus on the happy times, but it's sometimes easier said than done."

"I imagine your life was hard after you moved away."

"The first few years were difficult. Mom worked to make certain I had an education. Fortunately, I was able to obtain scholarships. And she remarried several years ago. David takes good care of her, and they're happy together."

"That's good. Mother never married again. She never got over losing Dad, despite all his faults. I often feared she would die of a broken heart, but she's a strong person."

Stephanie and Brian continued their conversation long after the server brought their meal. She was surprised to learn they had many things in common, not the least of which was losing their fathers much too early in life.

Brian wasn't the same person she had known in school. He was kind, considerate, and thoughtful. But then again, like everyone else, he was older and more mature. Much to her surprise, she discovered she enjoyed his company.

When he got ready to leave the restaurant, he said, "I'll see you around. I'm building the house across the street from Helen's. Since you're going to be in town for a while, maybe we can get together sometime."

"Thanks, I'd like that," she said. "Coming back has been easier than I anticipated. So far, no one has indicated they hold anything against me or act as if they want me to leave."

"I told you things had changed."

When she returned to her car, she saw a piece of paper stuck beneath the windshield wiper. Thinking it might be a flier for tonight's game or some fundraiser, she placed it on the seat beside her and started the car.

Although the daytime temperatures had cooled from triple digits to the lower nineties, the heat inside the car was almost unbearable. She turned the air to high.

While waiting for the car to cool, she picked up the piece of paper. She gasped as she read the words. It was a note—written in calligraphy—same as the other two messages.

Be careful about asking questions. This town has eyes and ears.

Chapter Eleven

Stephanie regretted she didn't accept Matt's invitation to attend the Friday night game. Whoever was responsible for leaving the notes was watching her. The message confirmed it. How else had they known she was in town today?

The idea of being alone in the house tonight didn't appeal to her. She reached for the phone to call Matt when it rang.

"Stephanie, this is Christine. I know this is short notice, but I wondered if you'd like to have dinner tonight. Kyle has to cover the game, and Emily is spending the night with a friend. I thought this would be a good time for us to get together."

"I'd love to. I wasn't wild about the idea of staying home alone tonight."

"Really? What's up?"

Stephanie took a deep breath and exhaled slowly. "Maybe I'll tell you at dinner. Where do you want to meet?"

"Do you remember where Fisherman's Cove is on Lake Brewster? How about if we meet there at eight? We'll have more privacy than any place in Driscoll Lake."

"Sounds great."

"Good. I'll take care of the reservation."

"I'll see you then."

***

Stephanie arrived at the restaurant a few minutes ahead of Christine. Located on a quiet cove, the peaceful ambiance and scenery made it a popular place.

When Christine arrived, the hostess seated them at a table that offered a view of the lake. "I requested a lakeside view," Christine said. "I love the relaxing atmosphere."

"I agree. I used to come here a lot with my parents. Dad always asked for a table near the windows. Sometimes the two of us would come here without Mom." Stephanie's eyes misted.

"You still miss him, don't you?"

"I miss what we once had." Stephanie looked out the window. The last rays of sunlight shone on the calm waters of the lake. The sky had changed to deeper hues of pink, orange, and purple. She turned back to Christine. "It's hard to grieve someone who destroyed your life."

"I can't imagine what you went through. People like me didn't make things easier."

"I won't pretend it didn't hurt. But what Dad did to us was even worse."

A waiter appeared at their table. "Can I interest you ladies in a glass of wine?"

"Just iced tea for me," Christine said.

"I'll have a glass of Sauvignon Blanc."

"Very well," the waiter said. He handed each of them a menu. "Our special tonight is cedar plank grilled salmon served on a bed of wild rice with grilled vegetables. I'll be back in a few minutes with your drinks and to take your order."

"I didn't know you liked wine," Christine said after the waiter left the table.

Stephanie raised her eyebrows. "We were fourteen the last time we saw one another."

"This is true." Christine grinned, but her smile quickly faded. "I felt guilty for the way I acted two. After high school, I wanted to contact you. I even asked for your address and phone number, but I was afraid to call. I thought you would push me away. It's what I deserved."

"It's time to put the past behind us and start over."

"I didn't think I would ever see you again. Thought you'd never come back here."

"I didn't plan to. When Nell Bradford called to say Aunt Helen asked for me, I said 'yes' before I had time to think. If I had stopped to consider the matter, I probably wouldn't have come."

"Helen asked for you?"

"Yes. It was an unusual request because she never asked me while she was still alive. She left a letter addressed to me with Miles Parker dated three weeks before her death. In it, she said she understood my reasons for not wanting to return. It must have been shortly afterward that she found one of Carol's journals."

"What would that have to do with you coming back?"

"She began to question my father's guilt because of something Carol wrote." Stephanie explained the journal entries and told Christine about the man Carol saw in South America.

"That is strange."

"Yes. And Carol died in a plane crash before she had a chance to talk to someone. Aunt Helen questioned if the crash may not have been an accident."

"It does sound suspicious. Especially if she wrote about seeing someone who she linked to Driscoll Lake. What do you think?"

"Carol alluded to the possibility of my father being innocent."

"A lot of people couldn't imagine your father as a killer."

The waiter returned with their drinks and took their order. Stephanie waited until he left before continuing.

"I went to see Carlos Gonzales this morning. He was understanding, but Carol's journal writings aren't enough to reopen the case. I've decided to stay a while longer and do a little digging on my own. However, I'm beginning to believe someone doesn't want me here."

"Why do you say that?"

"I've received three notes warning me to leave or face possible consequences."

"What?"

"I found two at the house. I thought they might have been pranks. You may not know this, but a few days ago, I was on a nationally syndicated talk show and 'declared' my father's innocence. The reporter asked me questions about why I'd never returned here, and I figured someone saw the show and meant them as a joke."

"Not a funny one."

"Dan Bradford told me there had been some similar incidents in the neighborhood involving teenagers. Today I found one on the car windshield not long after I spoke with Carlos. Someone has been watching me."

"Do you think the same person wrote all three notes?"

Stephanie nodded her head. "All were the same style and written in calligraphy."

Christine raised her eyebrows. "Calligraphy?"

"Yes. So it's not likely the person is a teenager playing a practical joke."

"But why would anyone not want you around?"

"I can only assume it has something to do with my father. Someone who doesn't want me to learn the truth. Whoever wrote them is wasting their time. Once I make up my mind about something, I'm not easily dissuaded."

"You should still be careful."

Stephanie took a sip of wine and set the glass on the table. "That's enough about me. Let's talk about you. I was a bit surprised when I learned you married Kyle Lawrence. You didn't like him when we were in school together."

"No, I didn't. I thought he was arrogant and self-centered—a carbon copy of his father. Kyle changed after you moved away. I think what happened with your father affected him somehow. He became a more thoughtful, serious person."

"He was one of my biggest supporters in school, but how would what happened with Dad affect him?"

"Kyle's father is a greedy person. Always wants more money and prestige. He insisted upon Kyle attending law school. The Judge even had a wife picked out for him. He thought Kyle should marry Rachel Jackson. I'm convinced it was because he knew she'd eventually inherit the Cameron money."

"That's interesting."

"Anyhow, after your dad died, I think Kyle saw what the love of money could do to a person."

"Yeah, that's what a lot of people said about Dad." Stephanie looked away.

"I'm sorry. I was talking about The Judge—not your father."

"It's okay. Money affects different people different ways."

"Kyle contacted his mother. She's a poet and a writer—married to an artist. Sort of a Bohemian type, and not very affectionate toward her son. Lives the kind of life Curtis Lawrence detests. She walked out when Kyle was a small child and The Judge divorced her. I think Kyle chose journalism to spite his father."

"She doesn't seem the type of person The Judge would marry."

"Again, it comes down to money. Her family is wealthy. The Judge wasn't happy when Kyle decided against law school. Refused to help with the tuition."

"He sounds ruthless."

"Curtis Lawrence acts like the perfect father and grandfather in public, but he's a sorry excuse for a father."

"I didn't know."

"Most people don't realize what a two-faced hypocrite he is. Want to know the sad thing? Kyle still craves his acceptance."

***

Stephanie and Christine talked until most of the other customers had left the restaurant. When Stephanie looked at her watch, it was after ten-thirty.

"Hey, I guess we'd better go. The restaurant will close soon."

"We did lose track of time." Christine signaled for the waiter to bring their check.

Stephanie started to reach for her wallet, but Christine held up her hand. "No. Dinner is on me. It's the least I can do after twenty years."

After Christine paid the bill, they walked outside together. When they reached their cars, she embraced Stephanie in a warm hug. "I've missed you, friend."

"I missed you, too. Let's do this again before I leave town."

"I'd like that."

Stephanie watched Christine drive away, then got into the rental car and started the engine. Her cell phone rang, and her mother's number flashed on the screen.

"Hi, Mom. You're calling rather late."

"I'm on the west coast. David had a business trip, and I came along. I wanted to check on you. Are you back in Denver?"

"No, I'm still in Driscoll Lake. In fact, I plan to stay a while longer." She turned the ignition off. It wasn't wise to drive and talk on the phone at the same time, especially on unfamiliar roads.

"Why? Wasn't the funeral Wednesday?"

"Yes, but I've decided to stay to take care of Aunt Helen's business." Stephanie chose not to tell her mom that she also planned to look into her father's death.

"You know how I feel about that place. I don't like the idea of you being there."

"I told you I can make my own decisions."

"I know honey, but—"

"Mom, please. We're not going to agree on this, so let's change the subject. Did you call just to check on me, or did you have something else to talk about?"

They spoke for twenty minutes when Stephanie realized the restaurant had turned off the outside lights. The street lamp at the far end of the lot did little to fend off the darkness. She saw a dark colored pickup truck parked across the street and shivered in a wave of uneasiness.

"Mom, I'll call you tomorrow. I'm sitting in the parking lot of a restaurant, and they've already closed. It's dark around here. I need to get on the road."

"Are you okay?"

"Yes, I'm fine. I just want to get home."

"Okay, honey. I'll talk to you tomorrow."

Stephanie slipped her phone into her purse, started the car, and pulled out of the lot. She couldn't shake the uneasy feeling. When the lights of Driscoll Lake came into view, she welcomed them.

She drove through town and was almost to the turn off for the lake when she saw headlights coming up fast. The vehicle pulled up close behind her. Its high beams glared in the rearview mirror.

"Dim your lights, jerk." She slowed the car slightly, hoping the vehicle would pass, but the driver continued to tailgate. She accelerated. They accelerated. She thought it might be a drunk driver, but they weren't weaving. Every move seemed deliberate.

There were no other cars around. Stephanie broke into a cold sweat and glanced at the seat beside her. She tried to reach for her cell phone, but couldn't take her attention off the road—there was a sharp curve ahead near the Taney Creek Bridge.

She tried an old trick she learned a long time ago and tilted the rearview mirror, so the headlights reflected back into the driver's face. The vehicle moved to pass, but as it came even with her car, the driver veered to the right. He was trying to force her off the road.

Another set of headlights appeared in the distance and the truck beside her accelerated and passed. Soon it was out of sight. Stephanie was unable to read the license plate but could tell it was a dark, extended cab pickup—the same kind parked near the restaurant.

She arrived home a few minutes later, shaken from the ordeal. A cup of chamomile tea would soothe her nerves and help her to sleep. She parked the car and entered through the front door.

Whiskers was asleep on the sofa. He rose, stretched, and followed her into the kitchen. The message light on the phone was blinking.

She pressed the button on the machine. The digital voice said, "You have one new message. Friday, 11:30 p.m."

Stephanie looked at her watch—the call came only ten minutes ago. She listened to a muffled male voice. "How did you like my little warning tonight, Stephanie? The next time, I won't be so nice." The line went dead.

She gasped. It must have been the person driving the truck. She scrolled through the caller ID log, but the number was blocked.

No one would be foolish enough to call and leave a trail. But the person knew the phone number and knew she was staying in Helen's house. Although this was a gated community, someone could easily circumvent the security measures and get inside the gates. It could even be someone who lived nearby. First notes, now phone calls. Stephanie feared what might happen next.

Chapter Twelve

Christine was already on her second cup of coffee before Kyle got out of bed. Most mornings he was awake first, but he'd got in late the night before—a long time after the game ended.

She was already in bed and asleep when he arrived home. She had opened one sleepy eye to glance at the clock when he came into the bedroom. It was well after midnight.

"Good morning sleepyhead," she said when Kyle stumbled into the kitchen.

He poured himself a cup of coffee and sat down at the table before responding. "You're in a good mood. I take it your meeting with Stephanie went well."

"We had a wonderful time. I feel as if someone lifted a heavy weight from my shoulders."

"Good. You've carried the guilt way too long."

"We've put it behind us now."

"I'm glad the two of you worked things out."

"We plan to get together again. Now that Stephanie intends to be here a while, we'll have plenty of time."

"So it's true? She's staying in Driscoll Lake?"

"How did you know?"

Kyle shrugged his shoulders. "You know what it's like to live in a small town. I overheard talk."

"Meaning you heard Madge Sinclair talking. That woman is a gossip. I don't know why Pat Turner puts up with her."

"I think it's because Pat feels sorry for her. Madge can tell a pretty sad story about how she can't afford to retire."

"And acts as if she's the only one who suffered when Cameron closed its doors. I'll make breakfast." Christine went into the kitchen and opened the refrigerator. "Bacon and eggs?"

"Sure. So why is Stephanie staying?"

"To deal with her aunt's estate, but also to learn more about what happened to her father. She's beginning to doubt his guilt."

"Oh? She should be careful about digging around in the past. She could get hurt."

"Hurt? By whom? Even you believe there are unanswered questions. Do you know something you're not telling?"

"What's that supposed to mean?"

"Well, you do work for the newspaper. I just thought—"

"No. I don't know anything. All I'm saying is whenever people start digging in the past, they're bound to learn some things they wished they'd left uncovered." He got up from the table and left the room.

Kyle had been acting strangely the past few weeks. And why was he out so late last night? Christine often thought he knew more than he was willing to admit about the Harris-Denton case. But what? Like her, he was only a teenager at the time.

She busied herself with preparing breakfast and tried not to think about the possible reasons for Kyle's behavior.

***

They sat on a park bench in the coolness of the early morning. A light, gentle breeze rustled the leaves of a nearby willow tree. Rays of sunlight filtered through the pines and sparkled like diamonds on the waters of the lake.

The peaceful scene made it hard for Stephanie to imagine that only a few hours ago, someone threatened her. She hated to spoil the moment and decided not to say anything to Matt.

"What are your plans today?" he asked.

"I need to return the rental car. There is an agency in Brewster where I can take it. It doesn't make sense to pay for a rental when I can drive Aunt Helen's car."

"If you need a ride home, I can help."

"Would you mind? I planned to ask your mother, but she may be busy today."

"Most likely she'll spend the day packing and getting supplies ready for the motor home. My sister called and invited them for a visit. Dad says he's going to stay away until the weather cools here. They may be gone a while if the long-range weather forecast is correct."

"She said something about taking a trip. They seem to enjoy those getaways."

"Yes, they do." Matt smiled. "I'm glad they're able to go whenever they please. One of the benefits of retirement."

"We always took family vacations every year. Dad used to say when he and Mom retired, he wanted to travel around the country in a motor home. Mom preferred the big cities, but Dad enjoyed nature. He especially liked our visits to the National Parks. I think he's the reason I love the outdoors so much."

"But you've lived in cities most of your adult life."

"Part of the reason was due to my job at the travel magazine. Later, I did it to be close to my editor. When I moved to Denver, I had the convenience of a larger city, but close enough to the mountains and places where I could hike and enjoy the outdoors." She reached to tuck a strand of hair behind her ear.

"I was wrong about you the day you arrived. You looked every bit the part of the spoiled, rich city girl who wanted nothing to do with anyone in Driscoll Lake. I shouldn't be so quick to judge others. Why do people do that?"

"Human nature, I guess. I do the same thing."

Matt glanced at his watch. "I need to go to the station for a while. What time did you want to meet at the rental agency?"

"Is ten okay? I'd like to have the entire afternoon to write."

"Sure," Matt stood up. "I'll meet you there."

Stephanie watched as he turned and ran back toward his side of the lake. Matt wasn't the only one who'd misjudged. She wondered how she could have been so wrong about him.

***

After she returned from the car rental agency, Stephanie spent most of the afternoon writing. The words flowed smoothly. Satisfied with the day's work, she saved the file and closed her laptop. She was well ahead of her word count and had no doubt she would finish the first draft on schedule, if not early. Now she could get down to the business of dealing with her father's situation.

She had known it was useless to go to the police with Carol's journal. After her visit with Detective Gonzales the day before, she decided it was best to leave her father's case in the past where it belonged.

But after last night's incident with the pickup truck, along with the phone call, she reconsidered. Someone didn't want her in Driscoll Lake. She couldn't think of any reason why unless it was because of her father.

Stephanie sat down at the desk, pulled a legal pad from the drawer, and began to make notes. She wanted to find Lisa Duncan and also talk to people who might have some knowledge of the events leading up to the night of the murder.

Brian's mother, Dorothy Nichols, had been her father's secretary. Brian said she resided in an assistant living facility. Stephanie made a note to speak to him about visiting his mother. She began to make a list of others who worked at the factory at that time.

Madge Sinclair had been employed for Cameron as the receptionist, but she was a notorious gossip. If Stephanie even hinted that she was looking into the case of her father, Madge would spread it all over town. Stephanie quickly nixed that idea. She would talk to Madge only as a last resort.

She searched her memory for other names but came up empty. She considered calling her mother, but she wasn't happy about Stephanie's decision to remain in Driscoll Lake. Best not to say anything just yet.

Finding Lisa Duncan was another matter. If she was still in journalism, she could be anywhere, since she was a foreign correspondent. Stephanie sighed, put down the pen, and looked out the window. She saw Nell entering their motor home. An idea sprang into her head. Helen may have mentioned Lisa to Nell or Dan.

She put on a pair of sandals, walked next door, and stuck her head inside the opened door of the RV. "Nell, do you have a minute?"

Nell turned from the closet where she was storing things. "I always have time for you. Want to go in the house for some lemonade?"

"No thanks. I just have a quick question. Did Aunt Helen ever mention someone by the name of Lisa Duncan?"

Nell frowned. "Can't say that she did, but the name sounds familiar. Why?"

"I found Carol's journal, along with some notes Aunt Helen made. Carol wrote it when she lived in South America. She made mention of her roommate, Lisa Duncan.

"I can't recall Helen ever saying anything. Wish I could be of more help. Do you know anything else about her?"

"Only that she was also a journalist."

"Sorry. Dan and I leave tomorrow, but if I remember anything, I'll give you a call."

"Thanks. It was a long shot. I guess Google may become my best friend."

***

When Stephanie left Nell's house, a dark blue extended cab truck pulled into the driveway of the construction site across the street. Brian Nichols got out, smiled, and waved at her.

It was the perfect time to ask about visiting his mother. "Brian, do you have a few minutes?" The sounds of hammers and saws made it difficult to hear over the noise.

"Sure," he yelled back. "I'll come to you."

He smiled as he walked up to her. "What's up?"

"I'd like to talk with your mother. You said she had some health issues, and I wonder if she would be up to seeing me."

Brian's smile faded. "Why do you want to talk with her?"

"I'd like to ask her about my father. I want to know if she noticed anything unusual in his behavior prior to his death. I'm also interested in her opinion as to his guilt or innocence."

"You don't think he was guilty?"

"I didn't say that. I never wanted him to be, of course. I'd also like to know what the police asked your mother. I came across something Aunt Helen wrote—she didn't think the police did a thorough investigation."

"Why don't you ask Matt? He's chief now. He could review the file."

"I've already spoken to Carlos Gonzales."

"And?"

"He said without new evidence there's nothing they can do."

"Then that settles it. Talking to Mom wouldn't solve anything. Besides, I don't think it's a good idea to remind her of the past."

"Why not? I don't want to bother her, but if I could see her for only ten minutes—"

"You stayed away from this place for twenty years. Why the sudden interest now?"

"Wouldn't you want to know the truth if it was your father? What would it hurt if I ask a few questions? You are the one who told me people had moved on with their lives."

"Some people have, others haven't. I fight every day against the reputation my father had. My actions as a teenager don't help matters. If you start asking questions, people might— I'll just say I would hate to see you get hurt again. Best to forget the whole thing."

"Why?"

"Suffice to say some people can be unforgiving. There are times it's best to leave well enough alone. There's nothing Mother can say that will change what happened." He turned and walked away.

Stephanie watched him leave. After their initial meeting, she thought she could trust him. His mother had been one of her father's strongest supporters. Why was Brian so reluctant to let Stephanie talk with her?

Maybe he was concerned about her health, but she couldn't shake the feeling there was something more behind his reasons.

She went inside the house and took a bottle of water from the refrigerator. Her eye caught the phone sitting on the counter, and she remembered last night's message. *How did you like my little warning? Next time, I won't be so nice.*

The caller knew her name. He was aware that she was staying at Helen's house. Someone in a dark-colored pickup tried to force her off the road last night.

A sudden chill enveloped her. Brian drove a dark extended cab pickup truck. Then again, so did Matt.

***

Brian watched Stephanie return to the house. Her request to talk with his mother had taken him by surprise. Why the sudden need to question a crime committed twenty years ago?

He hated to tell her no. Hated seeing the disappointment on her face. She was right—if it had been his father, he'd want to know the truth.

But he couldn't allow her to see his mother—at least not yet. Not until he talked to her first.

Chapter Thirteen

The longer Stephanie thought about Brian's refusal, the angrier she became. Who was he to dictate who visited his mother? She'd asked him out of courtesy, but unless Dorothy Nichols had visitation restrictions, Stephanie could have easily gone without his permission.

She was running out of options. Finding Lisa Duncan was more important than ever. She sat down at the desk and rummaged through the drawers, hoping to find an address. There were old bank statements, utility bills, a ledger, and Christmas cards from the previous year, but no address book.

She looked at the return addresses on the cards but didn't find one from anyone named Lisa. Inside the ledger was a piece of paper containing several passwords—including the one to unlock Helen's computer. Stephanie booted it up and signed in, thinking perhaps there might be a list of addresses in an online file.

Stephanie quickly dismissed that thought. Aunt Helen always resisted her attempts to convince her to use email or Skype. The fact she even had a computer was surprising. Helen was fun loving, but reluctant to use modern technology.

Lisa's contact information wouldn't be on the computer. Whiskers sat on the desk with his eyes fixed on her. In a few short days, Stephanie had learned his tactic for letting her know he wanted food.

"Hey, buddy. I guess you're ready to eat. I'm a little hungry myself."

She went into the kitchen and filled the cat dish before peering into the refrigerator. There was still some lasagna, but the thought of eating leftovers again didn't appeal to her. She didn't even have the makings for a good salad. Frowning, she looked in the meat compartment. A ham and cheese sandwich would have to suffice.

Stephanie placed the sandwich on the breakfast nook table and turned to pour a glass of iced tea when the phone rang. Nell's number flashed on the screen.

"Hello?"

"I remembered why I recognized the name Lisa Duncan. She's a weekend news anchor on one of the Dallas stations."

"Think it's the same person?"

"Don't know, but it's worth a try. It's cable channel fifteen if you want to see her. The station's website probably has more information."

"Okay, thanks, Nell." Stephanie hung up the phone and reached for the remote. The woman behind the news desk appeared to be around the same age Carol would have been. But why would someone with her experience as a journalist settle for a weekend anchor position at a local television station?

Stephanie shrugged. It wasn't for her to guess. Learning if she was Carol's former roommate was all that mattered. She opened her laptop and found the station's website.

It didn't take her long to find the information she needed. Lisa Duncan had been a foreign correspondent who at one time lived in South America.

Stephanie found her social media links and decided to send her private messages through Facebook and Twitter.

You may have been a roommate to my cousin Carol McKenzie. Would like to speak with you. I await your message.

An hour later, she received a reply.

Yes, I knew Carol. Will be glad to talk. Is there a better way to contact you?

Stephanie messaged back, entered her phone number, and eagerly awaited the call. When her cell rang, she answered immediately.

"Hello?"

"Stephanie? This is Lisa Duncan."

"Thank you for contacting me. I'm sure you're wondering what this is all about."

"I confess to being a bit surprised at your message."

"Carol's mom, my aunt, recently passed away. I came across Carol's journal along with some notes Aunt Helen left—that's how I got your name."

"I'm sorry to hear of her death. I only met Mrs. McKenzie once, but she seemed like a very nice person. So how can I help you?"

"Did Carol ever tell you about my father, Robert Harris?"

"Yes, she did."

"She wrote some things in her journal that led me to believe he may have been innocent. I think you were aware she had PTSD."

"I was."

"You may think it strange, but I had hoped to talk to you in person. I'd like to know a little more about Carol's state of mind just before her death. There are some things I'd rather not discuss by phone."

"I don't think it's strange at all. I'm not sure how much I can help, but I'd be willing to talk with you."

"If you're free sometime next week, I can drive to Dallas. Perhaps we can meet somewhere?"

"Sorry, I leave tomorrow morning for Tennessee, but if you're in Driscoll Lake, I'll be passing through on the interstate. I plan to get an early start. We could meet for breakfast—say around 9:00?"

"That would be great. There's a restaurant on the service road of the Driscoll Lake exit. I've never eaten there, but it's always crowded. Food must be good."

"Sounds great. I'll see you in the morning."

***

Lisa Duncan stood and extended her hand in greeting when Stephanie arrived at the restaurant.

"Thanks for agreeing to see me," Stephanie said as she took her seat. "It didn't occur to me until later you might be suspicious of such a request from a stranger."

"Not at all. I'm familiar with your work and knew you were related to Carol."

Stephanie glanced around the restaurant. She didn't want anyone to overhear their conversation. However, most of the people sitting closest to them were families with young children. She doubted any of them would be behind the notes or the threatening phone call.

"I guess you've wondered why I was anxious to meet with you. You said last night Carol had told you about my father."

"Yes, we often talked about him. Carol said she lived here when he died."

"Apparently Aunt Helen didn't read Carol's journal until recently. When I found it, I also discovered where my aunt made notes. She referred to the fact Carol might have seen something that would prove my father's innocence."

Lisa raised her eyebrows. "That's interesting. Carol always said she doubted his guilt, but didn't know how to prove otherwise."

"Wonder why Aunt Helen waited all these years to read the journal."

"I can explain at least part of that. After the plane crash, I had all Carol's personal belongings sent to her parents. The magazine I worked for reassigned me a few months later. When I closed up the apartment, I shipped several boxes of my things to my folks in Tennessee.

"When I relocated to Dallas last year, my parents brought some things I'd kept at their house. I found Carol's journal mixed in with some of my books. I have no idea how it got there. She took it everywhere, so I assumed she had it with her when she died."

"Did you read any of it?"

"No. After I discovered it belonged to her, I contacted your aunt and delivered the journal to her personally. That was almost a year ago."

"Carol wrote about seeing a man a few days before she died. Said it was someone everyone thought was dead. My first thought was her fiancé, but this person frightened her." Stephanie told her about the journal entries. "Did she try to contact you in the days before her death?"

"Not that I'm aware of, but I was in a remote area. It's possible she tried."

"She said you would understand and not think she was crazy."

"I would have believed her. There's no doubt in my mind Carol was sane."

"I wish I knew who the person was. She became convinced she saw the same person around the time my father died."

"What about her other journals? There may be some clues in one of them."

"Other journals? There was more than one?"

"Carol always kept one. She said they provided an outlet for her feelings and emotions. Not long before she died, she lamented about leaving some of them here."

"I haven't seen them, but I haven't started to sort through Aunt Helen's belongings. She had lots of books. I sure hope I find them."

"Are you sure you're ready for what you might find?"

"What do I have to lose? Most everyone thinks my father was guilty. If I find evidence to the contrary, that's good. If not, I haven't lost anything. I have to try."

"Stephanie." Lisa paused and took a sip of coffee. "I haven't been entirely honest with you."

Stephanie frowned. "Do you know something about the person Carol saw?"

"No. I wish I did. It's something Carol told me about your father. About allegations that he was having an affair with the woman he supposedly killed."

"An affair?" Stephanie spoke louder than she intended. The man at the next table glanced in her direction. She lowered her voice. "With Madelyn Denton? My father?"

"Your mother never said anything?"

"No. Maybe that's why Mom got me out of Driscoll Lake so soon after his death. She sent me to Atlanta shortly after Dad's funeral. I stayed with my grandparents until she moved there."

"Carol didn't believe it, but she said there was talk. She said probably because they once dated in high school."

"I didn't know that."

"Some people speculated your father killed Madelyn because of a lover's quarrel. If you find her other journals, you'll likely find where she wrote about it."

Stephanie looked out the window. She blinked back the tears that threatened to fall.

"I'm sorry. I probably shouldn't have mentioned it. I feel like a gossip."

"You're not gossiping. I asked you what you knew. Thanks for being honest with me. Apparently, there were a lot of things about my father I didn't know."

***

Watching Stephanie Harris had almost become an obsession for him. He didn't stalk her every move, but it was important to keep up with her—who she talked with and where she visited. He couldn't afford for her to ask questions. There was too much at stake for her to learn the truth.

Friday night she met with Christine Lawrence. Perhaps it was nothing more than old friends meeting for a long overdue reunion, but no sense in taking chances. When he learned they planned to meet, he went to Fisherman's Cove and waited outside. He parked his truck in a place where he could watch but not be so close as to arouse suspicion.

Stephanie had sat in her car for a several minutes after Christine left. He followed her from a distance until they came upon a lonely stretch of road. As luck would have it, there were no other cars around. That's when he decided to give her a little scare. The phone call was an afterthought. The prepaid cell phone made it impossible to trace the call back to him.

It was only by chance that he saw her today. He often went to the restaurant on Sunday mornings for breakfast. He didn't recognize the person she met, but it wasn't someone he'd seen around Driscoll Lake. If he had been sitting closer to their table, it was possible he could have overheard their conversation. But it was better to remain unseen.

Maybe he was getting a bit paranoid. Yes, he'd seen Stephanie go to the police station on Friday, but he didn't know her reasons. He only assumed it was to talk to Gonzales. But he also knew she was getting friendly with Matt Bradford.

The phone calls made him nervous. Two this week. A subtle reminder that he would be implicated if the truth came out. He knew the consequences—prison or worse. He'd done the right thing by trying to frighten Stephanie away.

Chapter Fourteen

Stephanie couldn't help but feel disappointed Lisa wasn't able to provide more information. However, she was encouraged by knowing Carol kept other journals and hoped one of them could help identify the name of the person she saw. The key was to find those books.

She was also surprised to learn there had been other speculation as to the reason for her father's crime. To her mother's credit, she never mentioned the possibility of her father having an affair. Then again, if it were true, Kathryn may have been too ashamed to say anything.

Stephanie recalled how she felt when she learned her husband was cheating. How ashamed she'd been to tell anyone, even though she was angry with him. When they split up, she told her mother the marriage failed because she had to spend so much time away from home.

It was years before she told her mother the truth.

When she returned to the lake, she took a pen and paper from the desk and began to make notes about the various theories surrounding her father's crime. There seemed to be little doubt her father killed Madelyn and then turned the gun on himself. But why?

Some people claimed he killed Madelyn because she discovered the missing money and went to his office to confront him. If she could only talk with Dorothy Nichols. She might be able to provide information on how involved Madelyn was with company business.

Others speculated she suspected him in her husband's disappearance. Stephanie discounted this theory as mere gossip. Her father had an alibi for the time Phillip disappeared.

The idea that he and Madelyn might be having an affair was a bitter pill to swallow. Madelyn was soft spoken and refined and was always kind. Stephanie never noticed any animosity between Madelyn and her mother. But to know her father dated Madelyn in high school came as a surprise.

If they were lovers, did they plan to marry? If so, then why did her father steal the money? If he married Madelyn, he wouldn't need to take funds from her company. Too many ifs. Nothing seemed to make sense.

Stephanie was still hesitant about talking to her mother. Kathryn would only try to convince her to leave Driscoll Lake.

The deeper Stephanie probed, the more questions she had. She was determined to get some answers, and that required a visit with Dorothy Nichols. No matter what Brian said, Stephanie had to talk to her.

***

The idea came to her in the middle of the night. She awoke from a sound sleep, wondering why she hadn't already thought of it. There wasn't any doubt the newspaper article stirred up a lot of emotion for many people—including her. Kyle said other people had questions and showed interest. She would turn that interest to her advantage.

***

Many of the old brick buildings in Driscoll Lake had stood more than a century. Unlike the outskirts of town, which had newer businesses and modern architecture, the downtown area hadn't changed a lot in the past twenty years.

The familiar sites were comforting to Stephanie. She was also happy to know Pat Turner was still the editor of the *Driscoll Lake Reporter*. When the scandal involving Stephanie's father occurred, Pat reported the story in a fair and impartial manner.

Stephanie got out of her car and walked toward the door of the newspaper office. She didn't call ahead and hoped she hadn't made an unnecessary trip. She opened the door—surprised to see Madge Sinclair at the front desk. Stephanie guessed the former Cameron employee must be in her late sixties now.

She also knew Madge's reputation for gossip. People used to joke she knew things before anyone else. Stephanie guessed she probably chose to work for the local newspaper in order to keep abreast of all the latest news.

Stephanie despised gossip, but it wasn't wise to make an enemy of Madge Sinclair. The last thing she needed was for Madge to spread rumors about her. Nor did Stephanie want Madge knowing her business with Kyle. She'd find out soon enough if he agreed to her plan.

"Good morning, Mrs. Sinclair," she said. "I didn't know you worked here."

"I have to work. After someone stole my retirement money, I can't afford to quit."

Stephanie didn't miss the jab toward her father, but she chose not to reply.

"What do you need? We're rather busy around here, you know."

"I'm here to see Kyle. Is he in?"

"Not until later this morning. Maybe early afternoon. Guess you came for nothing."

"Madge! That's no way to speak to Stephanie or to anyone who visits this office. You are to treat people with respect—no matter what your personal feelings are toward them. Understood?" Pat Turner's brown eyes flashed in anger.

"Yes, ma'am." Madge's face turned red, and she turned away.

"Stephanie," Pat said. "How can we help you today?"

"I had hoped to see Kyle about a matter, but if you're not too busy, I'd also like to visit with you."

"I'm never too busy for you. Let's go where we can have a little more privacy."

"Thank you." Stephanie followed Pat into her office and waited for her to close the door.

"Have a seat," Pat said. "I apologize for my employee's rudeness. Rest assured I'll speak to her about her rude behavior."

Stephanie sat in a chair in front of Pat's desk. "She's always been a gossip. I wouldn't expect anything different from her. However, I'm not about to give her the satisfaction of knowing she struck a nerve when she mentioned the retirement fund."

"I am sorry."

"Not your fault. Madge Sinclair is no different from a lot of people in Driscoll Lake. They blamed Mom and me for Dad's alleged crime."

Pat took the seat beside Stephanie and reached to take her hand. "Not everyone felt that way. There were some of us who believed in your father."

Stephanie smiled. "I know that."

"By the way," Pat said. "About Kyle's story last week. I was out of the country and didn't know about it until I returned home. I hope Helen didn't see it. I would hate to think it caused her distress."

"There's no need to apologize. In fact, I think Aunt Helen would have approved."

Pat looked puzzled. "How so?"

"She wrote a letter about a month ago and left it with Miles Parker. She said that she had always hoped to find some evidence that would cause the police to reopen the case and prove my father's innocence. Kyle's article seems to indicate he had questions about the original investigation."

"So you're not upset?"

"I was at first, but I know he intended no harm."

"I wasn't sure how you'd react."

"Mrs. Turner, can I ask you something about my father?"

"Of course, dear."

"Did you ever hear rumors that he and Madelyn Denton might be having an affair?"

Pat took a deep breath and exhaled. "Yes, I did. But that's what they were. Rumors. It's ludicrous to think otherwise. Your father was devoted to your mother."

"There weren't any signs he might be interested in Madelyn?"

"None that I'm aware of. Those rumors got started after their deaths. People were looking for an explanation. It was only speculation."

"I recently learned they dated in high school."

"They did for a while. I think your father took Madelyn to the senior prom. It wasn't a long-term relationship."

"That's it?

"That's it. However, it infuriated Curtis Lawrence, as I recall."

"How so?"

"He always had his eye on Madelyn. I think it was more for the money than anything else. Her father, William Cameron, wouldn't have anything to do with the Lawrence's. There was a feud between the two families. It went back several generations."

"That's interesting. Thanks for setting the record straight about my father and Madelyn."

"Glad to help. If you have other questions, give me a call."

Stephanie wanted to ignore Madge Sinclair on her way out, but she couldn't resist rubbing a little salt in the wound. "You were mistaken. Mrs. Turner assured me that she had plenty of time for me." With that, she turned and walked out the door, not giving Madge time to reply.

Stephanie took a deep breath. She was relieved to know there wasn't any truth to the rumors about a lover's quarrel between her father and Madelyn. At least that was one theory out the window.

***

He watched Stephanie leave the newspaper office. There were benefits to small town life—it was easy to monitor a person's comings and goings.

What business did she have there? Did she want information? Was she questioning the validity of the story about her father? It could have been something as simple as placing an ad for an estate sale. He shook his head. It was far too early for that. Helen's will hadn't even been probated. Stephanie had other business, and he needed to know what it was.

He could ask Madge Sinclair. She was a veritable source of information. To ask her directly would look suspicious. He couldn't afford to have Madge gossiping about him. He would simply have to rely on his other source. He'd soon learn what he needed to know.

If his suspicions were correct, someone needed to take care of Stephanie Harris before she found out the truth.

She had walked down the sidewalk with her head held high. She was calm and cool now. It would be interesting to see how she acted when someone gave her a bit of what she deserved.

***

Stephanie was disappointed she hadn't been able to see Kyle. She didn't even know his cell number. But she didn't want to go back and face Madge Sinclair. She would wait until later and call him at the office.

She glanced at her watch. It was still early enough to grab a bagel and coffee. She'd been so intent on seeing Kyle that she'd forgotten to eat breakfast. The coffee shop was a short distance away, so she decided to walk.

The place wasn't very crowded today. Stephanie placed her order and sat at a table near the front. She had only been there a few minutes when Kyle walked in.

He smiled and spoke. "Stephanie, how are you?"

"Good, thanks. I'm glad to see you. I've already been to the newspaper in hopes of finding you there. Madge said you wouldn't be in until later. I want to discuss a matter with you."

"Sure. Let me grab a cup of coffee, and I'll be right over." Kyle placed his order and then joined her at the table.

"So what's up?" He took a sip of his coffee.

"I'd like you to consider writing another article about my father."

Kyle jerked his head in surprise. "Another article? Why?"

"I recently came across a journal that belonged to Aunt Helen's daughter, Carol."

"A journal? What does that have to do with your father?"

She wrote some things that lead me to question my father's guilt. Aunt Helen must have read it only recently because she also began to have doubts."

"Helen? How do you know?"

"From some notes she wrote." Stephanie told him about the man Carol saw and her suspicion it was the same person she'd seen years earlier. "Apparently, Carol kept other journals, but so far I haven't been able to find them."

"Why not just talk with the police?" Kyle asked.

"Because I've already spoken to Carlos Gonzales. He told me what I already knew—without some new evidence, they have no reason to reopen the case. I thought perhaps another story, or even a series of stories, might lead to someone coming forward with new evidence."

Kyle sighed. "I'm more than willing to help, but don't get your hopes up. I don't mean this in a bad way, but the musings of a woman who suffered from PTSD might not be enough. Have you mentioned this to Matt?"

"No. I realize I'll need something more than this, but what I want is to raise interest in the story. For instance, there's a matter of the stolen money. The FBI didn't find conclusive evidence to link the embezzlement to my father."

"Except for the fact he was an authorized signer on the account," Kyle said.

"Other people were approved to sign—including Phillip Denton."

"But records indicated it was your father who authorized the transfer to the overseas account."

"To another corporate account. After that, the money went to a bank in South America, and the FBI lost track. I realize I may be grasping at straws here, but something doesn't add up. My father was an honest man. He had a good job, a family, a home. Why would he want to risk all that? Would you at least consider writing another article? Perhaps this time talk about the embezzlement?"

Kyle hesitated for a moment before answering. "Okay, I'll do it. With Pat's blessing, of course."

"Thanks, Kyle. I appreciate it. In the meantime, I plan to look for Carol's other journals. Aunt Helen said she hoped to live long enough to see my father exonerated. I may never be able to prove his innocence, but I'm going to do my best to find out the truth."

"I would like nothing more than for you to find out your father was innocent. You can count on me to help."

"I appreciate it."

"I'd better get to the office. I'll let you know what Pat says." He got up from the table and turned to leave.

"Kyle, wait."

He stopped and turned around.

"Don't mention the journals. At least not yet."

***

Kyle hadn't planned to write a second news article, but after hearing Stephanie's story, he couldn't say no. She, along with the rest of Driscoll Lake, deserved to know the truth. There would be consequences. Of that, he was certain. But he would do what he could to help her.

He parked his car in the lot behind the office and entered through the back door in the hope of avoiding Madge. She would feign interest and ask questions, all a ploy to have something else to gossip about.

If he wrote the article, Madge would know soon enough. Kyle went straight to his office and closed the door. Pat gave him a lot of liberties with his stories, but after her hesitation last week, he wanted her approval before he proceeded. He picked up the phone to call her office when someone knocked on his door.

"Come in." He grimaced when Madge walked through the door.

"Someone was here to see you this morning." She paused as if waiting for him to ask the person's identity.

"I know. I saw Stephanie at the coffee shop."

"What did she want? I informed her we were very busy around here."

"If she had wanted you to know, she would have told you. Do you need something, or merely digging for information?"

"I'm just doing my job." Madge walked away, slamming the door behind her.

Kyle shook his head. Madge had nerve—he'd give her that much. He reached for his phone and dialed Pat's extension. "I need to talk to you about something in private. Can I come to your office?"

"Sure. Come on in."

Twenty minutes later, he emerged from Pat's office. She agreed to the story. He looked toward Madge's desk, inwardly amused at the expression on her face. The suspense was killing her, but for now, he wasn't going to give her the satisfaction of knowing his business.

Chapter Fifteen

Pat Turner had served as a member of the Driscoll Lake City Council for ten years. Although she supported growth, she also saw the need to preserve the town's historic buildings. Not all the council members liked change, wishing Driscoll Lake was the same small community from years ago.

On the other hand, a few of them wanted the town to grow no matter what the cost. At least one member was for anything that brought new business and increased tax revenue. Curtis Lawrence repeatedly demonstrated he couldn't care less about the past. To him, the historical commission was a hindrance to progress.

Pat considered herself a moderate—a mediator between the two opposing forces. She'd had several occasions to intervene in some heated discussions during her years of service.

She arrived at the Monday night council meeting to find Curtis embroiled in an argument with long-time resident and councilman, Henry Garrett. She could feel the tension in the room before the meeting even began. Curtis Lawrence's temper was hotter than the Texas sun.

"Henry, things will never be the same. We're living in the twenty-first century, but you you're stuck in the nineteenth," The Judge said.

"I know what century it is. I happen to think this town has changed enough. I, for one, would like to see a bit of our history preserved. If you had your way, we wouldn't have any historical sights left."

"You seem to have forgotten I supported the preservation of the downtown area. History doesn't put dollars in the bank—or provide tax revenue for the city."

The two of them stopped talking when the mayor entered the room and called the meeting to order. Pat hoped it would be brief. The main item was a proposed tax abatement for a logistics company that wanted to relocate near the interstate.

She looked at the audience—some residents always attended the open meetings, others came when the council voted on something that was of interest to them. Kyle had arrived early to cover the story for the newspaper and sat near the front of the room. She was surprised to see both Brian Nichols and Rachel Jackson in attendance—and seated together.

The first order of business was the tax abatement. It was more of a formality to bring it to a vote since all members had previously indicated they were for granting the reduction. They moved through the remaining agenda items quickly. When the mayor asked for any open discussion, Pat was surprised when Curtis Lawrence spoke.

"I'd like to bring up a matter of concern several citizens have brought to my attention, and that is the condition of vacant, unkempt buildings. They're eyesores to our town. Worst of all, some of them could pose a danger due to their state of disrepair. I propose an ordinance whereby the owners of these properties are required to maintain the structures or face the possibility of having them condemned. The owners would be responsible for the expense of having them torn down."

"Curtis, there aren't that many vacant buildings around anymore," Henry Garrett said. "You should know, with all your push for progress and growth."

"At least one comes to mind—the old Cameron Manufacturing site. The buildings have sat vacant for almost twenty years. I doubt the factory building is structurally sound. It should be demolished."

"What? It's a part of our history. That building is over a hundred years old—one of the oldest in this town. Need I remind you of the part Cameron Manufacturing played during World War II? I think the historical society would have something to say about tearing the place down."

"And stand in the way of progress? At any rate, I have it on good authority a company is interested in buying the property. The current owner is willing to sell. A new business would benefit the local economy and bring in new jobs. The new owners should have a say."

Rachel Jackson stood up. "I agree with Judge Lawrence. It's time to do something about the place. He's correct in saying the owner should have a say in the matter."

Curtis looked pleased. "You see Henry, even Ms. Jackson agrees with me."

Henry frowned, obviously not pleased with the turn of events.

"Mr. Garrett, you can put your mind at ease," Rachel said. "I've already sold the property. Why don't we hear what the new owner has to say?" Rachel sat down and nodded toward Brian.

He stood and faced the council members. "Rachel is right. I do have an interest because I am the new owner."

Everyone in the room gasped in surprise. Pat glanced around. Some people in the audience acted pleased, while others seemed uncertain. Curtis Lawrence looked at Brian with an incredulous look on his face.

Brian continued. "And although I care about progress and growth, I also believe we need to preserve our past. The factory building does look hopeless, but it isn't beyond repair. I hired an inspector to examine it, and he agrees with me. I'm not prepared to divulge all my plans at this time, but I will say my plans should satisfy the concerns addressed from both sides tonight."

In the end, the council tabled the judge's proposal. When the meeting adjourned, Curtis Lawrence left without speaking to anyone. Pat noticed Kyle's amused look—he didn't often see his father defeated. As expected, Henry Garret was elated over the turn of events.

Pat wasn't sure what to make of what transpired. Did Curtis Lawrence have prior knowledge of Rachel's intent to sell the property? Why were both Rachel and Brian at the meeting? They must have had some insight as to the judge's proposal—otherwise they wouldn't have known to come prepared for questions.

Pat shook her head. It was hard to keep secrets in a small town.

***

He hurried from the building, got into his car, and peeled out of the parking lot. How dare Rachel Jackson sell to that son of a drunken fool? He'd wanted that property for years. Now he'd lost the chance. It seemed as if the Cameron family would always be a thorn in his flesh.

He needed to call his business associate. There was no reason to wait. He pressed the speed dial number and waited.

"Hello?"

"We lost the property."

"The factory? How? She decided not to sell?"

"She's already sold it to someone else. A resident by the name of Brian Nichols. He owns a construction company."

"Oh, yeah? What's he going to do with the property?"

"Says he has big plans for the area, but wouldn't reveal it tonight. You can bet it doesn't fit our agenda."

"Is the sale final?"

"Afraid so. I almost didn't go to tonight's meeting, but a source told me something was going down."

"Don't sweat it. We'll look somewhere else. Other properties will serve our needs."

He hung up the phone. Sure, he could buy something else, but that wasn't the point. He wanted the Cameron place—no matter what the cost. Now that a new owner was in the picture, he'd have to come up with another way. He'd think of something. Sooner or later, he always got what he wanted.

***

Stephanie spent all day Monday and most of Tuesday morning clearing out Helen's closets. She had been practical in many ways—the house wasn't fancy, and its furnishings were simple. But when it came to clothes, Helen spared no expense. Her wardrobe was extensive.

Helen also had a passion for books. She used to joke she owned a small library. After seeing her vast collection, Stephanie tended to agree. Tuesday afternoon she started emptying the bookshelves. She had already glanced at them in hopes of finding Carol's other journals.

So far, she hadn't had any luck. Maybe Carol had been mistaken about leaving them here. Stephanie hated to think she might have misplaced them during one of her many moves.

Mid-afternoon the doorbell rang and Stephanie hurried to answer. She was surprised to see Brian standing at the door.

"Hope I'm not intruding," he said.

"No. Please come in."

"Thanks, but I can't stay long. I wanted to apologize for the way I acted on Saturday. I spoke with Mom. She said she would be glad to talk to you and will answer any questions you have."

"Thanks, Brian. I appreciate it. I promise not to say anything that might upset her."

"Mom's tougher than I give her credit for. Guess I jumped the gun the other day. She's looking forward to the visit."

"I look forward to seeing her. I'll never forget her kindness to mother and me when Dad—" Stephanie blinked her eyes, not wanting to show emotion. "Your Mom's future was at stake, but she acted more concern for our welfare than her own."

"Yeah, she's like that. If you know when you plan to visit, I'll call ahead and tell her you're coming."

"Tomorrow morning?"

"She plays bingo then. The afternoon would be better."

"I'll go around two."

"Sounds good. Guess I'd better get back to work."

Stephanie watched Brian as he walked back to the construction site and wondered what made him change his mind. Both he and Matt were an enigma. One day they acted as if they didn't want her around, the next they were all too willing to help.

What was it with people in Driscoll Lake? Stephanie shrugged. At least Kyle Lawrence hadn't questioned her motives.

**

Dorothy Nichols was a shadow of her former self. Stephanie tried not to show her astonishment at seeing the frail body. It grieved her to see the hands that once typed many a letter with speed and efficiency now twisted and gnarled by arthritis.

Her once brown hair was now a shade of silvery gray. It was hard to believe this woman was only a few years older than Stephanie's mother. At fifty-six, Kathryn was still vibrant and youthful.

Dorothy's illness was likely the reason she looked much older. She sat in a wheelchair and looked out the window.

"Mrs. Nichols?"

She turned and smiled at the sound of her name. Stephanie remembered the same warm smile and the sparkle in her blue eyes.

"Stephanie! It's so good to see you. When Brian told me you were in town, I hoped you'd come for a visit."

"I couldn't leave without seeing you. You were always so kind to me." A lump formed in her throat.

Dorothy patted the back of Stephanie's hand. "I worried about you after you moved away. Helen kept me up to date."

"You were so unselfish. What happened affected your life also—losing your job, your retirement. I know things weren't easy for you in those days."

"Life is often hard. We can choose to sit back and wallow in self-pity or move forward. I've never been one to feel sorry for myself. Overall, I've had a good life."

Stephanie admired the inner strength of this woman. If anyone had cause to be bitter, she did. But she refused to allow adversity to dominate her life.

"Brian said you wanted to ask me some things about your father."

"Yes, I do. For years, I struggled with not wanting to believe Dad was guilty and knowing what the evidence indicated. While sorting through some of Aunt Helen's things, I came across something that caused me to doubt his guilt."

"I see." Dorothy propped her elbow on the arm of the wheelchair. She looked away for a moment—pensive.

"I never wanted to believe Robert was guilty," she said as she turned back to Stephanie. "He was one of the kindest men I ever knew. He was not only my boss, but I considered him a trusted friend."

"I think he felt the same about you. He always held you in high regard."

"He understood when I had to take time off because of my husband. Then Brian started getting into trouble." She shook her head. "Thank God he didn't turn out like his father."

"Mrs. Nichols. I'm going to be blunt. Do you think my father stole the money?"

"His signature was on the checks, but Phillip Denton had to co-sign them. Robert didn't often deal with the financial part of the business. We had an accounting department. The second signature was supposed to be a check and balance system, but we often used signature stamps."

"So you're saying anyone could have 'forged' their signatures?"

"It's possible for someone who had access to the accounts. If I had been investigating, I would have looked a little deeper into Karen Fulbright."

"Who is she?"

"Phillip Denton hired her as controller about a year or so after he took over the business. She showed up one day looking for a job, and he hired her on the spot."

"Strange."

"Phillip did whatever he pleased. I know almost everyone in this town thought of him as a model citizen, but I wasn't one of them."

Stephanie raised her eyebrows. Dorothy Nichols was the first person she'd heard speak of Phillip Denton in an unfavorable manner. "Oh really? Why?"

"A lot of things changed after Mr. Cameron died. I believe Phillip was as much to blame as anyone for the company's downfall. When he took over as CEO, we started to lose major contracts. Employee morale dropped to an all-time low—including your father's."

"Dad never talked about it, but he was never one to bring his problems home from the office. Tell me more about Karen Fulbright. I remember several of Cameron's employees, but not her."

"She was dedicated to her job. I'll give her that. Never missed work and always acted in a professional manner. But she wouldn't allow anyone to get close to her—she didn't attend the company picnics and Christmas parties. The only person she seemed to warm up to was Phillip."

"Think there was anything between them?"

"I often wondered, but I tried to stay away from office politics and gossip."

"What happened to her? Did the FBI question her about the money? It seems to me she would have known what was going on."

"She died in a car accident near the Taney Creek Bridge."

"Died? I don't remember that either. Did it happen after I left Driscoll Lake?"

"No. It was two months before your father's death."

Stephanie frowned. The events of 1991 had all the makings of a novel. Except this was real life. "There was a lot of tragedy involving Cameron employees that summer. If I were a suspicious person, I'd think the place was cursed."

"It would sure seem that way."

"Mrs. Nichols, was there any talk around the office about my father being involved with Madelyn Denton?"

Dorothy paused as if to consider her words before answering. "Not that I'm aware of, but as I said, I stayed away from office gossip."

"I see."

"Madelyn rarely came to the office before Phillip disappeared. Afterward, she often called your father and even came to the office several times. It made sense she would want to discuss things about the business, so I didn't think there was anything unusual about it."

"So you believe the meetings were business related?"

"Yes. In fact, Madelyn came to see your father earlier that day."

"The day they died?"

"Yes. That's why I thought it was strange she went back in the evening."

"Do you know what they talked about? Did either of them seem angry or upset?"

"They met in your father's office, so I can't say for sure, but I didn't hear any loud voices. Both acted worried about something. After Madelyn left, your father instructed me to send out a memo calling for a company-wide meeting for the following Monday. He said Madelyn would be present."

"Did he give any indication of his reasons for calling the meeting or give you an agenda to type?"

Dorothy shook her head. "Nothing. He said it was mandatory for all employees to attend. He indicated the company's future was at stake, but both he and Madelyn were dedicated to ensuring the company would survive."

"That doesn't sound like someone who was planning to commit suicide or who stole money. Did you tell this to the police during the investigation?"

"Investigation? That's almost a laugh. Joe Rivers sent a couple of people to dust for fingerprints. They took a few pictures, bagged the so-called suicide note, and sent the bodies for autopsies. A couple of weeks later they announced the case closed. Said it was a clear-cut case of murder-suicide.

"When auditors discovered the missing money, they called in the FBI to investigate the embezzlement. An agent questioned me several times. He was a complete professional. If Joe Rivers had applied even a tenth of his resources to the murder investigation, we might have had some answers as to your father's—" Dorothy cleared her throat. "Let me just say I thought Joe should have done more."

"You're not the first person who expressed concern. The more I learn, the more complicated this case seems."

***

Dorothy watched Stephanie walk from the building to her car. She hoped Stephanie was satisfied with her answers. It was true she didn't want to believe Robert Harris was guilty, but she had questions. There were things she'd never told anyone, such as the conversation she overheard the day he and Madelyn died.

She had been at lunch when Madelyn arrived. When she returned, Robert's office door was ajar. She couldn't help but overhear part of their conversation.

"I regret the day Phillip Denton came into my life. I made a mistake in marrying him. It should have been you in his place."

"Don't berate yourself. We all make mistakes."

"If I find him, it's over between us."

"I don't think you'll ever have to worry about Phillip."

Not wanting to hear more, Dorothy quietly left her desk. However, questions remained with her to this day.

What had Robert meant when he said Madelyn wouldn't have to worry about her husband? Did he kill Phillip? Were Robert and Madelyn having an affair? Did she return later that night to meet him, knowing there wouldn't be anyone else around? Did they have a lover's quarrel?

It wouldn't serve any purpose to tell anyone now. It would only open old wounds. There was no need to inflict more hurt on Stephanie or for that matter, Rachel. She wouldn't say anything. The secret would remain with her.

Chapter Sixteen

"I don't suppose it would do any good to invite you to the game tonight," Matt said. He and Stephanie had finished their morning run. "Mom and Dad have reserved seats. It would be a shame not to use them."

Stephanie had come to enjoy the time she spent with Matt. He dropped by on occasion when he checked on things at his parents' house. She invited him to stay for dinner the evening before. Except for their initial encounter, he'd been friendly.

"Matt Bradford, are you asking me on a date?" Her mood was light-hearted. She couldn't help but tease him.

"And last night wasn't a date?" He grinned.

"That's different. Since I still have several frozen casseroles, with no way of eating them all."

"So what about tonight?"

"Okay."

"I understand how you must feel, but if you'll just give it a chance—"

"I said okay. I'll come to the game."

"You will? Why the change of heart?"

"I can't keep hiding from the past. Since I plan to stay in Driscoll Lake for a few weeks, I should get out more often."

He paused for a moment and looked at her, his expression thoughtful. "That's good."

"So what time does the game start?"

"At 7:00. I have to attend a late afternoon meeting in Brewster, but I'll still have a chance to pick you up."

"There's no need for you to come out here. I'll meet you at the stadium."

***

In spite of her initial hesitation when she walked into the stadium, Stephanie enjoyed the game. She couldn't recall the last time she had felt excitement over a sporting event. It had been too difficult to get past the memory of the night her father died.

After she moved from Driscoll Lake, Stephanie didn't become involved in many extracurricular activities, choosing to pour herself into her studies. For the first few months after moving to Atlanta, she kept to herself. She felt betrayed and didn't make new friends easily. She eventually mingled with others in her class, but never felt close to them as she once did toward her friends in Driscoll Lake.

Tonight, for the first time in years, she felt a sense of freedom. Free to enjoy herself. Free from worry about the past. Free to enjoy her time with Matt.

Instead of thinking about her father's death on that fateful night, she remembered how she looked longingly at the team's quarterback, butterflies in her stomach, wishing he would take notice of her. Recalling the moment when he turned and smiled at her.

Twenty years later, Matt's dazzling smile still had the ability to make her heart skip a beat—something she hadn't counted on happening. She wasn't sure how he felt about her, or even why she would consider the thought of them having a relationship.

Although she had extended her stay for a few weeks, eventually she would go back to Denver and would resume her life. Matt would remain in Driscoll Lake. She learned the hard way that long-distance relationships don't often work.

When the game ended in victory for the Driscoll Lake Panthers, people stood to cheer for the team. Matt put his arm around her shoulder and leaned close. "Unless you need to leave we might as well wait for the crowds to clear."

"I'm not in a hurry." She liked being with Matt, no matter if it was a football game, a morning jog, or an impromptu meal.

"I didn't eat dinner. Want to go to Mary's for a burger?"

"Sure. I'd like that."

Although she had a few reservations about deepening their relationship, she wasn't ready for the evening to end.

***

He was surprised to see Stephanie at the football game. She was getting content with life in Driscoll Lake, blending in with the crowd, resuming old friendships. She seemed especially comfortable with Matt Bradford.

There appeared to be more than friendship between the two of them. He didn't miss the look in her eyes. When Matt placed his arm around her shoulders and whispered something in her ear, he didn't mistake the shared look of intimacy between them.

Matt Bradford wasn't a pushover. Neither was Carlos Gonzales. They were smart. Trained. Professional. It wouldn't take long for either of them to spot some discrepancies in the original investigation.

With Stephanie Harris still asking questions, she could easily persuade Matt to reopen the case. It was possible they would want to talk with him. He couldn't afford to have that happen.

**

Mary's Diner was a long-standing business located near downtown. Although several nationally known chains had opened restaurants in the area, Mary's remained a popular place with locals because of her home-style meals and mouth-watering burgers. She stayed open late after home games, and the place was always crowded.

When Matt and Stephanie arrived, they learned it would be at least a half-hour wait for a table.

"Do you want to wait?" Matt asked. "We could pick up a pizza and take it back to the lake."

Stephanie looked around the crowded room. "Maybe that would be best."

"Matt, Stephanie!"

They looked up to seek Kyle Lawrence approaching them. "Want to join us? We can grab a couple of chairs and make room." He nodded toward a corner booth where Christine sat with Brian Nichols. Stephanie was surprised to see Heather Stevens from Miles Parker's office seated next to him.

"What do you think?" Matt asked.

"Sure," Stephanie said.

After Matt and Stephanie sat down, Christine asked, "Do you know Heather?"

"We met a few days ago in Mr. Parker's office. Nice to see you again."

"Would you mind autographing *Forgotten Memory* for me? It's not every day I meet a famous writer."

Stephanie felt her face grow warm. She'd autographed hundreds of books for fans—it was part of being a well-known author—but she felt a little embarrassed in front of friends. Brian rolled his eyes. Stephanie wasn't sure if he was annoyed or embarrassed by Heather.

"Of course, I'll sign it. I'm sure I'll see you sometime before I leave town."

Christine said, "I guess you all know Stephanie is staying here for a while."

"What made you decide to stay?" Heather asked.

This time Stephanie didn't mistake Brian's annoyance. "Don't be so nosey, Heather. Her reasons could be personal."

Heather lowered her head.

"It's okay," Stephanie said. "It didn't make sense to return to Denver when I need to settle Aunt Helen's affairs."

"Gone twenty years and now you don't want to leave. Some people would find that strange," Kyle said.

"Kyle!" Christine protested.

"I'm only kidding. Some of us can't seem to get away from here."

Stephanie paused for a moment and looked at Matt. "I never thought I would say this, but I've enjoyed being here."

"What made you decided to write those articles about Stephanie's father?" Heather asked Kyle. "Didn't you think it would be hard for her to relive those times?"

Heather was persistent when it came to wanting information. Stephanie recalled the day she was in Miles Parker's office. She suspected Heather had tried to overhear the conversation between Brian and Miles. Her actions tonight seemed to confirm that.

Everyone at the table grew quiet. Kyle paused before answering. "It was the twentieth anniversary of the event. I had written it before her aunt passed away. I never imagined Stephanie would be here to read the story."

"I asked him to write the second one," Stephanie said.

It was hard to tell who was the most surprised by her statement. Christine's eyes grew wide. Brian had a look of astonishment on his face, and Matt's gaze narrowed.

Stephanie chose her words carefully. She didn't want everyone to know about Carol's journal. Even though the restaurant was noisy, someone could overhear. "I spent most of my life believing my father was guilty. However, I wonder if Mom and I got the full story. I hope the articles will generate interest in the case. Maybe someone might remember something significant and come forward with the information."

"I guess your life has been something like one of your books," Heather said.

"You could say that. Except, in my books, someone always learns the truth. And if I have my way, I'll learn the truth about my father."

"Doing a little detective work on your own?"

"Why all the questions, Heather?" Brian admonished her.

Stephanie cleared her throat. "I'm sure you all didn't come here tonight to discuss a twenty-year-old murder case. Why don't we change the subject?"

"Good idea," Brian glared at Heather, as if daring her to say anything more.

***

Rachel Jackson sat near the front of the diner and tried to pretend interest in her date's conversation. Part of her new resolve to move forward in her life included getting out in the community more often, but she wondered why she agreed to attend a football game with Alan Davis.

Many women would be flattered to go out with the handsome lawyer. Rachel had turned him down several times, but he'd been persistent. He seemed nice. Miles Parker trusted him enough to make him a partner in the law firm. But something made her hesitate. Before tonight, Rachel hadn't been able to pinpoint what it was about him that bugged her.

It didn't take her long to learn. She should have listened to her instinct. His ceaseless chatter left her weary. If he wasn't on his cell phone negotiating "important business," he rambled on about himself. There would be no more dates with Alan after tonight.

Her gaze wandered to the table where Kyle and Christine sat with Brian Nichols and Heather Stevens. When Matt and Stephanie walked in together, Rachel found it difficult to concentrate on anything else.

Stephanie appeared to have adjusted to being back in Driscoll Lake in the short time since she'd been here. Rachel didn't miss the possessive look in Matt's eyes—something seemed to be developing between them.

She nibbled at a French-fry. Mary still had the best burgers and hand-cut fries around, but Rachel had no appetite. She kept her eyes on Brian, looking for any indication of his feelings toward the attractive young woman seated next to him.

Rachel longed for male companionship, but not from someone like Alan. She wanted a man more like her father. Ron Jackson was what people would call a self-made man. He came from a low-income family and worked throughout high school to earn money for college. His excellent grades helped him to obtain scholarships and acceptance into medical school.

Unlike her mother, who was born into a privileged family, her father knew what it was to be a working man. Brian was like that. He'd overcome odds and worked hard to establish himself as a respectful building contractor.

Rachel often thought her mother might be alive today if her parents hadn't divorced. At least Madelyn wouldn't have married Phillip Denton. She never cared for the man and believed he took advantage of Madelyn when she was still vulnerable over the divorce.

Rachel had never thought Phillip's disappearance and presumed death was any great loss. Madelyn didn't live long enough to grieve his disappearance—not that she would have done so.

Rachel had suspected for some time their marriage was failing. She overheard arguments—most of the time over money. At least her mother had the sense to keep the family trust fund out of Phillip's hands. Giving him control of the business had been bad enough.

"Rachel? Did you hear me?" Alan's words brought her back to the present.

"I'm sorry. What did you say?"

There was a burst of laughter from the other side of the room. Rachel's gaze drifted toward the table where her former classmates sat. Alan turned to look in that direction.

"Do you know those people with Heather? We could go over and say hello."

"No. I need to leave." She stood up from the table.

Alan glanced at the uneaten burger and fries. "But you've hardly touched your food."

"I'm not hungry. And I have an early shift at the hospital tomorrow. Please take me home."

***

It was almost midnight when Matt looked at his watch. "Guess we'd better get out of here. Mary will close soon."

"Man, I didn't realize it was this late," Kyle said. I need to stop by the office for a while."

"At this hour?" Christine asked.

"Something I forgot to do earlier. If you don't want to wait, I can take you home first."

"We can drop you off," said Brian.

"You sure it's no trouble? That would be great," Christine said.

Matt and Stephanie lingered in the parking lot after the others departed. "Sorry about the crowd," Matt said. "I should have known. Mary's is always busy on Friday nights after games."

"It's okay. It was nice to visit with some of my high school friends." Stephanie took a deep breath of the night air. "I'm glad I went to the game. I wasn't sure how it would be, but I felt a sense of freedom tonight. Maybe I'm finally getting over the past."

"But you still have questions. Otherwise, you wouldn't have asked Kyle to write a second story."

"Yes, I do. I realize the outcome probably won't change, but I have to try." She tried to blink away tears that threatened to fall. "I didn't mean to get emotional."

Matt wiped a tear from the corner of her eye. "Look, I know tonight wasn't a real date, but how about dinner tomorrow? Just the two of us. We can go someplace in Brewster."

Stephanie smiled. "I'd like that."

"Good." He leaned down and placed a light kiss on her lips.

Impulsively, Stephanie took her finger and traced the scar on his chin. "How did you get this?"

Matt took her hand and pulled it aside. Something flickered in his eyes. Pain? Hurt? Anger? Something else?

"It happened a long time ago. It's getting late. You're probably ready to go home."

She jerked her hand away from his. "Maybe tomorrow night isn't such a good idea."

"Stephanie, I—" The ringing of his cell phone interrupted Matt's words. He took it from his pocket and looked at the caller ID. "Damn. It's the station. I'd better take this." He spoke into the phone. "Bradford here."

Stephanie crossed her arms and turned away while Matt took the call. She regretted mentioning the scar, but how was she to know he was so sensitive about it? He made it obvious he didn't want to discuss the matter. She waited for him to hang up the phone.

"No, don't bother him. I'll be right there." Matt ended the call. "Something's come up, and I have to go to the station. I wanted to follow you home, but—"

"I don't need an escort. I'm perfectly capable of seeing myself to the house."

"Look I—"

"You're right. It's late, and I'm tired. Now isn't the time to talk."

"Guess you're right. Will I see you tomorrow?"

"Maybe. You'd better run along."

Matt sighed and shook his head. "I'll call you.

Stephanie watched him walk to his truck before getting in her car and driving away. Something seemed to be developing between them. She couldn't deny her feelings anymore. This wasn't a schoolgirl crush like the one she had years ago. She was a mature woman.

Maybe she was assuming too much. Matt asked her to dinner. Period. The kiss was only a light brush on the lips. Nothing more. His feelings may never go deeper than friendship.

Stephanie was so engrossed in thought she paid little attention to her surroundings. She was vaguely aware of a vehicle behind her, but it followed at a safe distance. However, when she neared the Taney Creek Bridge, the driver accelerated, turned the headlights on bright, and pulled up near her bumper.

Her pulse quickened. "Not again." Traffic was sparse at this hour. She took a deep breath. Stay calm. You'll get through this.

She reached for the rear-view mirror to reflect the headlights back into the driver's face, but as she did, the truck pulled around to pass.

Stephanie gasped. It looked like the same truck that tailgated her a week ago—a dark extended cab Ford. She couldn't see the driver, but the truck edged closer.

He's trying to force me off the road.

She floored the accelerator, but Helen's small car was no match for the Ford's bigger engine. The bridge was just ahead. She wouldn't make the curve unless she slowed down. When she eased off the gas, the truck moved closer.

As she reached the curve, the pickup hit back of her car. She fought to maintain control, but the car hit a guardrail and left the road. As it rolled down the embankment, she saw a large pine tree directly in front of her. She jerked the wheel in a last-minute attempt to avoid hitting it head on.

Karen Fulbright died at this same spot.

It was the last thought Stephanie had before everything went black.

Chapter Seventeen

Where was she? Why did her body ache all over? Stephanie opened her eyes to see the shattered windshield and deployed airbags.

Someone forced me off the road.

How long had she been here? Did she lose consciousness? Her head throbbed, and something warm trickled down the left side of her face. She recognized the metallic smell of blood and reached to wipe it away, wincing with pain when she tried to move her wrist.

She attempted to call for help, but the words came out in a whisper. A loud silence enveloped her. There was no one around. She was all alone. A terrifying thought came to her. What if the driver came back? Checked to see if she was still alive? He might try to finish what he started.

She heard voices. Someone was shouting.

"There's a car down there. Near the creek."

"Hurry. Call 9-1-1 and stay here until help arrives. I'll check on the occupants."

She heard footsteps draw close and a beam of light shone through the shattered window.

"Ma'am, can you hear me? Are you all right?"

"Head hurts. I think it's bleeding."

"My wife has called for help. Someone will be along shortly."

Stephanie wanted to sleep but tried to stay awake by forcing herself to remember details of the accident.

Think. You were on your way home. It was a black pickup truck. Probably the same one from the week before.

The man called out to someone standing at the top of the embankment. "There's a woman inside. She's alive but hurt. I can't get the door open."

Stephanie heard the sound of an approaching vehicle. A car door slammed. Another voice.

"What happened?"

"A car went off the road. I've already called 9-1-1. My husband's down there. A woman is inside. She's alive, but banged up."

More footsteps. Someone was running. The steps came closer.

"Glad you're here, sir. She has a nasty bump on the head and some cuts."

She heard Matt's voice. "Oh, Dear God! Stephanie? Please be okay."

"I'll be all right," she whispered.

She must have blacked out again. When she came to, she was lying down. She opened her eyes to see a paramedic sitting beside her.

"We'll be at the hospital soon," he said.

Someone barked orders. Something about x-rays, CT scans, and blood work. "We'll need to clean that wound. It could have shards of glass inside."

"Where...where am I?"

"You're at Memorial Hospital ER. I'm taking you to x-ray now."

Everything was a blur. She was back in the emergency room. Heard voices. Probably a doctor.

"There's no sign of internal bleeding. She has a concussion and a small laceration to her head. There is also a deep gash on her upper left arm, and her left wrist is severely sprained. She's lucky. Things could have been a lot worse."

Another male voice. "So you're saying she'll be okay?"

"Yes. We've cleaned, sutured, and dressed the wounds. I want to keep her overnight for observation. If all goes well, she can probably go home tomorrow."

She was in a strange room. It was dark, except for the dim light that shone from beneath the bed. Her head and wrist ached. An IV line was in her right arm. She raised her head slightly to look around. A man sat in a chair in the corner, feet stretched out, and his head leaned back.

She touched her forehead and felt a bandage on the left side. When she shifted in the bed, the sleeping man awakened. It was Matt.

He stood up and walked to her bedside. "Stephanie? How are you?"

"I hurt all over."

"Don't try to talk now. You need rest."

"But, I…" Still groggy, she closed her eyes and fell back asleep.

***

Matt awoke before daylight. His tall frame made sleeping in a chair difficult, but he refused to leave Stephanie alone. From the looks of her car, she was lucky to be alive.

He stood up, stretched, and glanced at his watch. Six-thirty. Stephanie was sleeping. A nurse had come in at six and administered more pain meds, so he figured she would sleep for a while longer. He needed coffee. A short walk outdoors would get his circulation going.

Now would be a good time to contact the officer who investigated the accident. Dugan would go off duty at seven. Matt wanted to talk with him before he left.

When he was outside the building, he pressed the speed dial button to the police station. "This is Matt. Is Dugan still around?" He waited for the young officer to pick up.

"Dugan here. What can I do for you, Chief?"

"Tell me what you know about Stephanie Harris's accident."

"She's a lucky woman. I'd like to talk to her, but I understand they kept her in the hospital overnight."

"Yeah. I'm here with her. The doctor may send her home this afternoon. I'll see if she's up to answering some questions later today."

"I'm going off duty in a few minutes, but Carlos is aware of the situation. We found evidence another car was involved."

"What?"

"Someone hit her from behind. We found black paint on the rear bumper. There's also broken glass from a headlight at the edge of the road. We bagged it and will try to match it with the type of vehicle. Most likely it will have additional damage. I'll put out the word to the body shops around this area to look for a black vehicle with a dented front bumper and broken headlight."

"Thanks, Dugan. I'll talk with her as soon as she's awake to see what she remembers. Tell Carlos I'll call him later."

Matt placed the phone back in his pocket and went inside. Stephanie must have been terrified. She could have died. He shook his head, not wanting to consider that thought.

Having a cup of coffee wasn't important now. He needed to get back to Stephanie and be with her when she woke up.

***

Daylight filtered through the vertical blinds when Stephanie opened her eyes. She blinked and tried to remember where she was. She had a vague recollection of being in the emergency room, of doctors talking about a concussion, and of seeing a man sitting in her room during the middle of the night.

Then she remembered the accident—the fear she felt when the truck pushed her off the road. Her thoughts about Karen Fulbright. Was it a mere coincidence Karen's accident happened in the same spot?

It was over in seconds, yet it seemed as if everything happened in slow motion. Stephanie closed her eyes, not wanting to relive the incident, but knowing she must. When she opened them, she saw Matt was still sitting in the chair. This time he was awake.

"Good morning," he said. "How do you feel?"

"Sore." She managed a weak smile. "Have you been here all night?"

"Someone had to keep an eye on you. You had an accident. Do you remember?"

"Yes. Some of it, anyway."

"Do you feel like talking?"

Stephanie nodded, wincing with pain. She'd think twice before doing that again.

"What do you remember? Your car ran off the road near the big curve by the Taney Creek Bridge."

"I was—"

There was a soft knock. A nurse opened the door and walked into the room.

"Ms. Harris? I'm here to get your vital signs."

Stephanie waited for the nurse to complete her duties. She shifted to sit up in the bed and flinched when she tried to push up with her left hand.

"Are you in pain? I can give you something."

"A little, but I don't want any medication right now."

"Okay. Use the call light if you need anything." She smiled, turned, and left the room.

"What can you tell me?" Matt asked.

"I was on my way home. A pickup truck came up behind me driving fast. The headlights were on bright, and I couldn't see."

"You missed the curve?"

"Yes. But the driver forced me off the road."

"Did you see anything? The driver? What type of truck it was?"

"Couldn't make out who was driving, but it was a dark extended cab pickup. A Ford. I'm certain it was the same one as last week."

"Last week? What are you talking about?"

"I was on my way home after having dinner with Christine. A pickup tailgated me. It happened almost in the same spot. It stayed on my bumper a while, but sped up and passed me."

"Why didn't you say anything?"

"I should have, but I wasn't sure if the notes and the phone call were related."

"Notes? Phone call? What are you talking about?"

"Someone has been leaving notes for me."

"Notes? When? Where?" Matt stood up and began to pace the room.

"Warnings. Threats. Hard to say. I found the first one on the kitchen counter the day I arrived. Someone slipped a second one beneath the front door a couple of days later. I found the third one on the windshield of my car when I was in town one day."

"Why haven't you said anything?"

"I thought it was someone's idea of a joke at first. Your father said there had been some incidents of criminal mischief at the lake."

Did you keep them?"

"Yes."

"There were phone calls also?"

"Only one. Someone left a voice message. It was on Aunt Helen's answering machine when I arrived home after the tailgating incident."

"Stephanie, you should have told us. We could have investigated. This is serious."

"I know that now."

"I'm going to call Carlos. We already knew another car was involved last night. From what you said, the driver deliberately forced you off the road. It seems as if someone doesn't want you around."

***

After her conversation with Matt, Stephanie fell asleep. When she awakened again, it was almost noon. The pain in her head had subsided, and she was starting to feel restless.

"When can I get out of here?" she asked when the nurse came into the room.

"The doctor will be by to see you soon. If you feel like eating, I'll have your tray brought in."

"Sure." When the nurse left, Stephanie turned to Matt. "I'd rather go home."

"You probably will. Listen, I don't want you to be surprised when the doctor comes in. It's Rachel Jackson."

"Rachel? I'm surprised she would want me as a patient."

"She's a professional, Stephanie. She'd never let any personal feelings interfere with doing her job."

"I realize that, but I don't want her to feel awkward."

"Nor should you."

"I'm tough. I can handle Rachel. Or anyone else for that matter."

***

Rachel came to Stephanie's room shortly after noon. Matt had left to eat lunch in the cafeteria. To her credit, Rachel acted professionally.

"Good afternoon, Stephanie. How are you feeling?"

"I'm sore, but feeling better. Can I get out of here?"

"I don't see any reason to keep you any longer. The soreness will last for a few days. You didn't have any broken ribs, but you'll have bruising where the seatbelt restrained you. There was no internal bleeding. You have a severe sprain to your left wrist, but no fracture."

"That's good to know."

"I'm going to send you home with pain meds. It's a narcotic, and it will cause drowsiness, so no driving."

"Okay."

"You're very fortunate. Your injuries were relatively minor, considering the magnitude of the accident. You do have a mild concussion, so you'll need rest."

"I'll take it easy."

"You need to do more than that. I mean complete rest until Monday. Matt tells me you're a runner, but I don't want you to exercise until you follow-up with a primary care doctor. It's also a good idea not to use the computer for extended periods of time. Allow your brain to rest. Your nurse will go over your discharge instructions before you leave. If certain symptoms appear, you need to seek medical attention right away."

"If I have so many restrictions, what can I do?"

"Not much of anything at first. Someone needs to stay with you at least tonight to monitor for any warning signs. I don't want you to be alone. If no one's able to stay, then I'd like to keep you another night."

Stephanie sighed. Nell was out of town "I'm not sure. Maybe I could ask—"

"I'll take care of her," Matt said as he walked in the room.

"Good," Rachel said. "I'll write the discharge orders, and you can be out of here soon."

"Thanks, doctor."

"Please. We can dispense with the formalities. Call me Rachel." She smiled.

Stephanie took a deep breath and exhaled. "Okay. Rachel."

"I'll leave the discharge instructions with your nurse and have her disconnect the IV. It's okay for you to get out of bed now."

Stephanie looked at the hospital gown. "I would like to take a shower. Where are my clothes?"

"I'm afraid they got blood on them," Matt said. "There's a shopping center nearby. I can buy you something. Maybe jeans and a t-shirt and I guess you'll need..." His face colored.

Stephanie couldn't help but smile at Matt being embarrassed over the thought of buying her underwear. She and Rachel looked at one another and laughed.

"Why, Matt Bradford," Rachel said. "You're blushing."

Stephanie grinned. "You're right, Matt. I will need—"

"How did I get myself into this?"

"Never mind," Rachel said. "You're a man. You'd get it all wrong. Stephanie, I think we're about the same size. I keep a complete change of clothes here. You're welcome to wear them. I'll bring them to you."

"Thanks, Rachel. I appreciate it."

"No problem." Rachel looked at Matt. "And you. Go make yourself busy while she takes a shower."

"Sure. I need to make a phone call anyway." He hurried from the room.

"There's something I've wanted to say to you," Rachel said. "I didn't treat you right all those years ago. I'm sorry for the way I acted."

"Thanks, but you never did anything to me. I can't recall that we even talked after..." She found it hard to say the words.

"But I didn't do anything to stop how others treated you. What happened wasn't your fault or mine. The way some people turned against you wasn't right."

"It did hurt. Mom and I weren't responsible, but people acted as if we were. I'm older now. I'm moving on with my life. Coming back here has brought a degree of healing."

"I'm glad you came—even though it wasn't under pleasant circumstances. I think you'll find most people don't hold a grudge against you. You weren't responsible for your father's actions."

"I've come to believe Dad was innocent."

"How can you say that? He killed— I'm sorry, I didn't intend to bring that up."

"He killed your mother. That's what authorities said, but my father wasn't a violent man. Did you know the day they died, he and your mother had a meeting to discuss the company's future?"

Rachel shook her head. "No, I didn't."

"They also scheduled a company-wide meeting for the following Monday. Your mother planned to attend."

"A meeting? How did you find out?"

"I talked to Dorothy Nichols. She told me. Said the police never questioned her about it and felt they did a shoddy investigation."

"But the autopsy reports stated... Can't you just leave it alone? Don't you think we've all suffered enough without having to relive everything?"

"Rachel, what if your mother had been accused of killing my father? Would you have doubts? Wouldn't you want to know the truth?"

"Yes." Rachel's voice was almost a whisper. "I would."

Chapter Eighteen

Matt helped Stephanie into the house and made sure she was comfortable on the sofa. "Do you need anything? Something to drink?"

"No, I'm fine. You can go home. I promise to get some rest."

"I'm not going anywhere. Rachel said you needed someone to look after you for a day or two."

"Matt, I'm okay."

"I said I'm staying. You're not going to get rid of me that easy."

Whiskers came out of the bedroom. His loud meow left no doubt he was hungry.

"Okay. If you want to help, you can feed the cat. His food is in the pantry."

"At your service. Come along, Whiskers." He grinned and went into the kitchen.

"And his litter box probably needs to be cleaned." That should do it. She couldn't imagine him cleaning up after a cat, especially since she last cleaned the box the day before.

"No problem."

Stephanie rolled her eyes. Deterring Matt wouldn't be easy. She heard a clinking sound as he poured food into the stainless-steel dish, followed by running water.

"His water dish was almost empty. Where's the litter box?"

"In the laundry room. There's a box of fresh litter on the shelf." It wasn't as if she didn't appreciate Matt's offer of assistance, but she wasn't accustomed to having someone wait on her.

A few minutes later, he came back into the den. "Whiskers is a happy cat now. The minute I finished with the litter box, he decided to use it."

"He often does that. Most of the time he watches and waits while I clean it."

"Are you hungry? I can make dinner later, or we can order pizza."

"Matt, why are you doing all this? I can take care of myself."

"You heard the doctor's orders."

"But don't you have other things you need to do?" Stephanie yawned. "I'm going to take a nap."

"Right now, nothing is more important than looking after you. I asked Carlos to come by later to pick up the notes. Think you'll be up to talking to him?"

"Yes, I'll be okay."

"Good. Think you'll be okay for a few minutes? I need to grab a change of clothes at the house. Shouldn't be gone longer than ten or fifteen minutes."

Stephanie knew it was useless to argue. "I'll be fine, but aren't you concerned with what people might think if you stay overnight? After all, this is still a small town. Full of gossips."

"I don't care what anyone thinks. I'm staying."

***

It was almost six before Carlos arrived. "Thanks for allowing me to come, I don't want to tire you, but I do have a few questions about the accident."

"I'm fine. I'll tell you everything I remember."

"You said the vehicle was a dark, extended cab pickup."

"Yes, it was either a black or dark blue Ford. I wasn't able to get a license plate number, but I think a man was driving."

"Was he old? Young? Anything about him that stood out?"

Stephanie shook her head. "I couldn't see him well enough. Heck, I don't even know for sure it was a man. I'm just assuming it was after the phone call last week."

"Tell me about that call. Matt says this wasn't the first encounter you had with the pickup truck."

"No, it isn't. The Friday before, I had dinner with Christine Lawrence. It was late, and I was on my way home. The same pickup, at least I think it was the same one, came up behind and tailgated me. I was able to arrange the review mirror so the headlights would reflect in the driver's face."

"Good thinking. What happened then?"

"The driver sped up and passed. When I got home, there was a message on the answering machine."

"Did you keep it?"

"No, I erased it. Foolish of me, but I got tired of seeing the message light every time I walked by the phone. As expected, the caller ID showed a blocked number."

"Was the caller male or female? What did the message say?"

"The voice sounded muffled, but I'm certain it was a man. He said something about warning me and the next time he wouldn't be so nice."

"And he wasn't," Matt said.

"I believe you also received some notes."

"Yes, they're in the lap drawer of the desk. I'll get them." Stephanie stood up.

"No, wait. We may be able to lift some prints. Do you mind?" Carlos slipped on a pair of gloves.

Stephanie shook her head. "No, go ahead. They should be on top."

Carlos looked at each note before placing them in a zip-lock bag. "I'm glad you kept these. Some people would have thrown them away. Not sure if we'll be able to get any prints from them, but we'll try."

"You'll find mine. I didn't think about handling them."

"It's okay. If we find anything, we'll check to see if the prints match anyone in the database."

"I'd be glad for you to take my prints if necessary to compare."

"As soon as you're able, stop by the station."

"Okay." Stephanie sighed. "Not much to go on, is there?"

"The vehicle that hit you will have some damage. We've already sent word to all the body shops here and in the surrounding towns. I hope we'll learn something."

"Detective Gonzales," Stephanie asked. "Could this have anything to do with my father? I mentioned to a couple of friends that I had questions and wanted the case reopened. I also told them I had begun to pursue my own investigation. I'm not worried about them, but you know how word gets around in a small town."

"Hard to say at this point, but we can't rule out the possibility. I've kept you long enough. If you wouldn't mind signing this report, I'll be on my way."

He handed her the paper and a pen. She grimaced as she took the pen in her left hand. "Kind of hard to write with my wrist in this shape. I'm left-handed—just like my father."

***

Matt walked with Carlos to his car. "You thinking what I'm thinking?"

"Yeah. The same driver was involved in both incidents."

"I think it's worth looking over the old files on Robert Harris. It seems to me that someone doesn't want Stephanie here. I can't imagine why, but if the word is out she's asking questions, this could all be related."

"I'm already on it. In fact, after the initial newspaper article, I pulled the file out of curiosity. I knew Robert from high school. The person I knew wasn't a murderer. In fact, Stephanie came to me a few days ago and asked if I would look at the file."

"Stephanie came to you? I wonder why she didn't ask me about it."

Carlos shook his head. "You got me. I told her there wasn't anything in the file that warranted reopening of the case, so don't say anything to her just yet. I don't want to get her hopes up. I'll take another look, but I doubt I'll find anything."

"If this isn't related to her father, what could it be?"

Carlos shook his head. "A deranged fan perhaps? Who knows? Stranger things have happened."

***

Rachel was weary after her twelve-hour shift at the hospital. It wasn't because of a high-volume patient load. She had known better than to stay out late when she had an early shift.

Going out with Alan Davis had been a mistake in more than one way. She had a feeling he wasn't easy to deter. He would call again. Probably want to take her on a "real" date. Eating at Mary's Diner was the second mistake. Seeing Matt, Stephanie, and other friends together confirmed what she already knew—she was lonely. There was more to life than a career. She needed to socialize more often.

When she arrived home, she changed into comfortable clothes and settled in a lounge chair in the den. She looked outside at the pool—the cool water would be refreshing, but she was too tired. She picked up a stack of mail that her housekeeper left on the table.

The latest edition of the *Driscoll Lake Reporter* was on top. Rachel hadn't read this week's edition. She opened it and was surprised to see the second story about Robert Harris. She quickly read the article.

Rachel was only fifteen when her mother died—too young to know or care about running a business. Although ownership passed to her upon her mother's death, the administrators of the family trust were quick to appoint a board of directors and hire qualified personnel to oversee management of the company. However, with the missing money, coupled with a downturn in the economy, the company failed to survive. Everyone, including her, blamed Robert Harris.

She thought back to her conversation with Stephanie. If what Dorothy Nichols said was correct, Harris's actions didn't sound like someone who planned to commit suicide. Had he discovered the missing money and alerted her mother?

Why didn't the police question Dorothy Nichols? And why, if Robert Harris took the money, didn't he simply disappear? Why bother to go to the trouble to steal it only to kill himself? It would have been easy to vanish.

What if Stephanie was right? Maybe Robert Harris was innocent. Had Rachel blamed the wrong person for her mother's death? But if Stephanie's father didn't kill her mother, then who did?

Chapter Nineteen

Stephanie was almost back to normal by Monday morning. She still had a few aches and pains but refused to take any more pain medication.

"It wipes me out, and I don't want to sleep during the day," she told Matt. "If the pain gets too bad, I'll take some over the counter meds."

Matt stayed with her two nights, leaving only long enough to check his parents' house or pick up things at his place. "I'll come by after work."

"You don't need to stay again tonight. I'll be fine."

"Are you sure?"

"Yes. I'm grateful for what you've done, but I'm okay."

Matt looked around the room. "It wouldn't be a bad idea to install a security system."

"I'm not even sure I'll keep the house."

"Even if you do decide to sell, it would be an added incentive for the buyer. It will also reduce the insurance premium."

Stephanie sighed. "Okay, I'll consider it."

"Good. I'll talk to Brian about having your locks changed."

"Change the locks? Why?"

"Those notes and your accident weren't a joke. It's apparent someone doesn't want you in Driscoll Lake. You found two of them inside the house. They didn't get here on its own. Someone could have known where Helen kept a hidden key."

"Which I now have in my possession."

"And someone could have made a copy before you had it."

"This is a gated community with round the clock security. Don't you think you're overreacting?"

Matt sighed. "Maybe I am, but since you insist on taking care of yourself, I'm still going to talk with Brian. No sense in taking a risk."

***

Monday morning was unusually busy at the police station. It was almost noon before Matt had a free moment. Knowing Brian often ate lunch at Rosa's, he decided to walk the short distance on the chance of meeting him there.

He stopped by Carlos's office before leaving the station. "I'm going over to Rosa's for lunch. Want to come along?"

"No, thanks. Maria made homemade tamales. I have plenty to share."

"Thanks, but I hope to catch Brian Nichols and discuss changing the locks at Stephanie's place."

"Good idea."

When he arrived at Rosa's, Brian was at the counter placing his order.

"Hey, Matt," Brian said. "I never see you here this time of the day. What's up?"

"Looking for you. I'd like to talk to you about something."

"Sure. I'll grab a place to sit. This place is always crowded during the lunch hour."

Matt placed his order and joined Brian at a table near the front. Brian appeared restless and kept checking his phone for messages. "Is something wrong?"

"An issue with a job. What did you want to talk to me about?"

"What would it take to replace the locks at Stephanie's house?"

"New locks? I changed them a few months ago when I did a remodeling job for Helen. If they aren't working properly, they would still be under warranty."

"They work. Just need to be replaced."

Brian frowned. "Okay. If I remember, she has three doors."

"Right. A front door, another leading into the carport, and French doors off the screened in porch."

"It would take me an hour at most to change them out. Has Stephanie already purchased new ones?"

"Not yet, but she will."

"I'll be out there this afternoon to check on the job across the street. I can stop by the house, look at the current ones, and see what she wants. I can purchase the new locks at a discount and won't charge her anything for the installation."

"Thanks. Sounds good. I'll let Stephanie know you're coming. When do you think you can install them?"

"If I'm able to purchase them locally, I should be able to do it by mid-week."

"I appreciate it."

They finished their lunch in silence. Brian acted as if he were eager to leave. Matt walked with him to the parking lot.

When they got to Brian's truck, he asked, "Want a lift back to the station? It's hot out here today."

Matt started to say yes when he noticed Brian's truck had a dented front bumper and broken headlight. "What happened?"

"I had an accident Friday night after I dropped Heather at her apartment. A car backed out of a parking space and hit me."

"I suppose you filed an accident report."

"It happened on private property, so I didn't call the police."

"You should have notified authorities."

"Since when did the police begin investigating accidents on private property? If I'd known that, I would have done so."

"We don't."

"Then what's the big deal?"

"Forget it. And never mind about Stephanie's house. I'll take care of it myself."

Matt stalked away. A dented front bumper? Broken headlight? Black extended cab pickup? It was too much of a coincidence. What reason would Brian Nichols have for wanting to hurt Stephanie?

He walked back to the station and immediately went to Carlos's office. "I may have something about Stephanie's accident. Brian Nichols drives a black extended cab Ford. I saw his truck. It has a broken headlight and a small dent on the front."

"Oh?"

"He claimed it happened in a private lot and therefore didn't call the police. But it's just too coincidental."

"Now wait a minute, Matt. You're talking about Brian Nichols. Why would he possibly want Stephanie to leave town? Do you honestly think he would try to kill her? Sorry, that's not the Brian I know."

"But that's just it. Maybe we don't really know him. His mother was Stephanie's father's secretary. She suffered along with the rest of the employees of Cameron Manufacturing. Could be out for revenge."

"Matt, you're too close to this case. You need to step back and let me handle it."

"What do you mean too close?"

"Your relationship with Stephanie has you blinded to the truth."

"My relationship with Stephanie? Up until two weeks ago, I hadn't seen her in twenty years. She's a friend— that's all."

"I saw the way you acted toward her on Saturday. I know you want to help her. I can't blame you for that, but take my advice and allow me to handle it. I promise to keep you up to date."

Matt sighed. "Okay. I'll let you do your job. I don't want to believe that about Brian, but I know what I saw. And for the record, Stephanie is just a good friend."

"Yeah, right," Carlos said. "Matt, can I say something to you? Not as a colleague, but a friend?"

"Of course."

"I understand your wife's death was hard to deal with. But it's been almost five years. You're still young. It's time you moved on. Stephanie seems like a decent person. Since she's come back home, why not pursue a deeper relationship with her?"

Matt sighed. "Carlos, this was her home, but it's not now. Once everything is settled with her aunt's estate, she'll leave here. I don't want to become involved only to lose her to the big city life."

"You're already involved, Matt. You just won't admit it."

***

By Monday afternoon, Brian Nichols wished he'd stayed in bed with the covers pulled over his head. The day started at the bottom and went downhill. First, the building supply company delivered the wrong windows for the house in Lakeview Estates.

He made a quick call to the supplier, who apologized profusely, and promised to expedite the order for the correct ones. However, it would be at least two days before they would arrive from the factory.

When Brian requested they pick up the wrong ones immediately, the supply manager said he wouldn't have a driver available until the following day. That meant forty of the wrong windows were sitting on the building site where anyone with a mind to do so could steal them.

"I won't be responsible for your mistake, and I can hardly ask one of my men to be a night watchman."

"I'll take full responsibility."

"I'm counting on it," Brian said. "Your error is costing us at least two days of work and we're already behind schedule."

Next, one of his best carpenters quit. Said he got a job offer from a builder over in Brewster who offered him more money.

Then the strange encounter with Matt. He acted friendly enough until they got to the parking lot.

Why had he suddenly begun acting like a lion with a thorn in his paw? Making a big deal over him not reporting the accident. What made him change his mind about the locks at Stephanie's house?

Matt sure acted strangely. Brian had already suspected there was something more than friendship developing between him and Stephanie. Maybe it was jealousy. Whatever the case, Brian had more important things to deal with.

After lunch, he received word he had lost the bid on a subsidized housing project when another builder underbid him. Next the insurance company for the person who backed into him called to say it would be a few days before an adjuster could review his claim. He had already suspected they would try to give him the run-around, and he would end up having to file on his on policy.

Yes, he would have been better off if he'd stayed home and in bed.

He stopped at the assisted living facility on his way home for a quick visit with his mother. Afterward, he stopped at Tso's for Chinese takeout. All he wanted to do was go to the house, relax in his recliner, and enjoy his dinner. If he were a drinking man, he'd drown his sorrows in a few bottles of beer or something stronger.

When he arrived home, he peered into the almost empty refrigerator. He needed to do better about keeping it stocked and not eat out as often. But it was hard to come home to an empty house every day. Almost two years had passed since his divorce, and he was ready for companionship.

Not someone like that airhead Heather. He regretted asking her to the football game. For the life of himself, he couldn't figure out why Miles Parker had hired someone like her.

Heather acted too much like a silly schoolgirl. Brian was interested in someone more mature. Someone who would appreciate him for who he was. Someone like Rachel Jackson.

He had seen her on Friday night at Mary's Diner. He didn't miss the fact that she looked his way several times. She was with Alan Davis, so he didn't attempt to talk with her.

He shook his head. What was he thinking? Rachel Jackson? She wouldn't be interested in someone like him. Yes, they had a business relationship, but it's likely that's all they would ever have.

He reached toward the back of the refrigerator, pulled out a bottle of water, and took it and the sweet and sour chicken into the living room. He sat down in his recliner and turned on the TV. When had his life come down to this? A day of work and stress only to get home to an empty house where the biggest excitement was watching the evening news.

Something had to change.

***

Kyle Lawrence pressed the button to end the call and threw his cell phone on the sofa. It was rare when he asked a favor of his father, and never for selfish reasons. He had thought Curtis Lawrence would be willing to help his only granddaughter. He was wrong.

"Kyle, who was that on the phone?" Christine walked into the room.

"The 'Honorable' Judge Lawrence."

"You're angry. What happened?"

"A few days ago, I asked him if he'd be willing to help take the things Emily's youth group collected to the fire station for the benefit auction. He agreed but called today to say something came up, and he couldn't help."

Christine shook her head. "I'm sorry. I can't understand why he treats you that way."

"I stopped allowing him to hurt me a long time ago. I just don't want his selfish actions to affect Emily."

"She's tougher than you think."

"I should have known better, but was hoping he'd be willing to use his pickup. It's not like he ever drives it. Now I'll have to figure out another way to get the things to the fire station."

"I'll help."

"I thought you had plans today."

"Nothing important. We can fold down the back seat of my van. Between that and your SUV, we should be able to take most of the things. If we have to make more than one trip, it's okay."

Kyle smiled. "Thanks, honey. Sometimes I wonder what I did to deserve you."

***

By mid-week, things were looking up for Brian. The supplier picked up the wrong windows and delivered the new ones. The insurance company approved his claim. He contacted a body shop and arranged for them to begin the repairs.

He was able to hire a new carpenter—one that had worked for a competitor several years. The guy said he liked Brian's work ethics and wasn't so sure his former employer was honest.

On Wednesday morning, Brian drove to the job site in Lakeview Estates to check progress. Stephanie was in her front yard, and he noticed the splint on her left wrist.

He smiled and waved. "How's it going?"

"I'm recovering," she said, raising her voice so that he could hear from a distance.

"Recovering? From what?"

"You didn't know? I was in an auto accident Friday night."

"Accident?" Brian hurried across the road so that he could talk to Stephanie without shouting. "What happened?"

"I was on my way home after we left the diner. Someone forced me off the road near Taney Creek Bridge. My car rolled down the embankment. The doctors say I'm lucky. I could have been killed."

"Someone forced you off the road? Who was it?"

"I don't know. The driver left the scene. A similar incident happened a week earlier when a pickup tailgated me. When I got home, someone left a message on the answering machine saying it was a warning, and the next time they wouldn't be as nice."

"Someone threatened you?"

"Guess it's the same person who left me the notes."

"Notes?"

"Found one the day I arrived, the second a few days later. The third one was on my windshield the day we ate lunch together at Rosa's. Anyway, the police are checking all the local body shops. The other vehicle will have damage—at least a broken headlight. It was a black or dark blue extended cab pickup."

Brian felt the anger well up inside him. His nostrils flared, and he felt sure his faced turned three shades of red. "So that explains..."

"What?"

"Never mind."

"Brian, are you okay?"

"Yes. No. Sorry, I've got to run. I need to take care of something right away."

He rushed back to his vehicle and peeled out of the driveway—leaving skid marks on the road. He had to see Matt and set the record straight. He'd give Mr. High and Mighty a piece of his mind.

He drove straight to the police station and rushed inside. "I need to see Chief Bradford right way."

"Is this an emergency?"

"You might say that."

"Perhaps someone else can help—"

"No. No one else. I want to speak to Matt. Immediately."

"I'm sorry, but he isn't here. He's away for the day. Are you sure don't want to talk to another officer or Detective Gonzales?"

Brian took a deep breath and slowly exhaled "No. No one else." He turned and left the station. It was just as well. As angry as he was right now, he wasn't sure what he would do if he saw Matt. Better to calm down first and then confront him.

He thought Matt was a friend, but friends don't accuse other friends of attempted murder. And when you got right down to it, that's what Matt had done. Brian should have known better. It seemed he would never overcome his past.

Chapter Twenty

Rachel walked to the parking lot and climbed into her SUV, dreading another evening alone. She had been on an emotional roller coaster since Friday and tried to convince herself it was due to the extended hours she'd been working, but she knew better. She'd worked much longer shifts during residency.

The outing with Alan Davis wasn't her idea of a date, but it made her realize she was missing a lot. She envied Stephanie's ability to ease back into life at Driscoll Lake. Then again, Stephanie had always been an outgoing person—at least before her father died.

Thinking of Stephanie brought something else to mind. Rachel sensed a change within herself. She fought it all week, but she couldn't get Stephanie's words out of her head. "What if your mother had been accused of killing my father? Wouldn't you want to know the truth?"

She dealt with her mother's death by accepting what the police said. It hadn't been easy, but her father and stepmother had done their best to help ease her pain. Her half siblings welcomed her—excited about having a big sister around.

She rarely spoke about the incident, as if that would make the pain go away. Other times, when her inward anger threatened to spill out, she turned it toward one person. Even though he was dead, in her mind she often lashed out at Robert Harris with hatred.

Rachel knew coming back to Driscoll Lake would stir up old memories, but she had run from the past long enough. She was angry when Kyle wrote the first article. He insinuated Harris was innocent. Rachel couldn't understand why he would do such a thing.

After talking with Stephanie and reflecting upon the past, she started to have second thoughts. No one could argue with the evidence, but for the first time in years, she allowed herself to remember the type of person Robert Harris had been.

Grandfather Cameron was fond of him. He often told a story of when he lost his wallet containing a large amount of cash. Robert Harris was only a teenager when found the wallet and returned it with everything inside. William Cameron offered him a part-time job at the factory and promised him a position upon his graduation from college.

Rachel trusted her grandfather. He was always a good judge of character. Her mother often said he thought of Robert as the son he never had. Throughout the years, her grandfather had nothing but praise for the man.

Lost in her thoughts, Rachel drove slowly through town. She wasn't ready to go home. The place had too many memories. Most were good, but others sad, such as the last time she saw her mother alive. It had been on Friday afternoon as Rachel prepared to attend the first home game of the season. She had been excited about her second year in the high school band.

"Mom, are you coming to the game?"

"I have something to take care of first, but I'll be there for the halftime show. I wouldn't miss seeing my daughter."

Her mother never showed up. Didn't live to see her daughter graduate high school, attend college, or become a physician. A cold-blooded killer made certain of that.

Rachel pulled into the parking lot of a local bar and grill. Dinner and a glass of wine were in order. She walked into the building and asked for a seat in the restaurant section, not wanting to sit in the bar. The last thing she wanted was for people to think she needed to pick up dates in bar.

From her table, Rachel could see people entering and leaving the restaurant. The waitress had just brought her glass of wine when Brian Nichols walked through the door. After speaking to the hostess, he turned around as if to leave when he looked in Rachel's direction. He smiled and she motioned for him to join her. Maybe it wouldn't be a lonely evening after all.

***

Brian didn't want to believe Matt suspected he was responsible for Stephanie's accident. Granted they ran in different circles in high school, but since Matt moved back to Driscoll Lake, he treated Brian as if they were friends. So much for that. Friends don't quickly jump to conclusions without hearing the facts.

He went back to the job site after leaving the police station, but every time he looked at Stephanie's house, he thought about Matt. The more he thought, the angrier he became. He left and went to his office to complete some long overdue paperwork. His workers didn't need him to hang around. They knew what to do without having him stand over them.

It was six-thirty before he finished entering data into the computer. His business had grown enough to hire an office assistant, but he kept putting off. Heather hinted about coming to work for him, claiming she was bored at Miles Parker's office.

Brian wasn't sure she could type a letter, let alone enter numbers into his accounting software. He also suspected she enjoyed gossip. He didn't need or want anyone like that around.

His stomach growled—a reminder he hadn't eaten since breakfast. He still had no food in the house, so it was a matter of deciding which fast food joint to stop at. He missed having a home cooked meal in the evenings. His mother was an excellent cook. Before she entered the assisted living facility, she often prepared dinner and invited him over.

Brian locked his office, got into his truck, and drove away. The idea of eating junk food wasn't appealing, so he decided to stop at a local restaurant. As expected, it was crowded.

"It will be a thirty to forty-five minute wait," the hostess said. "Unless you want to sit at the bar."

He looked in that direction. Several customers sat and sipped their drinks while watching baseball on the big-screen television. Some of them were there simply to relax and enjoy a drink after a long day. Others looked as if they were members of a lonely-hearts club.

With the mood he was in, Brian would fit into the latter category. It would be too easy to drown his sorrows.

It was the second time this week he'd considered that option. Whenever the urge to drink hit him, he thought of his father. Harold Nichols was once a successful building contractor until he began to hit the booze hard. After that, he slowly wasted away and lost everything he'd worked so hard to achieve. Had it not been for Brian's mother, they would have lost their house. She was the strong one who held the family together. Brian didn't want to become like his father.

"No thanks," he told the hostess. "Guess I'll just grab a quick bite somewhere else."

He turned to leave when he saw Rachel sitting alone at a table. She smiled and motioned him over. The evening had just improved.

***

"I'm glad you could join me," Rachel said as Brian sat down opposite her.

"Thanks for asking. I was about to leave. Didn't want to wait for a table."

"I haven't ordered yet. Decided to have a glass of wine first. Would you like one?"

"No thanks. I don't touch the stuff."

Rachel cocked an eyebrow. "Oh? Does that mean all the rumors about you in high school were false?"

Brian shook his head. "No, I drank in those days. Learned I had a low tolerance for alcohol, so I gave it up."

Rachel pointed to her glass. "I hope this doesn't bother you."

"No need to worry. I don't condemn anyone who drinks. It's a personal choice for me. You probably know my father was an alcoholic. I didn't want to become like him."

"I understand."

"To be honest, I felt like downing a few beers or something stronger tonight."

"What's wrong?"

"Everything. Nothing. It's been a rough week."

"Want to talk about it?"

"I wouldn't want to bore you."

"Try me."

"I was involved in a small accident last Friday. Did some damage to my truck."

"Sorry to hear that."

"It wouldn't have happened if I hadn't been out with that airhead. I mean, Heather."

Rachel laughed. "Tell me how you really feel about her."

"Wish I'd never asked her out, and I won't make that mistake again. But that's the least of my worries."

"What's the problem?"

"Matt found me at Rosa's on Monday to ask if I could change the locks on Stephanie's house. I told him I would. But when we walked to the parking lot, he acted strangely. Said not to bother, that he would change the locks himself."

"He gave no explanation?"

"None. Today I went to a job site across the street from Helen's, I mean Stephanie's, place. She happened to be outside, and I noticed her arm was in a sling. She told me she'd been in an accident last Friday night. Had you heard about it?"

Rachel paused. As a health care professional, she couldn't discuss anything about Stephanie's care or even mention she had treated her at the hospital. "Go on."

"Sorry. Didn't stop to consider you may have been her physician. Don't want to get you in trouble."

Rachel chose her words carefully. "It's okay. Word gets around in small towns. I heard about it."

"Someone forced her off the road and apparently, it wasn't an isolated incident. A similar thing happened not long after she arrived back in town."

"What? I figured the accident was because of a drunk driver."

"That's not what the police think. Stephanie also told me someone had left her some notes at the house. Someone who was able to get inside."

"Notes? What did they say?"

Brian shrugged. "Some sort of warning about what might happen if she stayed in town. She also received a threatening phone call."

"You're kidding. Who would care if she stayed?" Rachel glanced around the room. She felt a tingling sensation on the back of her neck as if someone was watching.

"Beats me," Brian said. "Stephanie thinks it has something to do with the fact she's been asking questions about her father's suicide."

"So Matt thinks you might have been involved?"

"I drive a dark truck. It has a dent on the front. Police determined the vehicle that forced Stephanie off the road was a dark extended cab pickup. Guess that's enough for him."

"Half the people in this county drive dark colored pickup trucks. Matt isn't thinking clearly. I think his interest in Stephanie goes deeper than friendship."

"I think so too, but Matt knows me better than to think I would hurt her. At least, I thought he did."

"Brian, try not to take it personally. The police will investigate every lead. I know it's a coincidence, but they have to look at things objectively."

He slammed his hand on the table. "What reason would I have for wanting to hurt Stephanie? I went to the station to talk with him, but he was out of town. Just as well. I was pretty angry."

"If he does think you're involved, he's got a thing or two to learn about people. The Brian Nichols I know wouldn't do anything like that."

"Thanks for the support. It means a lot."

"I'm sure it's all a misunderstanding. Matt probably doesn't blame you. Back to Stephanie. Who wouldn't want her in town? If this does have something to do with—" Rachel shivered.

"Something wrong?"

"Not exactly. Just felt like someone was watching me." She shrugged. "Anyway, if Stephanie's accident is related to her asking questions about her father, then maybe we don't know the whole story."

"What are you saying?"

"I've already considered the possibility that I've been wrong all these years. What if Robert Harris didn't kill my mother?"

"A lot of people were surprised by the incident— including my mother."

"I accepted what I'd been told. I hated Robert Harris for what he did. For a long time, I didn't consider how his actions affected Stephanie. I wasn't the only one to lose a parent." Rachel paused and looked out the window. For the first time, she allowed herself to consider what things must have been like for Stephanie.

"It must have been devastating for her—maybe even more so. At least people didn't think of me as the daughter of a murderer. I can't blame her for wanting to know the truth."

"I guess so. But maybe she should leave it alone. To drag up all that again would just open old wounds."

Rachel felt the tingling sensation on the back of her neck again. Brian's words were lost as she glanced around, trying to look nonchalant. She spotted the reason for her uneasiness sitting on the far side of the room staring intently at her and Brian. When she caught the man's eye, he quickly looked away.

She turned back to Brian. "I'm sorry," she said. "What were you saying?"

"Something is wrong."

"Don't turn around now, but Curtis Lawrence has been staring at our table. I don't like the look on his face."

"Why would he be interested in us?"

"He wasn't exactly overjoyed to learn I sold the factory to you. I can't imagine it being something personal to him but if looks could kill, you'd be dead right now."

***

Rachel enjoyed spending time with Brian. He had a sense of humor, but the devil-may-care attitude he had in high school was gone. She liked his plans for the factory and could tell he had a good head for business.

"Like it or not, Driscoll Lake has changed," he said. "We're more of a white-collar community now. The town doesn't have the type of workforce needed to support a factory. I believe those days are gone."

Talking with Brian made her realize she was still holding on to the past. There was no reason to keep the Cameron home place. When she awoke the next morning, she reached a decision. It was time to sell the house.

Feeling invigorated, she went for a quick swim. After a shower and light breakfast, she phoned a local real-estate office.

"Hamilton Realty, Debbie McDade speaking."

"Debbie, this is Rachel Jackson."

"Rachel. Good to hear from you. How may I help you today?" The agent's voice was friendly and cordial.

"I'd like to discuss selling my house and property."

"The home place?"

"Yes. It's bigger than what I need, and it will make an ideal location for someone who raises or trains horses. The stables are still in good shape. Seems a shame for them to remain vacant."

"Funny that you called. A couple of days ago, a firm in Florida phoned about properties with acreage. Specifically asked if your place might be up for sale. However, they're interested in obtaining the mineral rights."

"Mineral rights? That's crazy. Even with all the oil in Texas, they aren't likely to find any in Driscoll Lake. No one has yet."

"I think they're interested in natural gas. New drilling techniques make it easier to extract oil and gas from previously hard to reach places."

"Yeah, at a cost to the environment. I can't see this place with a lot of pump jacks on it. Mind if I ask the name of the company?"

"Just a minute. I have it here someplace. Here it is. C. R. Investments."

Rachel frowned. "That's the same company that wanted to buy the old factory. They made several offers over the years. The last offer was above the market value if they could purchase the mineral rights."

"I'd hang on to those if I was you."

"I plan to. But I'm curious about this company. Think you find out more about them?"

"I know someone who can. I'll contact her and let you know what she says."

"I appreciate it. Will you be in the office this morning?"

"I'm meeting another client at eleven, but I'm free until then. Why don't you stop by around ten?"

"I'll be there." Feeling confident she had made the right decision, Rachel hung up the phone.

Chapter Twenty-One

"Don't look so overjoyed. I thought you'd be happy about what the doctor said." Matt grinned as he said the words, but Stephanie knew he was serious.

"I am ready to resume my normal activities." She stared out the window of the car. Matt had driven her to her follow-up appointment, and they were now on their way home.

He glanced in her direction. "But?"

"It shows, huh? Guess I'm a little discouraged. I've had a lot of time to think the past few days. Was it a mistake to try to learn something more about my father? Maybe I should have left it alone."

"Is it because of the accident?"

"Not exactly. I guess I set my hopes too high. Nothing's come from the newspaper articles. Carlos told me Carol's journal wasn't enough evidence to open the case. Maybe I was wrong to think the man she saw in Columbia had a connection to Driscoll Lake. If only I could locate the other journals, they might tell me something."

"You searched the house?"

"Yes. I don't know whether Carol left all of them here. She moved around a lot because of her job. They could be lost forever. I think it's time to put it aside and move on."

"Don't be discouraged. Something could turn up." Matt slowed as the approached the curve near Taney Creek Bridge—the place where Stephanie's accident occurred.

"Pull over," Stephanie said. "I'd like to see it in daytime."

"Sure," Matt pulled to the shoulder of the road. After checking for oncoming traffic, he got out of the truck and walked around to open the door for Stephanie.

They stood together beside the damaged guardrail. Tracks were visible, and broken branches were strewn about.

"You came so close to hitting that large pine tree. If you had." Matt shook his head. "I don't want to think about what could have happened."

"I remember jerking the wheel at the last minute and thinking this was the same spot where Karen Fulbright died."

"Karen Fulbright? Who's that?"

"She was an accountant for Cameron who died a car accident not long before my father's death.

"The accident happened here?"

"That's what Dorothy Nichols said. I told her it seemed as if Cameron was cursed. Karen, Phillip Denton, my father, Madelyn. Everything happened within a few months."

"And twenty years later, your accident. I don't believe in coincidences—at least not in this case. The notes, the phone call. They have to be related."

"What are you saying?"

Matt didn't want to tell her that he and Carlos had already discussed the possibility of the accident being related to her father. "Apparently someone doesn't want you here."

"If that's the case, then someone is hiding something. Why else would anyone care if I'm here in Driscoll Lake?"

"I can't answer that. But I want you to be careful. Let us handle anything that comes along. Don't try to be a hero. If you find the journals, don't tell anyone other than Carlos or me."

"But—"

"Stephanie, please. We don't know who's behind this. It's best you keep quiet."

***

"Thanks for taking me to the doctor," Stephanie said as they pulled into the driveway. "Now that I can drive again, I need to see about getting another rental car."

"No need for that. I spoke to Mom last night. She wants you to use her car. She said it would just be sitting in the garage while they're away."

"That's kind of her, but I can't. What if someone else tries to run me off the road? I wouldn't want to be responsible."

"Stephanie, it's not a joking matter. You saw the accident scene."

"I'm not joking."

"Okay, but Mom insists. She also told me in a stern voice to take care of you."

"Take care of me? Matt, I've been taking care of myself just fine. I won't crawl under a rock. I was ready to give up before I saw the accident site, but now I'm more determined to learn the truth about my father."

"When you make up your mind, there's no stopping you."

"I've always been headstrong."

"I'm learning that." Matt shook his head. "I don't want anything to happen to you."

"I'll be careful." Stephanie got out of the truck and glanced at her watch. "Would you like some lunch?"

"I can't. Need to get to the station. How about if I pick up dinner tonight?"

"Okay. I'll see you later."

***

Stephanie was eager to resume her exercise routine but decided to wait until the following morning to go for a run. Although it was now early autumn, the afternoon temperatures still felt more like mid-summer.

She spent most of the afternoon working on her manuscript. The end was near, and she felt the familiar rush of excitement over completing another novel. Around five, she got up from the desk, stretched, and went into Helen's bedroom. Several boxes of books lined the floor.

Whiskers came into the room and hopped on the bed. Stephanie scratched him behind his ears.

"It's time this room stopped looking like a storage closet. What do you think? Bet you'd like to have your favorite spot on the bed."

The cat meowed softly.

"I need more boxes. Maybe Aunt Helen kept some around here someplace." She hurried to the carport and opened the storage room door.

Like everything else in the house, Helen kept the storage room organized. Boxes sat neatly on shelves. Stephanie doubted they were empty, but she would eventually need to sort through them. Might as well start now. She reached for the closest one and opened it.

The first three contained Christmas decorations. Some of them looked old, so Stephanie put them aside for later in case she wanted to keep them for herself. She remembered how beautiful Aunt Helen's tree looked every year.

A thin layer of dust had accumulated on the box tops, causing Stephanie to sneeze. Just what she needed — allergies. She found two more boxes of books and a set of dinnerware. One box remained on the top shelf. She stood on a step stool, reached for the box, and sat it on a lower shelf before carefully stepping down.

She frowned. Apparently, someone had opened this box recently, for there were smudges on the lid. She looked inside to find more books. These were different. All were leather-bound with leather strap closures.

"Could it be?" She picked up the top one and opened the inside cover.

Carol McKenzie — 1989

Stephanie felt a rush of excitement as she looked to see another one dated 1982.

She had found Carol's journals.

***

Stephanie took damp paper towels and wiped the dust from the top of the box before taking it inside to the den. She paused for a moment to consider what she'd found. As an author, she had stumbled upon a treasure chest of information. Knowing about Carol's extensive travels, she could glean many story ideas from the pages of these books.

There were probably fifteen or twenty journals in the box. Today Stephanie was interested in only one — the year 1991.

When the doorbell rang, she glanced at her watch, surprised to see it was after six. She hurried to answer, and Matt stood at the door.

"Hope you like Chinese," he said.

"Love it." They walked to the kitchen.

"Good. I brought sweet and sour chicken and shrimp fried rice."

"We can eat in the breakfast nook. I lost track of time. I could have brewed some iced tea." Stephanie peered into the refrigerator. "Not much to choose from here."

"Water's fine," Matt said. He opened the containers of food and glanced toward the den. "Looks as if you've been busy this afternoon. I thought you'd already been through Helen's books."

Stephanie sat plates and silverware on the table. "You won't believe it. I found Carol's journals today. They were in the storage room. I had just started to look through them when you came."

"Guess I don't have to ask what you'll be doing this evening."

"I plan to stay up late and read. Hopefully the one from 1991 will help me learn something."

Matt placed a serving of chicken on his plate. "Don't you think Carol would have told someone what she saw? Especially if she'd thought it might prove your father's innocence."

"I don't believe she realized the significance at the time. Remember she was recovering from PTSD. In her last journal, she wrote about being afraid to say anything for fear the doctor might put her back in the hospital. Thought she was having flashbacks."

"What made her think otherwise?"

"She became convinced the man at 'the lake' was the same person she saw in South America a few days before she died. She saw something and later felt it could prove Dad's innocence."

"Maybe you will find something. I just don't want you to get your hopes up only to be let down."

***

Stephanie pushed back from the table. "The meal was delicious, but if you don't stop bringing all this good food to me, I won't be able to fit in my clothes. Never mind the fact I haven't been able to exercise the past few days."

"You look fine to me." Matt stood up and began to gather the plates. "I'll take care of cleaning up. I know you're anxious to look at the journals."

"You don't mind? Sometimes I think you're too good to be true."

"Don't worry. I won't make this a habit." He grinned.

Stephanie went into the den and sat down on the sofa. All the journals were a similar style. Carol had written her name and the year inside each one. The first one she opened was dated 1980.

She paused for a moment before continuing. When she found Carol's final journal, she was anxious to learn what was inside. She didn't stop to think about reading someone's personal writings. After having time to think, Stephanie felt a twinge of guilt. Reading the journals was almost like an invasion of privacy.

But she also knew Carol had been like a sister to Robert and would have done anything to help him. She would have approved of Stephanie reading them.

She pulled each book from the box and arranged them in order by date. The earliest one was dated 1975, the last one 1992.

"That's strange."

"What's wrong?" Matt walked into the room and sat down opposite the sofa.

Stephanie looked at each book again. "It's not here."

"What?"

"There's a journal for every year from 1975 to 1992, except for 1991. Why would it be missing?"

Matt frowned. "What's the date on the one you read the other day?"

"1996. That's the year Carol died."

"So others are missing. What about '93 to '95?"

"Carol left here the year after Dad died. She moved to South America at the end of '95, so she probably had that one with her. Can't say for sure about the others unless they're packed away somewhere else."

"Then the one you want could be with them."

"I guess so, but don't you think it's strange the one I need is missing?"

"Maybe. Then again didn't you say Carol's accident in Kuwait happened that year?"

"Yes. That's when doctors diagnosed her with PTSD."

"She probably kept it with her as a reminder of how far she'd come in her recovery."

"You could be right. But, wait. Now that I think about it, the smudges could have been fingerprints."

"What are you talking about?"

"The box top was dusty, except for a few places. It looked like someone had recently handled it. I wiped it off before I brought it in the house."

"Maybe Helen looked through the box and took the journal."

"Then where is it? Besides, the box was on a top shelf. I had to use a step stool to reach it. Aunt Helen broke a hip a few years ago. I don't think she'd have risked falling."

"Helen had some repair work done on the house a few months ago. It's possible the workers had to move some things around, and they moved the box."

"That could be it. And I guess you're right. Carol could have kept the journal with her." Even as she spoke the words, she found it hard to believe. Something didn't add up.

Chapter Twenty-Two

Throughout his years as a homicide detective, Carlos Gonzales had worked countless murder cases. In most instances, a trail of evidence led to the killer. Eyewitness accounts and forensics played a significant role. Interviews with a suspect's family or friends often helped to determine a motive. In a perfect world, all cases would be simple to solve.

But there were times, in spite of the evidence, that Carlos's gut instinct told him something wasn't right. This time it had to do with Robert Harris. While there was no clear-cut correlation between Stephanie's accident and a twenty-year-old crime, Carlos couldn't help believe the incidents were connected.

After meeting with Stephanie, he looked at her father's case file again. Something she said caused him to believe he'd missed something in his initial review.

He replayed the conversation with her many times throughout the week, trying to remember what it was that aroused his suspicion.

His wife Maria noticed his demeanor at breakfast Friday morning. "Something's on your mind, isn't it? One of your hunches?"

"You know me too well," he said.

Maria placed two plates of bacon and eggs on the table and sat down opposite Carlos. "Want to talk about it?"

"Yeah. Something Stephanie Harris said a few days ago. I've tried to remember, but I can't help but believe there might be a connection to her father's case."

"You've looked at the evidence?"

"Humph. What little there is. Not much more than a suicide note and an autopsy report. They didn't even interview the family or employees as to his state of mind leading up to that time."

Maria took a sip of coffee. "But he did leave a suicide note. Isn't that enough to incriminate him?"

"That's the damning thing. I'm going to look at the file again today. No matter how long it takes, I'll figure out what's bothering me."

***

Carlos arrived earlier than usual at the police station and went directly to his office. A sense of anxiety enveloped him. The investigation of Stephanie's accident had yielded no suspects. Matt's suspicion about Brian Nichols had proved unfounded. An off-duty officer, who lived in the same apartment complex as Heather Stevens, confirmed Brian's accident happened in the parking lot.

The person who hit Stephanie may have been intoxicated and merely left the scene. However, with the similar incident that happened earlier, he doubted it.

If someone didn't want Stephanie around, she wasn't safe. But why would anyone care that she was here? She hadn't lived in Driscoll Lake for twenty years. Did someone know she was asking questions about her father? Was someone afraid she would learn something? Did a former Cameron employee want revenge?

He closed the door to his office and pulled the folder on Robert Harris.

Something in the file contained a clue. Carlos was certain of it. He read the suicide note.

I know this will cause pain for my family, but I can't go on this way. Kathryn, I'm sorry to put you and Stephanie through this. You both deserve better. Phillip is dead because he knew too much. I love you and Stephanie with all my heart. Take good care of her. Love, Robert.

The note was simple, yet in a sense, complex. Carlos read it again, studying it line by line. The first part was typical of someone who planned suicide, but the latter half baffled him.

Phillip is dead. It wasn't exactly an admission of guilt, but how else would Robert have known the man wasn't alive?

Because he knew too much. About what? The stolen money? Something else?

Carlos rubbed his thumb over his lower lip. The most confusing thing was what Robert didn't say. There was no mention of Madelyn. Did she surprise him with her visit to the office? Was that the only reason she died?

Someone tapped on his door, and he looked to see Matt through the glass. Carlos motioned him inside.

"You're here early." Matt sat down in front of the desk.

"Looking at this old file on Robert Harris again. Something Stephanie said has been nagging at me all week, and I can't figure out what it is."

"No word from any of the body shops?"

"Nothing here or in Brewster. Of course, the perp could have taken it to Dallas or somewhere else for repairs. There's no way we can search everywhere."

"Yeah, I know. I'm concerned for Stephanie's safety. I've tried to stay close, but yesterday the doctor told her she could drive again. She's headstrong and independent."

"Hopefully she'll exercise caution."

"I don't expect her to stay at the house. She'll probably be out and about asking more questions. Did you learn anything from the file?"

"No. Have you ever looked at it?"

Matt shook his head.

"Read this suicide note."

Matt took the paper from Carlos. "Typed? Do we know this is his signature?"

"According to the report, it was verified by a handwriting expert."

"The strange thing here is not what he said, but what he didn't say. He didn't admit to anything."

"My thoughts exactly. Do you know who worked for Cameron at that time? Someone who would be willing to talk to me. Maybe tell me something about Robert, how he acted in the days leading up to his death?"

"There are several, but I'm not sure who would talk. Lots of animosity with some."

"Hopefully none of them want to take revenge on Stephanie."

"For real," Matt said. "Wait a minute. Dorothy Nichols was Robert's secretary. As I recall, she was very supportive of him."

"I'd like to talk with her.

Matt stood up and walked to the door. "I'm sure she wouldn't mind."

"I may be grasping at straws, but I don't think this case had a proper investigation. I'd like to give it the attention it deserves. With your permission, of course. Otherwise, I'm willing to do it on my own time."

"If you feel that strongly, go for it."

After Matt left, Carlos turned his attention back to the file. He carefully read each document, coming to the autopsy report last. The coroner's report stated Robert Harris died of a gunshot wound to the head. The bullet entered the right temple at a slight downward angle.

That could indicate someone was standing above him with a gun. Carlos looked through the photos and read the coroner's summation. The cause of death was a self-inflicted gunshot wound to the right side of his head.

The right side.

"That's it!"

He remembered Stephanie's words. "I'm left-handed, just like my father."

Robert was left-handed. If he had shot himself, he would have used his left hand and pointed the gun at his left temple.

Robert Harris did not commit suicide. He was murdered.

***

Otis Wood made the ten-mile drive to his farm every day. He had endured many hot Texas summers in his sixty-seven years of life, but none of them this dry. As a young boy growing up in the 1950s, he remembered the seven-year drought.

However, this summer undoubtedly had to be the driest single year on record. August was one the hottest months in recorded history. Even though it was now late September, it still felt more like mid-July.

There had been only a scant amount of rainfall in the spring. Weather forecasters called for the drought to extend into the fall and possibly winter. Some scientists said it could last up to ten years.

He slowed to look at a large oak tree near the road. The leaves had already turned brown. There were at least a dozen trees nearby in the same condition. It would be spring before anyone could determine if they were dead or had merely gone into an early dormant state.

The grass in the surrounding hay meadows was short and brown. Ranchers were already looking at alternate methods to feed their livestock through the winter.

Otis realized he should probably sell the few head of cattle he owned—maybe even the farm. Although no one in the family had lived on the property since his grandfather died in the 1980s, he was reluctant to sell. The land had been in his family for several generations.

A wealthy plantation owner deeded his great-grandfather fifty acres to start a new life after the War Between the States. His family had faced many hardships over the years, but they farmed the land and built a new way of life.

About ten years earlier, Otis purchased a few head of cattle with the idea of building a new home on the land. He and his wife Cleo planned to live there after their retirement. When Cleo became ill, Otis set aside his dream of living on the family homestead to care for her. He was able to keep her at home the first few years, but the dementia worsened, forcing him to place her in a nursing home.

The land and the cattle became his refuge. When he visited the farm, he found peace and solace. It reminded him of his childhood and visits with his grandparents. So, unless the drought remained several years as some predicted, he would keep the cattle. He was fortunate in that he had a spring-fed pond that was much larger and deeper than most stock ponds. Although the water level dropped each week, the cattle still had adequate drinking water.

When he arrived at the farm, the small herd stood near the front gate, anticipating his arrival. He'd never had to feed hay in September, but the grass was like dry powder. His biggest fear was fire. Wildfires were rampant throughout the state. Although burn bans were in effect statewide, all it took was one irresponsible person to toss a cigarette, and the entire place could go up in flames.

Otis opened the gate and drove his pickup into the pasture. After throwing the hay, he went to the pond to check the water level. Submerged tree stumps were visible for the first time in many years. Last week, something toward the middle of the water had caught his attention. He was curious to see if the waters had receded more and if so, he might be able to determine what was there.

He first thought it might be a barrel, but was perplexed about how it came to be in the pond. Neither his father nor grandfather had been careless with trash and rubbish. They would never use a water source as a dumping ground.

He parked his truck on a level patch of ground and walked the short distance to the shore. The object was still there. It appeared to have been underwater a long time. It was metallic but much larger than a barrel.

Otis shook his head. The statewide drought had exposed many things hidden beneath once-deep waters. Someone recently found a part of the space shuttle, Columbia, in Lake Nacogdoches—eight years after the explosion. He doubted this object was from the shuttle since most of that debris fell further south.

Otis walked closer to the water's edge to get a better view. "What in the—?"

He couldn't believe his eyes. Someone needed to know about this. He reached into his pocket for his cell phone and dialed the local sheriff's office. "This is Otis Wood. I need someone to come to my farm. I just found a car submerged in my pond."

***

When Sheriff Dave Sanders received the call from one of his deputies about a submerged vehicle found in a stock pond north of Driscoll Lake, he decided to drive out to the area to see for himself. Deputies had already called for a dive team as well as a tow truck. There had been no word yet as to whether a body was inside the car.

When he reached the Wood's property, a deputy stood guard. He opened the gate to allow Dave inside. A crowd of spectators had already gathered near the entrance.

"Follow this trail and veer to the right over that ridge." The deputy pointed in the general direction. "The ground is relatively smooth, so you won't have difficulty."

The sheriff reached the pond as the divers emerged from their first dive. He got out of his car and hurried over to listen to their report.

"We didn't see evidence of a body inside. The car is covered in mud and silt, but it appears to be a late 80s or early 90s model Cadillac. We should be able to tell more when it's pulled from the lake."

"Could you see a license plate?" Sheriff Sanders asked.

"It was a bit rusty, but it's a Texas plate with an expiration sticker of March 1992. We'll get the number once the truck pulls it out of the water."

March 1992. That meant someone last registered the car in March of '91. It could have been in the water twenty years. He did a mental check of any missing persons. No one came to mind right away.

The deputy who was first on the scene came up to him. "I've taken Mr. Wood's statement." He nodded toward a dark maroon pickup parked beneath a tree. A man sat on the tailgate, watching the unfolding of events.

"The property has been in his family for generations, but he doesn't come out here all the time. He runs a few head of cattle, but that's it. Said if it hadn't been for this drought, he wouldn't have had cause to check the pond."

"Did he have any idea how the car may have ended up in there?"

"No. He was as surprised as anyone. He's a bit shaken up, but that's understandable."

"What's your take on the situation?"

"You might think I'm crazy, but did you happen to read the recent newspaper article about the Harris-Denton case?" Phillip Denton disappeared in Fort Worth, but he drove a 1991 Cadillac coupe. You don't suppose the car belonged to him?"

"You might be on to something. I'm going to call Driscoll Lake." He pulled out his cell phone and punched in the number of the police station. When the dispatcher answered, he identified himself and asked to speak to Matt.

"Matt, Dave Sanders here. I think you might want to come out to Otis Wood's farm. He discovered a car submerged in his pond this morning. It's an early model Cadillac, much like the one Phillip Denton was driving when he disappeared."

"Thanks, Dave. I'll be right there," Matt said.

***

Matt watched as the tow truck began to pull the car from the pond. Years of being underwater had caused rust on the exterior, but not to the extent of making the model indistinguishable. It was an early 90s Cadillac El Dorado— the same kind Phillip Denton drove.

"It must have been down there twenty years or more," Dave Sanders said.

Matt shook his head. "Never imagined something like this happening around Driscoll Lake."

"You know what this means. Without a body inside and with the doors and windows closed, someone had to push the car in the pond."

"Why Otis Wood's place? The pond is in the middle of a pasture—not anywhere close to a road. Is Otis a suspect?"

"No, he's clean. The property has been in his family for generations, but no one's lived here for a long time. He's at a loss to explain it."

When the tow truck dragged the car to the banks of the lake, the trunk came open. Deputies scrambled to look inside.

One of them called out. "There's a body inside."

Chapter Twenty-Three

"Matt, I'll keep your department posted on what we find," Dave Sanders said. "We're taking the car to an impound lot and have called in a forensics team. Don't know if they'll find anything. We're sending the skeletal remains to Dallas for a forensics exam."

"Thanks, Dave."

"Fort Worth PD has already confirmed the license plate number belonged to the car Phillip Denton drove the night he disappeared."

"I called Carlos Gonzales. He has the old file on Robert Harris and can assist in giving you any information you need about the case. If the skeletal remains belong to Denton, it puts a new light on Harris."

"Yeah." Sheriff Sanders shook his head. "Guess there's not much more we can do here today. The press is already on this. I'm not prepared to answer questions right now and I've instructed my deputies not to comment. I'll call a press conference for later this evening. I'd like you or someone from your department to be there. They'll likely have questions about the Harris case."

"I'll be there. Just let me know the time."

Matt got into his truck and called Carlos. "Heard back from Fort Worth?"

"Talked to an investigator a few minutes ago. They never considered Robert Harris as a suspect. After the items belonging to Denton were found northwest of Fort Worth, they focused their investigation there. But now that Phillip's car was here..." Carlos's words faded.

"It means he made it back to Driscoll Lake."

"Right."

"I need to tell Stephanie. The press is already aware. I don't want her hearing about it on the news. I guess someone needs to tell Rachel Jackson. After all, Phillip was her stepfather."

"I'll talk to Rachel," Carlos said. "Go be with Stephanie."

***

Stephanie sat at her computer, typing the final sentences of a scene. The words flowed freely. The chapter she wrote had a lot of action and suspense. She managed to put aside any thoughts of her father, Carol, and the missing journal.

She was so engrossed in her work that she failed to hear the sound of an automobile in the driveway. When the doorbell rang, she jumped in surprise. She got up from the desk and hurried to answer.

"Matt! What are you doing here?"

"Can I come in?"

"Sure. Is something wrong?"

"Let's sit down." He followed her into the den and sat beside her on the sofa.

"I wanted to be the one to tell you before you heard it on the news. Authorities found Phillip Denton's missing car today."

Stephanie gasped. "His car was found? Where?"

"In Otis Wood's stock pond."

Her jaw dropped, and she put her hand to her mouth. When she regained her composure, she said, "You're telling me Phillip's car was right here in Driscoll Lake?"

"Yes. Otis drove out this morning to feed his cattle. When he checked the pond, he saw something suspicious. The drought has caused the water level to drop enough to make the car visible. It has been underwater for a long time."

"Are they sure it belongs to Phillip?"

"Yes. Fort Worth police confirmed the license plate number."

"Are you telling me Phillip drove into the pond?"

"No. Someone had to push the car into the water. There was a body in the trunk. They're sending it to Dallas for DNA testing. Most likely, it's Phillip's body."

"Then it could mean my father also killed him." Her voice broke. She stood up, clutched her arms, and walked to the patio door. She stood for a while in silence and looked toward the lake.

After a few minutes, she spoke. "All this time... so close." Tears ran down her face. "I didn't want to believe my father was guilty. I kept hoping there was some explanation. How could he have done this? Why?"

Matt hurried to her side and took her in his arms. She laid her head against his chest and wept.

***

For the second time in a week, Brian Nichols peered into his almost empty refrigerator. The thought of spending another Friday evening alone was disheartening, but considering the week he'd had, some down time would do him good.

After his dinner with Rachel a few nights ago, he decided not to approach Matt. It's possible he was wrong about Matt believing he was responsible for Stephanie's accident. If Rachel was right, Matt's feelings for Stephanie clouded his judgment.

He'd probably act the same way if it happened to Rachel. Was he kidding himself? He and Rachel didn't even travel in the same social circles.

He was foolish to think they could ever have anything more than a business relationship. Rachel's family was wealthy. She was a professional. He came from a working middle-class family—complete with an alcoholic father. Yes, he was a business owner and had worked hard to build up his reputation, but he was still a laborer. Water and oil don't mix.

Brian reached near the back of the fridge for a can of root beer and then went into the living room. At least he had something other than water to drink with his pizza.

"Another night in paradise." He picked up the remote and turned on the television.

The six o'clock news was on. He was about to change the channel when the news anchor announced a breaking story. Brian turned up the volume.

"The long Texas drought continues to reveal more secrets from the deep when a Driscoll Lake resident found a car submerged in his pond outside of town. Live on the scene is channel ten reporter Kim Blair. Kim, tell us more."

"Thank you, Don. The property owner, Otis Wood, spotted the submerged car this morning. Sources say the early model Cadillac belonged to missing businessman Phillip Denton, who disappeared in 1991. The source also told us a body was inside the trunk. Police haven't confirmed, but it's likely the body is Denton."

"With the body's location, foul play must have been involved. Any word on suspects?"

"Not from officials. However, some area residents believe Robert Harris, the man who killed Denton's wife, was involved. Sheriff Sanders has called a press conference for seven o'clock."

Brian switched off the TV. Years had passed since he'd been near Otis's place. As a teenager, he and some of the rowdier high school bunch would go out to the pasture to drink beer. It was the last place he ever took a drink.

He recalled the August night. It was somewhere around the time Phillip Denton disappeared. Brian was hanging around the city park when Kyle Lawrence came by in his new convertible. They didn't run in the same circles. Kyle's father insisted he maintain a certain social status and didn't want him associating with "riff raff" like Brian. The invitation surprised him.

"Want to go out to the Wood's place?"

"Don't have any beer."

"I know where some is stashed. And I also have something better." Kyle reached into the back seat and held up a bottle of whiskey.

"Sure." Brian climbed in the car.

Kyle drove north out of town and pulled off the road at Taney Creek. "Stay here and watch." A few minutes later, he came back with two cold six-packs.

When they got to the farm, Kyle hid the car in a wooded area. They went behind an old barn. After they'd had a few beers, Kyle reached for the whiskey.

Before that night, Brian had stayed away from hard liquor. It didn't take long for him to discover he liked the sweet, smoky taste.

"Better go easy on that stuff," Kyle said.

"I can handle it."

It was the last thing Brian remembered until the following morning. He woke up in his own bed, having no idea of how he got there.

Kyle asked him about the incident at school a few days later. "I want to talk to you about Friday night."

"What about it?"

"Do you remember anything?"

"I don't even know how I got home."

"I took you. Your mother wasn't there, but I helped you to your room. Can't believe you don't remember."

"The last thing I remember is drinking the whiskey. And if you're afraid I'll say something to your old man, don't worry. We're not exactly on speaking terms."

"No, it's not that. Just making sure."

"Why do you keep asking?"

Kyle's face flushed and he looked away. "Nothing. Never mind."

"I get it. You had a girl out there. Who was she? Don't tell me you—"

"I get it. You had a girl out there. Who was she? Don't tell me you—"

"Forget it. This time I'm not going to kiss and tell. Let it go." He shook his head and walked away.

Brian couldn't help but think Kyle was hiding something. Who was he trying to protect? Not that it mattered. Brian swore he'd never again get drunk enough that he wasn't able to remember things.

A few days later, Kyle asked him if he'd like to go back to Otis's place. "I got some more stash. Going back out there this weekend. Want to come?"

Brian shook his head. "No more booze for me. Not after what happened last weekend. I don't want to end up like my old man."

Kyle looked away, lost in thought. "Yeah," he said slowly. "I don't want to be like mine either."

***

He switched off the television and threw the remote across the room. After all these years, they found the car. If it weren't for this blasted drought, it might have remained unseen forever.

Too late to think about that now. He should have listened to his instinct long ago and disposed of the car far away from Driscoll Lake. Otis Wood's pond had seemed like the perfect place. It was deep, back from the road, and rather isolated.

Local reporters were already on the scene—even the Dallas stations had picked up the story. Phillip Denton's photo was all over the evening news.

It would take weeks, maybe even months, for the DNA results to confirm the identity of the body. There was already speculation Robert Harris killed Phillip. The police would likely reopen his case—at the least, they would review the file.

What if they wanted to talk with him? What would he say?

He took a deep breath. He was certain no one had seen him that night. Authorities wouldn't even know to question him.

They couldn't tie him to anything. The only other person who knew of his involvement wasn't going to talk. He took a deep breath. No reason to be overly concern. At least not yet.

***

Stephanie didn't remember Matt leading her to the sofa. When the dam broke, years of pent up emotions burst forward like a raging river. Matt sat beside her and placed his arm around her shoulders.

When the hiccupping sobs subsided, she heard a soft "meow" and felt Whiskers brush against her legs.

She reached down and rubbed his head. "It's okay, buddy. I'll be all right." She turned toward Matt. "I'm sorry."

He pulled her close and kissed her on the head. "No need to apologize. You needed to let it out."

"For years, I believed my father was guilty. I was angry with him. Angry he would do such a thing to us. When I came back and started to remember the good times we had, I couldn't see him killing himself and Madelyn. Now I know he not only killed her but Phillip as well."

"You don't know that. We don't even know for sure it was Phillip's body."

"Come on, Matt. Who else could it be? And who else but my father would be a suspect?"

Matt stood up from the sofa and walked to sliding glass door. "I don't know."

"I'm glad Aunt Helen isn't around to see all this. It would have devastated her. All these years, she wanted to believe he was innocent.

"I guess all that's left for me to do is have the will probated, put the house on the market, and get on with my life."

"A life in Denver?"

"There's nothing left for me in Driscoll Lake. The sooner I leave, the better for everyone. For me to remain here would be a constant reminder to the Cameron employees of what they lost."

"Stephanie, I." Matt sighed. "Just don't rush into anything."

"I'm not rushing. I didn't intend to come here in the first place. When I did, I thought I'd be in town for two or three days at the most. For a while, I was caught up in a dream of what might have been. Nothing like harsh reality to shatter our dreams."

The phone rang. Stephanie went into the kitchen to answer it. The caller ID indicated it was a local TV station.

"Guess the press already knows where I am. I'm not going to answer."

"You're likely to get more calls. The sheriff has called a press conference and asked me to be there. I need to get over to Brewster, but I'll come back. I can screen the calls."

"No!" she said.

Matt jerked his head in surprise.

"Sorry, I didn't mean to sound so abrupt. I appreciate the offer, but I need to be alone for a while. I'll turn off the ringer and let the answering machine pick up."

He sighed and shook his head in resignation. "Okay, but if you need anything, I'm a phone call away."

"I know. Thanks."

***

It was well after daylight when Stephanie awakened the following morning. She probably wouldn't have woken up then had it not been for Whiskers hopping on the bed and nudging her.

"Hey, buddy." She yawned and stretched. "Guess you're hungry." She got up, walked to the bathroom, and splashed cold water on her face. Her eyes were puffy and swollen. Sure wouldn't win a beauty contest looking like that.

She went to the kitchen, poured food for Whiskers, and turned on the coffee pot. The answering machine blinked, so she pressed "play" to listen to the messages. As she suspected, the first two were from local news stations. She deleted them.

The third message took her by surprise. It was a man's voice, but he sounded as if he was trying to disguise it. The message was short.

"Things aren't always as they seem. There are still unanswered questions. Don't give up. Keep digging."

The call had come at 10:18 p.m. Stephanie scrolled through the numbers on the caller ID, but as she suspected the number was blocked. She pressed the button to listen again. The voice was different from the last anonymous caller.

What was the caller talking about? The case against her father? Phillip Denton? What else could it be? And just who was this person?

Chapter Twenty-Four

When Matt arrived at the police station on Saturday morning, Carlos was already at his desk.

"Figured you'd be in the office today," Matt said.

"Couldn't sleep. Got here at six-thirty."

"I brought coffee. Much better than that watered-down stuff in the break room." He handed a large cup to Carlos and sat down opposite him.

"Thanks." Carlos took a sip of the hot liquid. "Strong and black. Just as I like it."

"Can't blame you for coming in early. I had a hard time sleeping with everything that happened yesterday." Matt shook his head. "Still find it hard to believe. Did you speak to Rachel Jackson?"

Carlos nodded. "Got to her barely before the press did. I have a feeling she wasn't overly fond of her step-father."

"Why is that?"

"She thanked me for telling her but didn't show any emotion. I might as well have been talking about a stranger. But she was a teenager when he died. Lots of kids aren't fond of their stepparents. How did Stephanie take it?"

"She was upset, to say the least. Mixed emotions—hurt, anger. What you might expect."

"I'm still not convinced her father is the killer."

"You mean Phillip's murderer?" Matt sipped his coffee.

"I don't think he killed Phillip or Madelyn. In fact, I'm almost sure he didn't commit suicide."

"What—?" A spasm of coughs interrupted his sentence.

"You okay, buddy?"

Matt cleared his throat. "Yeah, just swallowed wrong. What do you mean you don't think Robert committed suicide?"

"Something Stephanie said last week bothered me, and I finally remembered what it was. She signed the accident report with her left hand. It was hard because of her sprained wrist. She said she was left-handed—just like her father."

"So?"

"I looked at the autopsy report on Robert Harris. The fatal shot was on his right temple and entered at a downward angle. It would have been a physical impossibility to pull the trigger with his left hand."

"Maybe he was ambidextrous."

"I considered that possibility. There's also the business of Phillip Denton's bloody clothing found in King County. That's three hundred miles from here."

"And Harris was with his family the night Denton disappeared."

"Correct. However, we don't know when he died. Let's assume for a minute Harris met up with Denton and killed him. Why did he dispose of items in an isolated location far away from here?"

"To lead investigators in the wrong direction. No pun intended."

"Exactly. But why not ditch the car there also? Why bring it back here and risk being seen?"

Matt shook his head. "You're right. It doesn't make sense."

"Unless Denton made it back to Driscoll Lake, Harris killed him, got rid of the car, and then drove west to dump the items."

"If that's the case, he sure went to a lot of trouble."

"I agree." Carlos took another sip of coffee. "There is another possibility."

"What's that?"

"Someone else killed them both and tried to make Harris look guilty. Think about what he said in the note, 'Phillip is dead because he knew too much.' What if someone else embezzled the money and made it look as if Harris did it. Denton and Harris could have been onto them."

"What about Madelyn?"

"I don't believe the killer planned her murder. I'm guessing she went to the office that night, surprised the murderer, and died because of it. There's no mention of her in the note."

"But it did have Harris's signature on it."

"Yeah, I know."

"Where do we go from here?"

"I want to talk to both Stephanie and Rachel. I'd also like to visit with Dorothy Nichols. I'll keep other agencies informed, including the FBI. I don't want to make the same mistakes as Joe Rivers. If he'd sought outside help, we might have had answers years ago."

"You feel pretty strong about this, don't you?"

"I went to high-school with Robert Harris. I never believed he was capable of murder."

"Several people shared your views."

Carlos shook his head. "I don't know, Matt. We're missing something here, and for the life of me, I can't figure out what it is."

***

"I realized the past few days have been difficult for you," Carlos said as he followed Stephanie into the den. "I trust you're recovering from the accident."

"Physically, I'm much better. I'm not so sure about emotionally."

"I understand. I'm sorry to have to bother you."

"It's okay. Please, have a seat." She gestured toward a chair and sat down on the sofa.

"Considering the recent events, I am looking into your father's file. Multiple agencies are involved, but I assure you there will be full cooperation between each of them."

"Thank you."

"Is your mother aware of the recent turn of events?"

"No. I haven't spoken to her in a few days."

"Do you think she would be willing to answer a few questions if the need arises?"

Stephanie looked up at the ceiling and exhaled a long, slow breath. Pursed her lips and closed her eyes. Her mother had moved on with her life. She broke any connections to Driscoll Lake years ago. But Stephanie knew she would cooperate fully with any police investigation. She opened her eyes and looked at Carlos. "Yes."

"It may not be necessary. I realize you were young when your father died, but maybe you can answer a couple of questions. I apologize in advance if this is painful."

"Go ahead."

"Are you aware if your mother, or any members of the family, saw the suicide note?"

Stephanie shook her head. "We didn't. The police told us Dad apologized for his actions and expressed his love to us. Honestly, I don't think Mom wanted to see it. Guess it was too distressing."

"Are you aware of how much investigators questioned her?"

"They didn't ask many questions. I think they asked about Dad's gun. She verified he kept it in his car. The serial number of the murder weapon matched the gun belonging to him. But you'd have all that in the case file."

"Tell me about your father's mental and emotional state in the weeks or days before he died. Did he seemed depressed or give any indication he might be suicidal?"

"None whatsoever. After Mr. Denton disappeared, Dad began working longer hours. He seemed concerned about something, but he was never one to talk business at home—at least not around me."

"I see. One more question. You mentioned a few days ago that your father was left-handed. By any chance was he ambidextrous?"

"No. He did everything with his left hand. He used to joke about how clumsy he was with his right one."

Carlos rose from the chair. "I don't want to keep you. I know you've been through a lot. Thank you for taking the time to talk with me."

"Detective Gonzales, do you think my father was a killer?"

"The man I knew wouldn't have killed anyone."

"For years, I thought Dad was guilty. It seemed so cut and dry. But after returning here, I started to have my doubts. The father I remembered was a loving, caring person."

"I would love to be able to prove his innocence, but I need more concrete evidence to do that."

"I wish I had something more to give you."

Carlos reached into his pocket and pulled out a business card. "If you think of anything, call me. This has the station number as well as my cell phone. Don't hesitate to phone day or night."

"Thank you. It's nice to have someone in your profession who believes in my father."

***

Before he left the police station that morning, Carlos phoned Rachel Jackson and Dorothy Nichols. Both agreed to meet with him. He drove to Rachel's house after leaving Stephanie.

The large Georgian-style home sat on a hundred acres outside of town. It had been in the Cameron family for several generations. A large for sale sign stood near the entrance. Carlos drove through the gates and glanced toward the empty pasture and stables. Madelyn Cameron was once an accomplished equestrian rider. Carlos wondered if Rachel also shared her mother's passion for horses.

Carlos parked his car in the circular driveway, walked to the front door, and rang the bell. Rachel answered the door almost immediately, leaving him with the impression she had been watching for his arrival.

"Detective Gonzales, please come in." She led him into a large sitting room and gestured toward a sofa. "Have a seat. Would you care for some water or lemonade?"

"No, thank you. I'm fine. I appreciate you agreeing to see me today. The sheriff will probably ask you some questions, but I hope you're willing to answer a few for me."

"Of course."

"After locating your stepfather's missing car, we're taking another look at your mother's murder. I believe the cases may be related."

"Aren't they? Robert Harris was accused of killing my mother. Now it appears he may have also killed Phillip."

"I'm not certain about that. The case is still under investigation."

"I'll help in any way I can, but I don't understand why you've reopened the case on Mom. I thought the police concluded it was a murder-suicide."

Carlos chose his words carefully. "I have reason to believe Robert Harris may not have killed your mother."

"What?"

"I'm not certain Robert Harris murdered your mother, or that his death was a suicide. I ask that you keep this confidential. I don't want the press to get wind of it right now."

"I won't say anything."

"What can you tell me about your stepfather?"

"Please don't refer to him as my stepfather. I never thought of him in that capacity. He was my mother's husband. I never cared for the man."

Carlos raised an eyebrow. "Why do you say that?"

"I believe he took advantage of Mom when she was vulnerable. She and my father had recently divorced when he appeared on the scene. In my opinion, he was a smooth-talking con artist."

"A con artist?"

"I don't think Phillip Denton had a penny to his name when he first came to town. I believe he talked a good talk in order to get what he wanted—control of the company.

And he did whatever it took, including marrying my mother. I have no proof, so it's only my opinion."

"I understand."

"But what about Robert Harris? Do you have new evidence?"

"Let's say I don't believe the original investigation was thorough enough. I think there's a chance they missed some important clues."

"Detective Gonzales, I'll be honest with you. All these years I hated Robert Harris for what he did. Stephanie doesn't think her father was guilty. I wasn't thrilled about the news article dragging everything up again, but I've tried to put myself in Stephanie's shoes. And I understand how she must feel. If I were her, I would want to know the truth."

"That's what I want, also."

"Is there anything else I can help with?"

"I know you were young but was there any indication that your mother and Phillip may have been having marital problems?"

"Not really—I mean, not more than usual. The last few months before his disappearance, they pretty much lived separate lives. He spent all his free time at the office. Mom enjoyed social and charitable activities."

"Do you know if they ever discussed the business?"

"To her discredit, Mom pretty much turned control of it over to Phillip. After he disappeared, she was forced to become involved."

"Did she ever discuss company business around you?"

"No."

"Did she act upset or worried in the days before her death?"

"Not to me, but if she had been concerned about anything, she wouldn't have let me know. I'm afraid I'm not much help."

"On the contrary, you have been. May I call you again if I have further questions?"

"Of course."

Carlos rose to leave, and Rachel walked him to the door. "You've got a beautiful place here. Do you still have horses? I remember your mother was a good equestrian rider."

"I used to ride with Mom, but lost interest. I sold the horses years ago. Now I don't have time."

"Again thank you for seeing me."

"Detective?"

"Yes?"

"Please find my mother's killer. If it was Robert Harris, I accept that. If not, I want to know who it was, and I want them brought to justice."

***

"Thank you for agreeing to see me, Mrs. Nichols. I won't take up too much of your time."

Dorothy Nichols waved one arthritic hand in the air. "All I have is time. I'm more than willing to help clear Robert Harris's name."

"So you have doubts about his guilt."

"I always believed he was innocent. Robert had everything going for him. He was completely devoted to his wife and daughter and would have never done anything to jeopardize that relationship."

"I understand you worked for him several years. What was he like as an employer?"

"Couldn't have asked for a better boss. I was going through a difficult time with my son while trying to make ends meet. My husband didn't— He wasn't able to work. Robert helped me any way he could. He made certain I received a generous raise every year and put me in contact with a support group. Tried his best to help Brian, but you know how teenagers can be."

"I see. How long did you work at Cameron?"

"I began working there when Brian was a baby, so somewhere around sixteen years. I started out as a receptionist, but when the opening came as Robert's assistant, I got the job."

"He was a good person to work for?"

"The best. Not a thing like Phillip Denton. That man was a tyrant."

"What were your duties?"

"The usual things. I managed his calendar, scheduled meetings, made travel arrangements, and such. I typed all Mr. Harris's correspondence."

"What about email?"

"We didn't use it in those days. Didn't even have a word processor—used an IBM typewriter."

"Then he never typed any of his correspondence?"

"Humph. He used to joke I could type a three-page letter in the same amount of time he could hunt and peck for a sentence. He always wrote things out on a legal pad, and I would transcribe from his notes." She held out her gnarled hands. "Believe it or not, I once typed eighty to ninety words a minute."

Carlos smiled. "I believe that. Would you think it was strange the suicide note was typed?"

"Typed? Absolutely, I would think that strange. That alone would be enough for me to know he didn't do it."

"I see. Did you ever work directly for Phillip Denton?"

"No. He had several secretaries during his time there, but none of them stayed long. He was too arrogant and demanding. As bad as I needed a job, if I'd had to work directly for him, I would have quit. It would have been better to scrub floors or wait tables."

"What was Robert Harris's relationship with Denton like?"

"Amiable. Robert wasn't the kind of person who would talk bad about anyone—no matter how he felt. However, I don't think he cared for the man."

"What do you believe the reason was?"

"Robert was dedicated to his job and the company. Before Denton wormed his way in, many thought Mr. Cameron would name Robert as CEO when he retired. Denton didn't seem to care about Cameron, and it bothered Robert."

"Some people would consider that a motive for murder. You don't think there was any jealousy or animosity?"

"None at all. He wasn't that type of person. He was dedicated, but not greedy."

"Let's talk about the money. That investigation is not in my jurisdiction, but I'd like to get your thoughts."

"I never believed Robert stole the money. The FBI questioned me, and I told them such. I can't understand why they didn't focus more on Karen Fulbright."

"Who was she?"

"She was a stranger to Driscoll Lake. Showed up one day to apply for a job and Phillip Denton hired her as the controller. She didn't sign the checks, but had access to all the books."

"What happened to her? Do you know if she still lives around here?"

"No, she died in an automobile accident about a month before Phillip disappeared. Her car ran off the road at Taney Creek Bridge."

"I see. Did she—?"

"Excuse me, Detective Gonzales." Dorothy Nichols called out to a nurse who was walking by. "I haven't had my medication this morning. Is someone going to bring it to me?"

The nurse gently patted Dorothy's arm. "Mrs. Nichols, I gave you your medicine at nine. Like always. Don't you remember?"

Dorothy's cheeks colored and she hung her head. "Oh, yes. I remember now. I'm sorry."

"It's okay, honey." The nurse turned and walked away.

Carlos stood up. "I won't take any more of your time, Mrs. Nichols. You've been most helpful to me today."

"My pleasure. I'll do anything I can to help clear Robert's name."

Chapter Twenty-Five

Carlos was anxious to get to the office on Monday morning. After spending Sunday with extended family celebrating his father's birthday, he was ready to resume his investigation.

When he took the job in Driscoll Lake, he promised Maria he wouldn't work on Sundays. "Sundays are for family," she had said.

He understood why she felt that way. He'd spent far too many of them away from home during his years in San Diego. Crime didn't take a holiday.

A surge of adrenaline flowed through him as he entered his office. He was about to make a breakthrough. He wasn't sure how, but he felt it.

Carlos settled behind his desk with a cup of coffee. After one sip, he wished he had stopped at the coffee shop. Sandra was working dispatch today. It wasn't hard to figure out who brewed this mess.

He sat the cup aside and turned to the notes he made of the three interviews he conducted on Saturday. After talking to Stephanie, he was certain Robert Harris didn't shoot himself. The question now was who did and why? How did Marilyn come into play?

What about Phillip Denton? If the body turned out to be his, which Carlos felt confident it was, it was likely the same person killed him.

Rachel didn't have a favorable opinion of Phillip, but it had no bearing on the investigation. She was young and probably still trying to come to terms with her parent's divorce when Denton came on the scene.

Dorothy Nichols didn't like the man either, but her opinion had more to do with his style of management. Talking to her had been helpful. Her statement about Robert's typing skills, or lack thereof, caused even more doubt he committed suicide.

However, her actions toward the end of the interview disturbed Carlos. He'd seen the beginning stages of Alzheimer's disease. Maria's father suffered with it for years. What began with short term memory loss progressed into a debilitating illness that eventually claimed his life.

Still, Dorothy acted coherently when talking about the events at Cameron. He had no reason to doubt her words. In early stages of dementia, the long-term memory is still intact.

Three people were dead—four counting Karen Fulbright—even though she died as the result of a car crash. Each one had either knowledge of or access to company financial records. That meant each of them could potentiality identify the real thief.

Karen's death brought to mind other questions. Was it only a coincidence someone attempted to harm Stephanie at the same place Karen died? For that matter, was her death truly an accident?

Carlos shook his head. The more he studied the case, the more complicated it became. It was time to make a phone call. He picked up the phone, dialed the FBI satellite office in Brewster, and asked to speak to Special Agent Vince Green.

He didn't have to wait long before Vince answered. "How are you today, Detective Gonzales?"

Carlos and Vince's father attended the police academy together. The elder Green went on to be an FBI agent. Vince decided to follow his father's footsteps and studied criminal justice.

"Doing well, thank you. And yourself? I was happy to learn you'd transferred to Brewster."

"I'm getting settled in. I gather this isn't a social call."

"No, it isn't." Carlos told Vince of the recent events involving Phillip Denton and his re-examination of the Robert Harris file.

"Interesting. It does raise suspicion as to whether he committed suicide. If in fact, he didn't kill himself I would doubt he killed Madelyn Denton."

"I agree."

"So how can I help you?"

"I'm curious about any background information the department has on the key players—Karen Fulbright, Phillip Denton, and Robert Harris. Even Madelyn Denton."

"Sure. Give me a few days, and I'll get back to you."

"I appreciate it. Too many things don't add up. I believe there is a common link between the murder, embezzlement, and Karen Fulbright, but I don't think the link was Robert Harris."

"I'll let you know what I find."

***

Stephanie was surprised to hear the doorbell ring. It was mid-afternoon, and she wasn't expecting Matt. She looked through the peephole to see Rachel Jackson standing at the door and hurried to open it.

"Hope I'm not intruding," Rachel said. "I was in the neighborhood and thought I'd drop in to see how you're doing."

"You're not. Please. Come in."

Rachel hesitated. "I guess I could come in for a few minutes." She followed Stephanie into the den and walked to the French doors that led to the screened in porch. "This is a beautiful place. I love the view."

"That's one of the best things about it. The screened in porch is wonderful. There's usually a good breeze off the lake."

"It's tranquil here. I was in the neighborhood looking at property. I've decided to sell the house."

"The big house and all the property?"

"It's more than I need. Time to move on with my life. You encouraged me to do that."

"I did? How?"

"Even with the things that happened when we were younger, you moved on in life. You have a successful career—doing something that you love. Many people would have allowed themselves to become victims of the past. You didn't do that."

"Neither did you. You became a doctor. Not everyone can handle medical school. Are you not happy with your choice?"

"Yes. It's not that at all, but I stayed bitter too many years. I held on to the house because I felt it was the last connection with my mother. I realize now I don't need material things to remember her by. I'll always have the memories." Rachel turned away and wiped away the tears that ran down her cheeks.

"Rachel, I wish more than anything I could change what happened that night."

Rachel nodded. "I know you do. We both lost someone very precious to us. It changed both our lives."

Stephanie hesitated. "Did you hear about Phillip's car? Guess Dad also killed him."

"You don't know that."

"Well, Phillip didn't put himself in the trunk and push the car into the water."

"It could take weeks or months to identify the body and determine a cause of death."

"Do they have Phillip's DNA profile for a comparison? What about family?"

"Phillip claimed he didn't have any family. I'm sure they'll compare a sample with what they have on file. They should have a profile from the clothing they found back then. It will still take some time."

"I'm so tired of waiting. I've only been here three weeks, yet in ways, it feels like months. Sometimes I wished I hadn't come back."

"Don't say that. I'm glad you came. I needed to make things right with you. I'm sorry for what has happened since you've been here."

"Thanks for saying that. I also needed to make amends with a few people. I was bitter, too."

Rachel smiled. "I believe forgiveness allows us to begin healing. Something we both need. We'll both feel better when everything is settled and all this is behind us."

***

After speaking to Detective Gonzales, Special Agent Vince Green began to review the Cameron Manufacturing embezzlement case.

After the death of Robert Harris, agents made a thorough investigation of his financial records. They learned he made seventy grand per year. He lived in a modest three-bedroom home with a mortgage. His wife Kathryn wasn't employed but often did volunteer work within the community. They owned two automobiles—a 1988 Oldsmobile and a 1990 Suburban.

The Oldsmobile was paid for, and Harris had taken out a three-year loan on the Suburban. The family had a modest savings account, didn't spend money frivolously, and took family vacations each summer. He had no gambling or credit card debt, was current on both his mortgage and car loan, and had an excellent credit rating. His daughter attended public schools. By all accounts, the Harris family lived a comfortable, but frugal life.

Harris had no siblings. His parents died in a car crash when he was twelve years old, and afterward, he lived with relatives in Driscoll Lake. A background check of the McKenzie family, including their daughter Carol, was clean.

When Robert's cousin, Carol McKenzie, transferred to South America as a foreign news correspondent, the FBI placed her under surveillance. Again, there was no indication she had involvement with the stolen money. She lived in a modest apartment, had a roommate, and didn't spend extravagantly.

Likewise, there was no evidence Kathryn Harris, as well as any other family members was involved in the embezzlement scheme. In fact, other than his signature on the checks, investigators couldn't find any concrete ties between him and the money. Robert Harris did not fit the profile of an embezzler.

He graduated from Driscoll Lake High School as valedictorian and later attended the University of Texas at Austin, where he received a master's degree in business administration.

There wasn't as much information on Phillip Denton, but upon a cursory glance, Vince didn't see any red flags. Denton moved to Texas from Chicago six months before his marriage to Madelyn Cameron Jackson. He was born in Southern California, attended UCLA, and received a degree in business management.

Karen Fulbright was born in the Pacific Northwest. She attended Oregon State University and graduated with an MBA in accounting. She lived in the Seattle area until she moved to Driscoll Lake five years before her death.

Fulbright had a job with a prestigious firm and lucrative salary in Seattle. It wasn't certain why she left, and no one knew of any friends or relatives she had in Texas. An agent interviewed her former co-workers as part of the embezzlement investigation. She didn't give a two-week notice when she left Seattle. Just walked in one day and announced she was moving to Texas. No one knew if she had a romantic involvement, and everyone said she was a very private person.

One co-worker suspected Karen was having an affair with a married man, but it was only a hunch based on a couple of phone conversations she'd accidentally overheard. Likewise, her co-workers in Driscoll Lake didn't know much about her personal life. No one indicated she had anything other than a professional relationship with Robert Harris.

If Vince were a betting man, he'd place money on Karen Fulbright. Why would anyone leave a high-income job and move to a relatively unknown town where she had no apparent connections?

Karen Fulbright had access to all the company's financial records. Karen Fulbright had the answers. But Karen Fulbright was dead.

***

Rachel had long since pushed aside any thoughts of Phillip Denton. Although he never mistreated her, she hadn't liked the man. She'd been a young girl, still reeling from her parent's divorce, when he came on the scene.

Today, she could think of little else. The body in the car was almost certainly Phillip. If only identification didn't take so long. Like Stephanie, she was ready to put the past behind her.

Rachel turned onto the quiet country road that led to her home. She would miss the wide-open fields and the tree-lined stream that ran through the property. In the springtime, whippoorwills called out each evening from beneath the flowering dogwoods that lined the banks of the creek. But it made sense to move to a smaller place. She'd seen several suitable houses in Lakeview Estates.

When she slowed to turn into her driveway, she saw her neighbor, Jesse Kimball, at his mailbox. The aging Korean War veteran had lived in the small house across the street most of his life. He walked with a cane now, and Rachel couldn't help but notice the slight stoop in his posture. She lowered the car window and called out to him.

"Good evening, Jesse. How are things with you?"

"Doing okay. Life is good. I'm sure going to miss you when you move. Just got used to seeing you again."

"I won't be far. I promise to come by on occasion to see you and Ms. Liz."

"She'd be mighty disappointed if you didn't."

"You tell her not to worry."

Rachel smiled as she drove up the long driveway leading to her house. So many of Jesse's generation were dying. She saw them on a weekly basis at the hospital — Korea, World War II, and even Vietnam vets who had faithfully served their country.

Vietnam. That was it. Phillip claimed he was wounded there.

She parked her car and hurried inside the house. It was almost five, but she hoped to catch Carlos. She called the police station and asked to speak with him.

"Rachel, how can I help you today?

"I have some information that might assist in determining if the skeletal remains belong to Phillip."

"Go on."

"Phillip said he caught some shrapnel in his left leg and knee which shattered his kneecap. He had surgery before he and Mom married. He told Mom the surgeon used both wires and screws to repair the knee, but he still walked with a limp. Not long before he disappeared, he saw an orthopedic surgeon in Brewster. He hoped another surgery would help him walk better."

"Thanks, Rachel. This could certainly help expedite the identification process. I know it was a long time ago, but by chance to you know the surgeon's name?"

Rachel rubbed her forehead. "I'm not sure, but my guess would be Dr. Nick Carson. He's with the Brewster Orthopedic group and has a reputation for being one of the best around. Knowing Phillip, he would have insisted on the finest."

"Do you know if he scheduled the surgery?"

"No, he didn't. The surgeon said it wouldn't help. He planned to seek a second opinion from someone in Dallas. That was just before he disappeared."

"Thank you for your time, Rachel. I'll relay this information to the sheriff."

"Please call me if you hear anything. Stephanie isn't the only person who is anxious to learn the truth."

Chapter Twenty-Six

Carlos phoned the sheriff's office immediately after he hung up with Rachel.

"Good to hear from you, Carlos," Dave Sanders said. "Any news?"

"Yes. Glad I caught you before you left the office. I just got off the phone with Phillip Denton's stepdaughter, Rachel Jackson. She gave me some information that may prove to be useful in determining if the body found in the car belongs to Phillip. Did you look at the skeletal remains?

"Yes, I did. Any particular thing I should have noticed?"

"Phillip Denton had a surgical procedure on his left kneecap. Apparently, he was injured in Vietnam, so there may also be bits of shrapnel in the bone. The surgeon used screws and wires. Do you remember seeing anything like that?"

"I don't recall, but I didn't look that close. Do you happen to know who did the surgery?"

"No, it happened long before he moved to Driscoll Lake, but Rachel said Denton saw an orthopedic surgeon in Brewster about the possibility of a second surgery. She thinks it may have been Dr. Nick Carson."

"I'll phone the lab in Dallas. If necessary, we can obtain Denton's medical record to assist in identification."

"Thanks, Dave."

"I'll be in touch."

***

"The end." Stephanie breathed a sigh of relief and closed her laptop. She always felt good when she finished the first draft of a manuscript, but she was particularly happy to complete this one. Maybe it was because so much had happened in her life the past few weeks.

She had spoken to Miles Parker the day before. He filed the application for probate of Helen's will. The entire process could take at least three months. It was now a matter of waiting.

Stephanie had also come to terms with the fact her father was probably guilty. She couldn't do anything else to clear his name. It was time to go back to Colorado.

"But today I'm going to celebrate," she said to Whiskers. He hopped on the sofa and nudged her arm with his head. Stephanie scratched him behind the ears. "You're spoiled. Guess you know it."

Whiskers purred, stretched, and lay down beside her with one paw touching her arm.

Stephanie glanced at her watch. She really wanted to get out of the house. She'd spent a lot of time indoors the past couple of weeks—first recovering from the accident and then dodging questions about her father. If only Matt were home.

An idea sprang into her head. She jumped up from the sofa and went to the front window. Brian's truck was at the construction site across the road. She opened the door and went to meet him.

"Hey, what's up with you?" he asked.

"I thought I might visit your mother again today."

"Oh?" Brian wrinkled his brow.

"This time for fun. No questions. I thought about taking her to dinner. That is if you think she'd enjoy getting out."

"She'd love it. I'll give her a call to say you're coming."

"Tell her I'll be there around six and to pick her favorite restaurant."

***

Stephanie decided a fresh bouquet of flowers would be a lovely gift for Dorothy. She pulled into the parking lot of the local supermarket and went inside to the floral section.

She lingered for a few minutes over the colorful arrangements before selecting Gerbera daisies. When she started toward the checkout, she couldn't help but overhear a conversation between two women standing near the deli. She stopped at the sound of her name.

"Stephanie Harris is still in town?"

"Oh, yes. She came here for her aunt's funeral almost a month ago and has been busy stirring up trouble."

"How so?

"You remember all that business with her father. She won't leave it alone. Trying to convince others he was innocent."

"I thought they said he was guilty."

"Of course he was. That's my point. Stephanie has also been cozying up to Matt Bradford. Guess she's trying to get the law on her side. Speaking of Matt, I overheard Nell tell someone he was responsible for his wife's death."

"No. I can't believe that."

"Of course, Nell and Dan tried to keep it hushed. Wish I had more details, but I'm sure I could find out. I also heard he had an affair. Now this business with Stephanie. He's spent several nights at her house. We don't need someone like him for our police chief."

Stephanie had heard enough. She turned and walked toward the women. "Madge Sinclair. I might have known it was you since you have nothing better to do than gossip."

The woman standing beside Madge colored in embarrassment and dropped her head.

"Here's some truth for you Madge. You're the perfect model for a new character in my next novel. The setting is a small town, complete with gossips and cruel people. That ought to give you something to talk about."

Madge's jaw dropped.

Stephanie had never seen her speechless. Before Madge could recover, Stephanie turned and walked away. Now she understood why her mother had been so eager to leave Driscoll Lake. She realized the sooner she finished her business and left here, the better.

***

Stephanie was still seething when she reached the nursing home. Madge had a lot of nerve to gossip about her and Matt. Even worse was the fact she was spreading rumors about him being responsible for his wife's death. How dare she accuse him of having an affair? Ridiculous.

Or was it?

She turned off the ignition and took a few deep breaths. No way would she allow Madge Sinclair to ruin her evening with Dorothy. Once she felt composed, she got out of the car and went inside.

She started across the lobby toward Dorothy's room when she saw an older black man pushing a woman in a wheelchair. When Stephanie drew nearer, she recognized the couple. It was Otis Wood and his wife Cleo. The woman's far away gaze left little doubt that she suffered from Alzheimer's or another form of dementia.

"Mr. Wood?"

"Stephanie. It's good to see you."

"Likewise to you and your wife."

"She's not doing well." Otis shook his head. "Her mind doesn't work like it once did."

"I'm so sorry to hear that. She was my favorite teacher. She encouraged me both in and out of the classroom."

"Cleo was proud of all her pupils, but I think she always held a special place in her heart for you."

"Really?"

"Oh, yes, and when she heard you'd written a book, she was as proud as if she'd written it herself. Told everyone what a good student you were. She read all your books until." His voice quivered with emotion. "Until she was no longer able."

"Oh, that means a lot to me."

"Hardest thing I've ever had to do is to put her in this home. But they take good care of her."

"I'm sure it was difficult. Do you think she'd know if I spoke to her?"

"Can't ever tell, Miss Stephanie. Some days she acts as if she understands, but those are rare. She hardly ever tries to speak."

Stephanie sat her purse and the vase of flowers on the floor and knelt beside the wheelchair. She took the elderly woman's delicate hand. "Mrs. Wood, this is Stephanie. I just want to say you were a big influence on my life. Without your encouragement, I may never have become a writer. I want to thank you for caring about me."

Cleo turned her head and looked into Stephanie's eyes. Her hand squeezed Stephanie's—ever so slight. For a few seconds, Stephanie thought she could see a hint of recognition. Just as quickly, the blank stare returned. The moment of lucidity had passed.

Stephanie stood up. "I thought she recognized me for a moment, but probably not. She hadn't seen me since I was fourteen.

"It's possible. She kept up with you through your aunt. Helen used to show her photos of the two of you together."

"That's nice. I wish I could have talked to her before—I'll never forget the kindness she showed me.

"It's okay, Miss Stephanie. She would understand."

***

As Stephanie made her way to Dorothy's room, she thought about the two encounters she'd had within the last hour.

Madge Sinclair. Angry. Bitter. Rumormonger. Probably lonely. In some ways, Stephanie felt sorry for her.

Cleo Wood. Loving. Caring. Kind. Always a positive influence to those around her. Stephanie recalled how she used to say, "Always look for the good in people. It's there. You might have to dig a little, but you'll find it. Sometimes all it takes is to reach out to someone with love."

She often spoke about forgiveness. "It's not always easy, but always best."

Cleo Wood lived by her words. She was a positive influence to everyone around her.

Cleo would tell Stephanie to forgive Madge.

Chapter Twenty-Seven

"I think you need to get out this evening," Matt said as he and Stephanie finished their morning run. "You've been cooped up in the house too long."

"I went out last night. I took Dorothy Nichols to dinner."

"But you weren't with me. I'll make dinner reservations for us."

"Matt, you don't have to do that."

"I know I don't have to, but I want to. You've been through a lot the past few days. Let's just say I'm your personal cheering up committee."

Stephanie laughed. "A committee of one?"

"Who else do you need?"

"Confident aren't you?" she teased. "Where are we going? I need to know how to dress."

"To the Riverbend Steak House near Brewster. They have the best steaks around. You can dress casually—jeans are fine. I'll pick you up around seven."

"I'll be ready."

***

After leaving Stephanie, Matt went next door to his parents' house. There was little to worry about. They had a modern security system, but his mother felt better knowing he checked the house from time to time.

He did a quick run-through. Satisfied there were no problems, he locked the door and walked back to his pickup truck. Noise from the construction site across the street drew his attention, and he looked up to see Brian Nichols.

Brian glanced in his direction but quickly turned away. He felt a twinge of guilt for the way he'd acted the previous week. It was ludicrous to think Brian was to blame for Stephanie's accident.

Matt walked across the street and waited for Brian finished speaking to one of his workers.

Brian's greeting was cold. "Kind of busy here. What's up?"

"I won't stay long. I owe you an apology for the way I acted last week. Stephanie's accident had me upset. It was wrong of me to think you'd be involved."

Brian's demeanor softened. "It's okay, man. I might have acted the same way if Ra— I mean, I understand."

"Thanks."

"She's special to you, isn't she?"

"Uh, yeah. She is. Guess that affected my judgment."

"It happens. Did you ever get the locks changed?"

"No. I planned to, but got busy and never did it."

"If you'd like, I'll take care of it. Might be a couple of days, though."

"Sounds good. Thanks, Brian. I hope there are no hard feelings."

"None."

***

Kyle phone Stephanie mid-afternoon. "I was thinking about writing another article," he said. "There's a lot of talk this week about finding Phillip Denton's car. This might be a good time to follow-up with a story about the journal."

"No," Stephanie said. "I don't want you to mention the journal. I wouldn't do anything to discredit Carol's memory."

"What makes you think it would?"

"Come on, Kyle. She was here recovering from PTSD. She'd suffered flashbacks. Everyone would assume that's all it was—a flashback. Or worse, that she was having hallucinations. I found most of her other journals."

"You found them? Did you learn anything?"

"Nothing. For some strange reason, the one from 1991 is missing."

***

Riverbend Restaurant sat far back from the road, surrounded by trees. The outdoor dining area was in back, and the land sloped away toward a small stream.

"It's beautiful here," Stephanie said as she took a sip of Cabernet Sauvignon. A cool breeze blew across her face. "I'm glad we decided to sit outside."

"I prefer the outdoors whenever possible," Matt said. "Deer will often come to drink from the creek in the evening hours. I find it relaxing."

"That it is. Not to mention the food is great. Can't remember when I've had a better steak."

"I'm glad you like it. It's always crowded on the weekends, so I prefer to come on a weeknight. More privacy that way." Matt's blue eyes gazed at her, unblinking.

Stephanie glanced away and took a deep breath before turning her attention back to him. "I spoke to Miles Parker on Monday. He's started the process of probating Aunt Helen's will."

"Why do I have the feeling I'm not going to like what you're about to say?"

"It's time for me to go back to Colorado."

"Do you have to leave?" Matt reached across the table and took her hand. "I'd really like you to stay."

"I live there, remember?" For some inexplicable reason, she couldn't bring herself to call Denver home. Sure, she missed the beauty of the Rockies and the crisp mountain air, but she'd come to enjoy the time she'd spent in Driscoll Lake.

She'd rekindled old memories—thoughts of happier times before her father's death. Not to mention her increasing affection for Matt. Although he'd never said anything, he seemed to be developing feelings for her. But she'd often noticed a faraway look in his eyes and wondered if he still hadn't come to terms with his wife's death. His mother said as much.

Before they could have any relationship, she had to make certain he had put the past behind him. She hated to admit it, but Madge's words from the day before left her wondering if any of them were true. Stephanie's ex-husband had been unfaithful. She didn't want to become involved in that type of relationship again.

Stephanie bit her lower lip. "I may be assuming too much, but before anything could happen between us, I have to know something. What happened to your wife?"

A muscle twitched in his jaw.

"I understand if you don't want to answer."

"It's okay. You need to know the truth. Tara's death was my fault."

Stephanie's eyebrows rose. "How so?"

When we married, she wanted children. A few years went by, but she was unable to become pregnant. It took a bit of persuasion on her part, but we both went for fertility tests. When we learned the problem wasn't with me, she became pretty despondent."

"I see."

"Tara came from a large family. It didn't help that her youngest sister had recently given birth to twins and another one seemed to get pregnant every time the wind changed. "I told her it didn't matter, that I still loved her, and if she wanted children we could always adopt."

"I gather that wasn't an option for her."

"Only as a last resort. Tara somehow felt less than a woman because she couldn't conceive. She sought a second opinion and found a doctor who believed a surgical procedure could correct her problems. When months went by and she still didn't get pregnant, our marriage began to suffer.

"No matter how many times I told her differently, she became convinced I couldn't ever love 'half a woman.' About a month before her death, I started working longer hours. Staying away from home late every night. One day a female co-worker asked me to go for a drink after work. She was also going through a tough time in her marriage, so I agreed."

Here it comes. He was having an affair. Stephanie took a deep breath. "Go on."

"It wasn't the wisest thing I ever did, but I swear there was nothing more than friendship. That evening Tara came by the station looking for me. Another officer knew where I'd gone and told her. She came to the bar and found me with Kay. When she saw us together, she ran outside.

"I rushed after her and caught up with her just as she got in the car. She was hysterical. I jumped in the passenger seat, and she started the engine and peeled out of the parking lot. It had rained that day and the streets were wet." Matt paused for a moment and looked away.

"I tried to get her to slow down, but she wouldn't listen. She ran a red light and collided with a delivery truck. She swerved to the right, but it hit on her side of the car. She died on impact."

"Matt, I'm so sorry."

"My injuries were minor—just a few cuts and bruises. The officer who investigated the accident said it was a miracle I walked away."

"That's how you got the scar on your chin?"

"Yeah. It wasn't until after the funeral I learned the reason Tara was looking for me. She'd just found out she was pregnant. Both my wife and baby died because of me."

***

Stephanie spent most of the drive home in deep thought. On the one hand, she was relieved to learn Matt didn't have an affair. She had no cause to doubt his words. However, she didn't want to compete with his dead wife's memory. Matt still had some issues to work through.

He seemed to sense her need to ponder the situation between them and said little. Stephanie appreciated his sensitivity.

They were almost at Helen's house when she spoke. "It wasn't your fault."

"What?"

"Tara's death. It wasn't your fault."

"How can you say that? If I hadn't—"

"What if? We can go through life paralyzed by the 'what ifs.' What if you hadn't gone to the bar after work? What if Madelyn hadn't gone to the factory that night? What if my father hadn't pulled the trigger or stolen the money? Those things happened, and we can't do anything to change them."

He parked in the driveway and turned off the ignition. "But I—"

"I'm not suggesting you forget Tara, but life is too short for us to be victims of our past. We can stay there and allow it to cripple us, or we can move forward. Coming back to Driscoll Lake made me realize I'd been doing the same thing."

Matt shook his head. "I guess you're right."

She looked at him and smiled. "I know it isn't easy, but take one step at a time. You have your whole life ahead of you."

"You're good for me."

Stephanie looked at the dashboard clock. It was nearly eleven. "Look, it's late, and you probably need to get up early. I'd better go inside so you can go home. We can talk again tomorrow."

"Okay. I'll walk you to the door."

She reached into her purse for the house key. Before she could unlock the door, Matt took her by the shoulders.

"Just so you know. Tara's memory would never come between us."

"Matt, I—" Stephanie looked down at the large pot of geraniums. "It's been moved," she said.

"What?"

"The geraniums. Someone has moved the pot."

"Are you sure?"

"Yes. You can see the water stain on the concrete where it once sat. Matt, you don't think someone could have been looking for the key, do you?"

"Wait here. I'm going in first." Matt pull a handgun from inside his jacket, took the key from Stephanie and unlocked the door.

Stephanie waited for what seemed like an eternity before he came back out.

"Everything looks okay."

Once inside, Stephanie looked around to ensure everything was in place. Whiskers had been asleep on the sofa. He yawned and stretched when she walked into the den. She breathed a sigh of relief. "No more hidden notes."

"I'm staying with you tonight."

"I'll be fine. I can call if I need anything."

"No arguing. I'm not leaving you alone."

Chapter Twenty-Eight

Stephanie overslept the following morning. By the time she awoke, Matt had already left. She was glad he stayed but didn't want to admit to him how much last night's incident unnerved her. Had someone known where Helen kept the hidden key? If so, what was the reason? To leave another anonymous note? Maybe Matt had been right. She should install a security system and change the locks.

She showered and ate a light breakfast. It felt strange not to have anything to do. She'd finished sorting and packing Helen's belongings. It was too soon to begin edits on her manuscript—she always waited a week or two after completing the first draft.

"What will I do today, Whiskers? I can't sleep all the time like you do." She opened her laptop to search for companies that sold security systems. The sounds of hammers came from across the street, and she looked out the window to see if Brian was around. When she saw him standing outside, she hurried to talk with him.

"Glad you came over," Brian said. "I wanted to tell you how much Mom enjoyed the evening with you. That's all she's talked about the past couple of days."

"I had a great time. I couldn't leave town without seeing her again."

"Leave? You're going back to Denver?"

"Soon. Nothing more I can do here until the probate hearing for Aunt Helen's will. I wanted to ask you about having the locks changed on the house."

"Matt asked me about them yesterday. Told him I could do it in a couple of days. Would Saturday be okay?"

"Sure. That will work."

"I'll call before I come."

When Stephanie turned to walk back to the house, she saw the door to Helen's mailbox partially opened. It was too early for the postman, and she was certain she closed it yesterday. She peered inside and saw a small package wrapped in plain brown paper. It felt like a book but had no postmark or return address. Someone printed "Stephanie" on the front.

Curious, she ripped off the paper. Inside was a plain, leather bound book—the same style as Carol's other journals. She opened it and looked inside.

Carol McKenzie, 1991.

The missing journal had found its way home.

***

Stephanie was anxious to read Carol's words and didn't stop to consider the significance of someone placing the package in the mailbox. She hurried into the house and sat down on the sofa, her hands trembling as she opened the book. As in the case with the others, Carol began a new journal each year.

She skimmed through the first part. Carol didn't write anything for several weeks around the time of her accident. When Stephanie came to the first entry for September, a few days before her father's death, she began to read.

September 1

I've been back in Driscoll Lake for two months. Coming home has certainly helped the healing process. Mom worries about me, so I try to placate her by staying with them most of the time. I come to the cabin as often as I can. I love Mom and Dad, but I need quiet. It's peaceful here—I feel the serene setting will help with my recovery. No television, radio, or loud noises. I can't bring myself to watch the news or read newspapers yet.

There aren't many houses around—only a few weekend cabins. Most of the summer vacationers have gone now that school has started. A few are here for the Labor Day weekend, but afterward most everyone will leave again.

September 2

Bob, Kathryn, and Stephanie came to the lake today, along with Mom and Dad. We had a nice cookout, but Bob seemed preoccupied. Guess it's because of the business with Phillip Denton. The company CEO disappeared a few weeks ago after returning from a business trip. He never made it home to Driscoll Lake.

September 4

Most days I think I'm getting better. Then something happens to trigger a memory of that awful day. Last night I had a nightmare about Kuwait. At least, I think it was a dream. It was so real. I felt as if I was living the incident all over again.

In the dream, I kept trying to reach Jeff. The acrid smell of the smoke was so real—just like it was that day. When I woke up, I was certain I could still smell it and thought I heard Jeff call my name. Doesn't make sense because he never had a chance to call out to me that day. Why did I hear his voice so clearly last night?

September 8

I saw him again last night, walking through the woods. This time it wasn't a dream. Why, why is this starting again?

Stephanie paused, took a deep breath, and closed her eyes. She had resigned herself to her father's guilt, but finding this journal gave her a new wave of hope. However, if Carol thought she saw her dead fiancé, would any of her words be reliable? She read on.

September 14

Something terrible has happened. Both Bob and Madelyn Denton are dead. The police say he killed her and then turned the gun on himself. He left a suicide note, saying he was sorry for everything. Mom called me last night. Kathryn and Stephanie were at the football game. The police came for Kathryn. Stephanie was with the band. I went to the stadium to pick her up. I had to be the one to tell her. It's one of the hardest things I've ever done. How do you tell a fourteen-year-old her father is dead?

September 16

I saw Dr. Hawkins this morning. I told him about the dream. He believes it was a flashback. He said the trauma of Bob's unexpected death could trigger more if them, so he increased my medication dosage. Contrary to what he thinks, Bob's death has caused me to face reality. I am getting better. I won't take more medication.

But don't most mental health patients believe they don't need their meds? I'm not crazy. Yes, I had a rough time dealing with Jeff's death. I know the accident wasn't my fault, but I should have been the one in that car. If only I hadn't switched places with him.

September 17

Bob's funeral was today. It's hard for me to believe he killed himself and Madelyn. He adored Kathryn and Stephanie. He would never put them through such grief. My heart aches for them. Kathryn sobbed openly at the funeral, but I've yet to see Stephanie shed a tear. Except for one outburst outside the football stadium, she's shown little emotion. I think she is still in shock.

Stephanie laid the book aside, got up, and walked outside to the screened-in porch. She needed a few minutes to compose her thoughts. Reading about her father's death and the funeral wasn't easy. Carol was right—she didn't show a lot of emotion. It was months later after she moved to Atlanta when she allowed herself to cry.

She looked out over the peaceful waters of the lake. Even with all the houses around, the area was still quiet. It was easy to see how Carol saw it as a place of respite. After a few minutes, she went back inside to read more of the journal. She needed to know the identity of the person Carol saw only days before her death. Whoever it was, there might be a connection to her father.

September 28

The incident with Bob has become even more bizarre. An outside firm is in the process of conducting an audit of the financial records of Cameron Manufacturing. Someone has taken large sums of money, including the employee retirement fund. They called in the FBI. Bob is the prime suspect.

The idea he embezzled money is ludicrous. Bob was one of the most honest people I know.

October 3

The lake has become my place of refuge after the events of the last month. Too much is happening. This used to be a quiet little town—now there is nothing but turmoil. The FBI has questioned Kathryn about the embezzlement. Dad advised her to get an attorney—even though he doesn't believe she was involved.

October 4

With everything that's happened, I forgot to write about this. I'm not having flashbacks! The man I saw in the woods was real.

On the night of Bob's death, after leaving Kathryn's house, I decided to come out to the lake. I went to bed, but couldn't sleep.

Around 3:00 in the morning, I got up and walked outside to the deck. The quiet atmosphere with only the sights and sounds of nature has a soothing effect on me.

A car pulled into the driveway of one of the cabins across the lake. A man went inside. A few minutes later, the porch light came on, and two men came out. One of them had a large duffle bag. Both men got in the car and drove away. Apparently, the man I saw in the woods a few times had been staying in the cabin.

I don't know who he is, but the cabin belongs to...

Stephanie gasped. She flipped the page back and forth. The next entry was two days later on October 6. When she looked closer, she saw a torn edge. Someone had ripped a page from the journal.

And someone must have taken the journal from Helen's house, then returned it. Were they responsible for the missing page? If so, who was it and what did they have to hide? She read on, hoping to find another reference to the person.

October 6

Things have quieted down around town—at least with the murder investigation. Joe Rivers says it's an open and shut case. The FBI is still questioning Kathryn about the money. They've even talked to Mom and Dad.

Stephanie and Kathryn are suffering. So called "friends" have turned their backs on them. There are rumors the factory may have to close. People are upset over their lost retirement funds.

Kathryn says she's leaving here as soon as possible. She spoke to a real estate agent about selling the house. Says she can't afford to keep it. Besides a modest savings account, Bob didn't leave lots of money. He had a sizable insurance policy, but they probably won't pay off since his death was ruled a suicide. Mom and Dad have offered to help until she can get a job.

I haven't had any more nightmares. I'm convinced it was a dream and not a flashback. I'm glad I didn't mention seeing the man to Dr. Hawkins. He would have insisted on stronger medication. Maybe would have wanted to put me back in the hospital. I can't have that happen. Mom and Dad need me.

October 8

I heard more rumors today. They are ludicrous. Some people say that Bob and Madelyn were having an affair. I don't believe it. Bob was completely devoted to Kathryn. He and Madelyn dated in high school, but that's it.

Kathryn sent Stephanie to live with her grandparents in Georgia. Guess she wants to protect her from all the gossip.

Stephanie spent the rest of the morning reading the remaining entries. There were no more references to the incident at the cabin, but Stephanie felt certain the man Carol mentioned in her last journal was the unknown man she saw at the lake.

It was time to phone Carlos Gonzales again.

Chapter Twenty-Nine

Carlos received a call from Sheriff Sanders on Thursday afternoon.

"I finally spoke to the Dallas lab and Dr. Carson this morning. Rachel Jackson is correct—the body doesn't belong to Phillip Denton."

"Did you notify Fort Worth?"

"Yeah. Why did someone else's body end up in Phillip Denton's car? Carlos, how much have you looked into his disappearance?"

"We don't have anything on file here. I only know what I found on the Internet except for what little the Fort Worth police told me."

"Didn't someone find items belonging to him?"

"You mean the blood-stained clothing? Thinking it may have been a ruse?"

"I wonder."

"The thought crossed my mind also, but the DNA match was positive. There was enough blood on the clothing for someone to have bled out. Phillip Denton has to be dead. Wherever his body is remains a mystery."

"Which leaves everyone back at square one. The press will be asking questions. I'm calling the Rangers for assistance. Someone is missing a husband or father. It's my hope we can identify the body and give them closure. I'll keep you updated."

Carlos hung up the phone, hurried to Matt's office, and knocked on the door. "Got a minute?"

Matt motioned him inside. "Yeah, what's up?"

"Just got off the phone with Dave. The body isn't Phillip's."

"What? You're kidding me."

"Wish I was. It would make things a lot simpler."

Matt's office phone rang. "Yeah, Macey. What's up?"

"Sorry to interrupt," the dispatcher said. "Stephanie Harris is on the line. She said it's important that she speak to you and Carlos."

"Put her through."

***

CHAPTER ONE

Matt and Carlos
***

Stephanie was glad to hear Carlos was in Matt's office so they both could hear what she had to say. When Matt answered the phone, she explained about finding the journal.

"You found what?"

"Carol's missing journal. It was in the mailbox this morning. Wasn't there yesterday."

"Someone mailed it to Helen's address?"

"No. There wasn't a postmark. It was in plain brown paper with my name printed on the front."

"What? When did you find it?"

"Early this morning."

"And you just now called me? Hold on a minute."

Stephanie heard muffled voices before Matt came back on the line.

"I'm going to put you on speaker so that Carlos can ask you some questions."

"Go ahead, Stephanie," Carlos said.

"I found the missing journal.

"Why didn't you call us right away?"

"Because I spent the morning reading it. There is a link to the person Carol saw at the lake the night of my father's death and the man she saw in South America. I'm sure of it. She planned to go to the police, but never got the chance. She died in a plane crash the following day."

"Stephanie, did she say who this person might be?" Carlos asked.

"She claimed she didn't know him. A page is missing so—"

"Missing?" Carlos asked.

"Yes. Someone apparently tore out one of the pages. Carol knew who owned the cabin. I think the missing page must have had the owner's name."

"Any other pages missing?"

"No, just the one."

"And you're sure she saw this person the night of your father's death?" Matt asked.

"Yes. Carol wrote she decided to go to the cabin after she left our house that night. She couldn't sleep and went outside to the deck."

"Do you know if she told anyone?"

"No, she didn't. In other entries, she wrote her doctor believed she was having flashbacks. She'd seen this man in the woods at night a couple of times. She didn't say, but I think she believed it was her dead fiancé. She was relieved when she saw the man together with whoever owned the cabin. In her last journal, she lamented over not telling someone."

"Stephanie, what time did you find it?" Matt's voice was somber.

"Around eight this morning. I walked across the street to talk to Brian and saw the mailbox door partially opened."

"You're positive it wasn't there yesterday?"

"Yes. I checked the mail shortly before you came to pick me up for dinner."

"Then someone placed it there while we were away or sometime during the night. I don't like this. Who else might have known about the journal?"

"I don't know. I mentioned them to a few people—Christine, Kyle, Dorothy Nichols. But I can't think of anyone who would deliberately keep this one from me."

"Somebody did. And for some reason, the person decided to return it—minus one page."

"Stephanie, one more question," Carlos said. "Was the printing on the package the same as the notes you received?"

"No. This one was plain print. I still have the paper. Honestly, I was so excited to see the journal it didn't occur to me until later to be suspicious."

"Okay. I may want to read some of the journal entries myself."

"I don't mind. Just let me know."

***

Pat Turner rarely watched the evening news, but tonight she decided to turn on the television while she prepared dinner. In light of the recent events regarding Phillip Denton's missing car and the skeletal remains, she wanted to hear of any new reports.

There was a lot of speculation. As usual, the gossips had their theories—including Madge Sinclair. Pat overheard her tell someone on the phone she was more convinced than ever Robert Harris killed Denton. She admonished Madge for using the telephone to perpetrate more rumors.

While Pat sautéed shrimp and boiled water for pasta, she kept her ear tuned to the news. Most of it was about the widespread fires across the state and the continuing heat and drought. Although the temperatures had cooled to the lower nineties, it was still too hot for early October.

She had just taken the pasta from the burner and placed it in a colander to drain when the television anchor announced a breaking news story. Pat reached for the remote to turn up the volume and listened with interest.

"There is another twist to the story of missing businessman Phillip Denton. A spokesperson for the Driscoll County Sheriff's Office confirmed the remains found last week are not those of Denton. Authorities had hoped the discovery of the body would put an end to his mysterious disappearance twenty years ago."

Pat picked up the phone and dialed Kyle. "Hear the latest about Denton?"

"Yes," he said.

"How did they confirm the remains aren't his? It's a little too early for DNA test results." Pat knew Kyle had a source at the sheriff's department who often told him things off the record.

"Denton had surgery years ago to repair a shattered left kneecap. There was no indication of a surgical procedure on the remains and the knee cap was intact."

"Okay, thanks, Kyle. Gets stranger all the time doesn't it?"

Pat hung up the phone, finished preparing the linguini and shrimp, and took her plate to the dining table. She preferred to eat her meals in silence. She'd heard enough about the drought, wildfires, and police investigations. But after eating a few bites, she felt that nagging sensation again—much like when she first returned from her vacation.

"That's it," she said aloud. "The man on the cruise ship."

She saw him for a brief moment when they first boarded. Something about him caught her eye—perhaps due to the fact his companion looked young enough to be his daughter.

As it turned out, he had the same dining table as Pat and her sister. The first night at dinner, his wife told everyone he was ill and decided to take his meal in the cabin. He must have had a major illness because she never saw him again. She later learned they departed early while the ship early was docked in Greece.

Pat remembered thinking there was something vaguely familiar about him. Now she remembered what it was.

"Impossible. You've read one too many suspense novels. But there was something about the way he walked."

Crazy at it seemed, she decided to call Carlos Gonzales. She glanced at her watch. It was too late today, but she made a mental note to phone him first thing in the morning.

***

Joe Rivers had a good career as Driscoll Lake police chief. During his twenty-five-year tenure, the crime rate was low, and most of the residents were law-abiding citizens. It made his job easier.

The growth of the town in recent years brought with it increased crime. He was glad he no longer had to deal with it. Matt Bradford was young but had the experience needed to run the department.

After his retirement, Joe and his wife bought a house on Lake Brewster so that he could pursue his love of fishing.

Most mornings found him on his dock or trolling the shoreline in his flat-bottomed boat. Life was good.

He kept up to date of the happenings of Driscoll Lake by reading the local newspaper and occasionally talking with a few old acquaintances. The recent newspaper article served as a reminder of something that had bothered him for twenty years—the one case in which he felt he didn't do right.

The deaths of Robert Harris and Madelyn Denton was the biggest crime ever to hit Driscoll Lake. Everyone, including Joe, was surprised when one of the town's most respected citizens killed one of its wealthiest.

Like many residents, he was at the Friday night football game when he received the call. He rushed to the factory, along with EMS and other emergency personnel. The young officer who was already at the scene confirmed everyone's worst fears. Two people were dead.

Joe instructed his lieutenant to drive to the stadium and arrange to meet with family members in a secluded area.

Deputies sealed off the crime scene and began to collect evidence. For cases like this, Joe wished he lived in a larger town with a bigger budget. If he did, he would have had the benefit of a coroner or medical examiner—someone who specialized in deaths. Instead, he had to call the local Justice of the Peace to pronounce the victims.

By then, the mayor and two members of the city council had gathered outside the building. They were eager to hear what happened, so Joe went out to talk with them.

"It appears to be a murder-suicide. Harris left a note. Lt. Rogers has gone to meet with the families now. The press will hear about this soon. We'll post officers here to protect the crime scene, but I think it's a good idea to hold a press conference away from this area."

"We can have it at City Hall," said the mayor. "I'll go ahead to make sure things are set up."

"Thanks, Mayor. I'll be there shortly to answer questions."

One of the council members left with the mayor, but the other one stayed behind. He waited until they were alone before he asked, "What really happened here?"

"It's as I said—an apparent murder-suicide. You know my resources are limited. I'd like to call in the Texas Rangers to investigate. They have more expertise."

"Why? You said there was a suicide note. The autopsies will confirm what we already know. The town doesn't need a lot of drawn out negative publicity. The sooner we get this behind us, the better for the families and everyone—including you."

Joe didn't mistake the threatening undertone. The council had the power to take away his job. He reluctantly agreed.

He felt somewhat relieved after the autopsy reports confirmed the investigation's initial findings. When auditors discovered someone had embezzled money from the company and the trail led to Robert Harris, Joe convinced himself that he had done his job.

Twenty years later, he still had reservations about the investigation. When he received a call from Carlos Gonzales, asking to meet and discuss the case, he welcomed the chance to tell his side of the story.

***

It felt a little strange to be back in Texas. He decided against staying in Brewster—it was too close to Driscoll Lake. Dallas was perfect. People there were too busy to ask questions, but it was close enough to be able to slip in and out of town unnoticed.

He made a couple of trips to familiarize himself with some things and learn some necessary information. Tomorrow night, he would go back and finish the job.

Life had been good. He had everything wanted, although it hadn't been easy to come by. He had to take risks to get where he was. He wouldn't allow anyone to stand in his way—including Angel.

She'd become a liability to him. It was time to take care of her. He pressed the speed dial button on his phone.

"I want you to make another phone call to our friend. Need to make certain of his whereabouts for tomorrow night. I don't have to remind you to be discrete."

"I'll take care of it."

"One more thing. Angel has to go. I don't care how you do it, but I don't want her around when I get home."

"You want her dead?"

"Whatever it takes." He pressed the button to end the call.

He'd taken a chance on coming back, but he didn't trust anyone else to do the job. It required caution and careful planning. He decided to carry out his mission on a Friday night. Getting a gun wouldn't be a problem. He knew exactly where to go. And just like before, he would make the crime appear to be a murder-suicide.

He would end it at the place it began—on a Friday night during a football game at the old factory. Some things in Driscoll Lake hadn't changed. Many of the town's residents would be at the stadium.

This time the police force was better equipped, but he had no worries. By the time someone found the bodies, he'd be far away. He would board a flight to New York, then Germany, and on to Italy. After tomorrow, he would never have to return.

Chapter Thirty

"I have to go to Dallas today," Matt said. He and Stephanie sat and looked at the lake after their Friday morning run. "But I'll be back for tonight's football game. Want to go? My parents' seats are still available."

"Yes, I'll go," Stephanie said. "In spite of what happened to me after the last game, I had a good time."

"I won't let anything like that happen to you tonight. I'll need to meet you at the stadium, but rest assured, I'll follow you home." Matt took her hand.

Stephanie closed her eyes. Being in Driscoll Lake with Matt felt like the most natural thing in the world, but she couldn't remain here forever. She thought a lot about what he told her about his wife. Perhaps someday they could pursue a relationship, but Stephanie sensed he still needed time to get over the guilt.

She took her hand away, stood up, and walked to the edge of the lake. "Matt, I've thought more about what I said the other day. It's time for me to leave Driscoll Lake. I've finished my business here. I may never learn the identity of the man Carol saw, and even if I do, there's no guarantee it will prove my father's innocence."

He got up from the bench and stood beside her. "There's nothing I can do to change your mind?"

"Not now. I'll come back for the probate hearing. By then, I'll make a decision on what to do with the house."

"What about us? I'd begun to think maybe we had a chance. Guess I assumed too much."

Stephanie turned her head and closed her eyes in an attempt to fight back the tears.

"Look, I know you have painful memories of this place. You don't have to leave Denver. I can—"

Stephanie held up her hand. "Wait. We're both carrying baggage from past relationships. Let's take it one step at a time."

"Meaning what?"

"Meaning we both need to deal with some things. I'm not closing the door, but I don't want to rush into anything. Up until a month ago, twenty years separated us."

"I'd never want to push you."

She smiled. "Thanks. I just need some time."

"I guess I'll have to be satisfied with that. When do you plan to leave?"

"Sometime next week. I haven't even booked my flight. In the meantime, let's enjoy the remaining few days I'm here."

***

When she arrived back at the house, Stephanie showered and changed into jeans and a pullover top. She phoned the airline, made a reservation for the following Tuesday, and arranged transportation for Whiskers.

Now that she'd set the departure date, it was time to say goodbye to some people. She wanted to see Christine again. Kyle had done his best to help—she should thank him.

Which brought to mind Madge Sinclair. Stephanie felt guilty about the way she'd acted toward her. Madge was a busybody and delighted in stirring up rumors. Still, she needed to do the right thing and apologize.

Doing it over the phone wasn't good enough. She needed to tell her in person. If Madge chose not to accept the apology, at least she'd done her part. She could leave town with a clean conscience.

***

Madge Sinclair sat behind her desk at the newspaper office. Stephanie wasn't surprised at her cold reception, but she couldn't blame her.

"I assume you're here to see Mr. Lawrence or Mrs. Turner. Neither one is in the office."

"I didn't come to see them," Stephanie replied. "I came to see you."

"Why? To gather more information for your next book?"

"No. I came to apologize."

"Apologize? To me? Why"

"For how I acted toward you in the supermarket. I have no intention to write a book using you as a character model. I'm sorry. There's no excuse for the way I acted, but I get a bit defensive when it comes to my father."

Madge's demeanor softened. "I suppose if it were me, I'd feel the same way."

"Make no mistake. I despise gossip. I still had no right to say what I did."

Tears ran down Madge's face, and she quickly wiped them away.

"I didn't mean to make you cry."

"It's not you. I just... It's not important."

Her words confirmed Stephanie's earlier suspicion. Madge was a lonely woman. Spreading rumors was her way of getting attention.

"Mrs. Sinclair, do you have any family around? Any close friends with whom you can visit?"

She shook her head. "There's no one except my niece, Heather. She's young and has her own life. As far as friends, I guess I wouldn't have any except for those who want to hear the latest rumors."

"You can change that. I went to the nursing home a couple of days ago. There are lots of lonely people there who would enjoy a visit from someone—anyone. Have you ever considered the possibility of volunteering there?"

Madge shook her head. "No, I haven't."

"I'd be willing to bet you know a lot of the history of Driscoll Lake. True history. Important facts. Some of those longtime residents would love to hear your stories."

"I've never thought of that. Yes, I do know some of the town's history. I've lived here all my life. My great-grandparents were early settlers. My father passed along a lot of stories to me."

"I'll bet some of the residents would welcome visits from you. Think about it."

"Maybe I will."

Kyle walked through the door. "Stephanie. What brings you here today?"

"I had a little business to take care of. Was about to leave."

"As long as you're here, can you come into my office? I'm hoping to change your mind about another article."

"I don't think so, Kyle. It's time for me to leave the past behind. I may never know the truth about what happened.

I can live with that. I have a few minutes to talk, but don't expect me to say yes."

As they turned to walk to Kyle's office, the phone rang.

Madge answered. "No, I don't know. You might as well stop asking. I don't care if you are family. You're not going to get any more information from me."

Stephanie smiled and winked at her. *Good for you, Madge.*

***

Kyle shook his head. "I can't believe you're quitting. You've come so far."

"I've done everything I know to do—spoke to the police, read Carol's journals, and talked with people who worked with my father. There's nothing else I can do."

"What about the journals? Helen said—"

Stephanie raised her eyebrows. "Helen?"

Kyle cleared his throat. "I thought you said Helen believed your father was innocent."

"She wanted to believe it. So did I, but this business with Phillip Denton's car puts a new twist on things. I'm sure my father is now the prime suspect in his murder."

"Then you haven't heard?"

"What?"

"The body doesn't belong to Phillip. It was on the news last night."

"I didn't know. Matt didn't say anything this morning. Strange."

"Why don't you reconsider?"

"This doesn't change my mind. Write the story about the car and the body, but leave me out of it. I'm going home to Denver next week, anyway."

Kyle sighed. "I guess you have made up your mind. You know I wish you the best."

"I appreciate all you've done. Not to mention you were my biggest supporter way back then. I want to keep in touch with Christine, so you'll be hearing from me."

***

"Why was she at the newspaper office? Did she talk to Kyle again?"

"I don't know."

"What do you mean you don't know?"

"Madge wouldn't say. She told me I wouldn't get any more information from her and was tired of being known as the town gossip."

"What's going on? Why the sudden change?"

"I don't know. Look, if it's so important to you, ask Kyle. I agree with Madge. I'm tired of being your source of information. From now on, you can find someone else."

"Do I need to remind you of how you got your job? If Miles Parker finds out you've been giving out privileged information, he'll fire you. It won't be so easy for you to get another job around town. It's not as if you have any special skills."

"I'll take my chances. Anything would be better than this." She ended the call.

He slammed the receiver. First the car, now this. Why did he suddenly have the feeling his world was about to come apart?

***

Pat Turner spent most of the morning debating whether to call Carlos Gonzales. She had no proof—only a nagging suspicion.

She replayed the incident on the cruise ship dozens of times.

There has to be some mistake. It just can't be who I think it is.

She'd phoned the office earlier to tell Madge she would be late. "I'm going to take a little time for myself this morning. Kyle can handle anything that comes up. I'll be there around noon."

She didn't want Madge to know the real reason for her absence. If Madge overheard what she had to say, the news would be all over town before nightfall.

Pat didn't want anyone to think she was foolish—or worse, becoming senile.

What was that famous quote about opening one's mouth and being thought a fool? What if there was a chance her suspicion was correct?

She picked up the phone, dialed the police station, and asked to speak to Carlos. "Tell him I'm calling as a friend, not a member of the press."

The dispatcher put the call through, and Carlos answered on the first ring. "Pat, what can I help you with today?"

"You may think I'm crazy, but..."

***

Carlos hung up from talking with Pat and immediately phoned the FBI office and asked to speak with Vince Green. When the young agent answered, Carlos told him everything Pat said.

"It may be nothing. Mrs. Turner debated over telling me, but in the end felt strong enough about the matter to call."

"I'm glad she did. Maybe this will give us the break we need. You said the ship sailed from Venice?"

"On August twenty-fourth. The woman went by the name of Angel Rossi. Don't know the husband's name, but she said they lived in Italy. Pat stated they departed early while the ship was docked in Greece."

"I'll obtain a passenger list from the cruise line. May take a few days. By the way, I found some interesting information on Phillip Denton in our files. Were you aware he had a twin brother?"

"No, I was not. According to his step-daughter, Denton claimed he didn't have any family. Maybe she was mistaken."

"Then she was also mistaken about his military service. Phillip Denton was never in the armed forces, but his twin brother did two tours in Nam. After the war, Roger Denton wandered from place to place—turning up at random times only to disappear again for months or a year or two at a time. It's been more than twenty years since anyone last saw him. Thought you might want to know."

"That is interesting. Wonder why Denton would lie about something like that? Thanks, Vince." Carlos hung up the phone and looked at his watch. It was time for his visit with Joe Rivers. With every fiber in his body, Carlos sensed the case was about to break wide open.

Chapter Thirty-One

Nigel had never questioned his employer's assignments. Each one had all been under the umbrella of surveillance— the term Jorge preferred to use. It was just a fancy name for spying on someone. The assignments had taken him to several different locations including the Caribbean, South America, Switzerland, and a few in the United States.

He first met Jorge fifteen years ago in France. Upon learning Nigel was once a private investigator, Jorge hired him to do a job. He had wanted someone to trail his wife.

"I believe she's cheating on me," he said.

It didn't take Nigel long to confirm Jorge was correct.

Jorge moved around a lot. He would call him from time to time to spy on someone, usually his current wife or significant other.

Many times, the suspicions were unfounded. Nigel decided the man was either paranoid or hiding something. He suspected the latter was true, but as long as Jorge paid him to do a job, he would follow through.

Throughout the years, he'd seen several women come and go. Most of them were around the same age, a couple of them a few years older. But they all had one thing in common—money. The current companion was much younger, at most in her early thirties, and didn't possess any wealth. Nigel figured she was likely a trophy to appease Jorge's ego now that he had grown older.

It was around five years ago when Jorge became obsessed with a small town in Texas. He telephoned Nigel, asked him to fly to the states, and gave him specific instructions on whom to contact.

"You are not to discuss anything about the past. Make certain your contact knows this up front. This job will be long-term. I'll tell you to call him with precise instructions. Under no circumstances are you to let him know my whereabouts and never mention my name. He'll know who I am."

After that, he would have Nigel call the other party on occasion, "Just to remind him of what I know." A few weeks ago, Jorge instructed him to report on the whereabouts of a well-known author as well as a local newspaper reporter. His curiosity aroused, he decided to conduct his own investigation.

Jorge had never asked him to kill before yesterday. Nigel had already learned enough information to know he didn't want any more association with the man. He wouldn't spend the rest of his life in prison for anyone. It was time to turn the tables. He talked to Angel and instructed her as to what she needed to do. He had one last phone call to make, and then his association with Jorge was over.

***

He'd kept a dark secret for twenty years. A secret that he'd often wished he didn't know. A secret that, if told, would destroy his life. He spent the first few of those years always on alert, constantly looking over his shoulder.

Years had passed before he heard anything from his former co-conspirator. He relaxed somewhat but never let his guard down. He knew too much. He would never be entirely safe.

About five years ago, he received an unexpected phone call. The man called himself Nigel, but he doubted that was his real name. Not that it mattered. He knew who Nigel worked for.

The instructions were always precise. "Buy a prepaid cell phone with cash, keep tabs on a particular person, get information about a certain situation." As long as he carried out the instructions, he felt reasonably safe. Until today's call.

"I thought you should know something."

The information the caller relayed frightened him.

"I trust you'll be at the football game tonight."

"I planned on it, but—."

"Stick to your routine. Probably best you're with a crowd. I've made a few phone calls, so hopefully you won't have to worry." The line went dead.

For the first time in years, he didn't feel safe, but he couldn't go to the police without incriminating himself. He considered staying home, but Nigel was right. It would be safer for him to be in a crowd. What had him worried was what might happen after the game.

⁕

Stealing Christine Lawrence's cell phone was easier than he anticipated. He followed her from a distance to a convenience store on the outskirts of town. She parked on the side of the building, which made it easier for him to be unnoticed.

She appeared to be in a hurry. That was to his advantage. She chatted on her cell phone as she went inside the store.

What was it with people and phones? Why did they feel the need for constant communication? He had a phone, of course, but only used it for business. Idle bits of conversation of any kind left a bad taste in his mouth.

He got out of his car and stood where he could observe her inside the building. When she paid for her purchase, he stood against the building and waited. He had to time his movement just right, but he'd done it with success many times.

When she rounded the corner, he moved and bumped into her. The contents of her purse and the package she carried spilled onto the sidewalk.

"I'm sorry," she said. "In too big of a hurry."

"My fault. Clumsy of me. Allow me to help."

The phone lay near a newspaper stand. When she turned to retrieve her wallet, he slipped the phone into his pocket.

"I believe that's everything," he said.

"Thank you." She hurried to her car, got in, and drove away.

He waited until she was out of sight before getting in the rental and driving in the opposite direction. He drove a few blocks and pulled into a parking lot to check the phone. Good fortune was on his side. Silly woman. Had the latest Smartphone, but didn't bother to use a passcode. It made everything so much easier.

His malicious laughter echoed in the car. With luck, she wouldn't discover her missing phone for a while. He never intended to harm her or her daughter. He would let them live. But like Kathryn and Stephanie Harris twenty years earlier, they would be without a husband or father.

His next point of business was Rachel Jackson. He knew her work schedule. She would leave the hospital around seven. He'd observed her for the past couple of days. She always parked on the upper level of the parking garage in the section reserved for employees and took the skywalk to the main hospital building.

Thanks to Christine, he was ahead of schedule tonight. He pulled up to the booth and took a ticket. There wasn't any reason to suspect him of anything. To the attendant, he was just another visitor. It would likely be a few days before anyone figured out someone had abandoned the car. Even then, no one would tie it to the passenger from Italy. He'd used a different ID for the rental. He drove to the second level, parked the car, and took the stairs to the top floor.

By this time of the evening, the daytime staff had left for the day and the night shift workers were already inside. It would be easy to slip in unseen and get inside her car. He remained in the shadows until he was certain the coast was clear, then took the Slim Jim and unlocked Rachel's door.

He climbed in the back and waited. It wasn't long before he heard footsteps. Rachel got in the front, fastened her seatbelt, and started the engine.

He waited until she was on the outskirts of Brewster before making his move. He quietly rose up and put the gun to the back of her head. He almost laughed aloud at her surprise gasp.

"Hello, Rachel. Glad to see me?"

***

Several days had passed since Brian visited his mother, so he decided to stop by after work on Friday. He found her sitting in a wheelchair in the lobby. She smiled when he approached.

"Hello, son. It's always good to see you."

"Sorry, I haven't been around. It's been a busy week."

"I understand. Did I tell you Stephanie took me to that new Italian restaurant?"

"Yes, you told me the other day."

"I did? Well, we had a marvelous time. She's such a sweet girl. So much like her father. He's always so generous and kind."

"Was."

"What?" Dorothy frowned.

"He *was* generous and kind. You're talking about him as if he were still alive."

The memory lapses began about six months earlier and were becoming more frequent. The doctor confirmed it was the early onset of Alzheimer's. However, her memories of the past were still sharp and clear.

"Don't be silly. I know Robert is dead."

Brian relaxed. Perhaps it was a slip of the tongue.

"What brings you here on a Friday night? Aren't you going to the game?"

"Not tonight."

"You work too hard. I wish you'd find a lovely young woman and settle down."

"I tried that once. It didn't work."

"You can't judge all women by your ex-wife."

"She wasn't to blame for our failed marriage. I was too busy trying to start a business. It's hard to make a marriage work when one spouse is never home."

"You can let go of some things. You've established your business. People know your reputation."

"Yeah," Brian said. "That's the problem."

***

Rachel drove slowly through the streets of Driscoll Lake, careful to obey the directions of her captor. She debated on running a stop light or do something that might attract the attention of the police, but dismissed the idea. That would only anger her kidnapper. She had no doubt he would pull the trigger.

"Where to?" she asked.

"The old factory, of course. Where it all began. Or in the case of your mother, where it ended." He chuckled.

Rachel clenched her teeth and gripped the steering wheel. She hated this man for what he'd done to her. He ruined Stephanie's life. He was the one who killed both her mother and Robert Harris. Two innocent people who happened to get in the way of what he wanted.

She started to turn onto the road that led to the deserted building.

"No, go the back way."

She crossed the old railroad tracks and turned onto the narrow road. She didn't like being there even in daylight. The road dead-ended past the factory. On the opposite side were woods and a thick growth of tangled vines and underbrush. Trains hadn't run this way since the plant closed. Rachel slowed the vehicle near the back gate.

"Don't stop here," he said. "Drive on."

"To where? There's nothing out here."

"Drive all the way to the end and pull your car off the road. We wouldn't want anyone to spot it quickly."

Rachel knew he planned to kill her, just as he killed her mother. He was a madman. She would play along and follow his instructions, but she needed to find some way of distracting him. Had to buy some time. "Look, if you want money, I can get it for you. I promise to remain silent."

"You must think I'm stupid. You'd go to the police the minute I let you go. If you think the Cameron fortune can buy your way out of this, you're mistaken. Now get out of the car and walk."

"Where? The woods? The railroad tracks?"

"Stop pretending to be dumb. I know you're not stupid. We're going inside the building."

She felt the muzzle of the gun against her back. They came to a break in the fence.

"Go through there." He directed her to the loading dock and through a missing door.

She didn't have much hope of surviving. No one would look for her tonight. It may be days before anyone found her body. They wouldn't even know she was missing until she didn't show up for work on Monday.

"What now?" she asked.

"We wait. Your friends will join you soon."

Chapter Thirty-Two

"I'm getting ready to leave," Madge said to Kyle. "Want me to lock the door? Pat's already gone home."

"Yes, please. I want to finish my article for next week. I plan to go directly to the game from here. Christine and Emily went early."

"I guess Emily is looking forward to being in high school next year."

"Yeah. She can't wait to march with the band."

"I was once in the high school band. Back in the dark ages."

"I didn't know that." Kyle smiled. "You've been in a good mood today, Madge. What's going on?"

"Let's just say someone helped me to see the light about some things."

"Oh, yeah?"

"You'll be seeing a new me from here on out. Guess I'll be going now."

"Okay, Madge. See you Monday."

***

After Brian left the nursing home, he drove to the restaurant where he'd seen Rachel the week before. As usual, his refrigerator was empty, and he couldn't drum up any enthusiasm for take-out fast food.

The restaurant wasn't crowded, considering it was Friday night. Most people ate an early dinner before going to the football game. Such was life in a small town.

Brian considered going to the stadium. It wasn't as if he didn't enjoy watching the local team. He was certain to see many people he knew—Kyle and Christine, Matt and Stephanie. Maybe they would decide to go out after the game and invite him.

Therein was the problem—he didn't want to be the fifth wheel. And there was no way he would go out with Heather Stevens again.

The hostess greeted him when he walked inside. "Good evening, sir. Would you like to sit at the bar tonight?"

"Uh." Brian hesitated and glanced in that direction. Several men and a few women were watching the major league playoffs. The mood was jovial. It would be easy to order a beer and ease into the conversation. He quickly pushed the idea aside. The thought of drinking had come up too many times of late.

"No, thanks," he said. "I'll sit in the restaurant."

***

Dr. Mark Jacobson tried for over an hour to reach Rachel Jackson. Although she wasn't on call the weekend, it wasn't like her not to answer calls or pages.

He went to the parking garage to make certain she was gone. One of the nurses had reported seeing a suspicious looking man hanging around the evening before, but he left before security was able to check. Last week someone robbed a woman at gunpoint at a nearby convenience store.

After satisfying himself that Rachel had left, he attempted to reach her again by phone. Again, the call went unanswered.

"That's strange."

One of the nurses was standing nearby. "What did you say?"

"Sorry. Just thinking aloud. I've been trying to reach Dr. Jackson for the past hour. Needed to ask her something about a patient. She isn't answering her phone or pages."

"That is strange. She always calls back."

"I checked the parking garage a few minutes ago. Her SUV was gone, so I at least know she left."

"I hope everything is okay."

"If she doesn't call back soon, I'll call the Driscoll Lake Police. I hope she hasn't been in an accident."

***

"The end."

Kyle saved the document and closed the word processing program. His weekly column was a bit different from usual. He wasn't sure why he'd decided to write a nostalgic column about small town life. Maybe it was everything that had happened in Driscoll Lake the past few weeks. Things that brought back memories of the past. Many of them were pleasant. Others brought a sense of guilt and fear, but for the most part, living here had been good.

The town wasn't perfect, but it had been a good place to grow up. Stephanie's memories of Driscoll Lake were tainted. He understood the reasons. He wanted her to know about that night. She was so close to learning the truth. If only he could tell her.

There was no way to do that without admitting what he'd known for years. But to do so would destroy his family.

Kyle looked at his watch. It was almost 7:15. The first quarter had already begun.

"I need to hurry." He stood up from his desk and turned to leave when the phone rang. He started not to answer but saw that it was Christine's number. She would be upset that he wasn't already at the game.

Wonder why she called the office instead of my cell phone.

"Hi, honey, I know I'm late. Leaving now."

"This isn't Christine. But if you want to see her and your daughter again, you'll do as I say."

The menacing voice sent a cold chill down his spine. The man sounded vaguely familiar. "Who is this?"

"A voice from the past. Listen carefully and do as I say."

"Where are Christine and Emily?" Beads of perspiration broke out on Kyle's forehead.

"They're safe. At least for now."

"If you hurt them, I'll—"

"You're not in a position to demand anything. If you do what I say, they won't get hurt. Call Stephanie Harris. Tell her to meet you at the old factory in an hour. Say you know the truth about her father."

"What if she won't come?"

"She'll be there. She's obsessed with wanting to know the truth. Tell her to go behind the building and enter on the side of the railroad tracks."

"Let me talk to Christine. I want to make sure she and Emily are okay."

"No. I already told you they're safe. One more thing—if you or Stephanie say anything to the police, you'll never see your wife and daughter again. I know Stephanie is friendly with Matt Bradford. Tell her not to say anything to him. Understand?"

"Yeah."

"Good. Time is short. Get to it."

Kyle jumped up from his desk and started toward the door, but turned back to his computer. He typed a brief email message to Pat, attached a file, and hit the send button.

Just in case something happens.

***

Brian ate his meal alone. He didn't recognize a single person who came into the restaurant. Driscoll Lake was growing, which made people like Curtis Lawrence happy. Brian curled his lip at the thought of the man. He was certain "The Judge" was the person responsible for the planning commission's delay on his proposal for the factory renovations.

He walked to the parking lot. The glow from the stadium lights shone brightly. Even though it was a half dozen blocks away, he could hear the marching band. He envied the people there—laughing and enjoying themselves as if they didn't have a care in the world.

Sure, he'd established his business. He had a good reputation among most people and had several ongoing projects. Being able to purchase the old factory was a longtime dream. The project would require a lot of time and hard work.

Brian knew his mother wanted him to marry again. Maybe even give her a grandchild. Time was short. Before long, Alzheimer's would destroy her memory.

He wasn't ready to go home, so he decided to drive around town and eventually arrived at the old factory. He parked, unlocked the gate, and walked toward the building.

It would take a lot of money to repair this old place.

Brian shook his head. In addition to the funds he borrowed, it would take a considerable chunk of his savings for the renovations. If his plans failed, it could destroy his business—everything he'd worked so hard to achieve. He couldn't allow that to happen.

***

Stephanie looked forward to tonight. A month ago, she wouldn't have dreamed of being back in Driscoll Lake—let alone attending a high school football game. She knew her excitement wasn't about the game, but because of spending time with Matt.

After Matt called at six to say he would be late, she hadn't been in a hurry to leave the house. "There's been an accident, and I'm stuck on the freeway in Dallas. I have the tickets with me, but I called the stadium to explain. Go to the ticket booth, tell them who you are, and they'll let you in the gate. I'll be there as soon as I can."

Stephanie took one last look in the mirror. She'd stopped in town earlier and purchased new jeans and a red and white t-shirt. Might as well be like everyone else and wear the school colors.

Satisfied her appearance was okay, she went into the bedroom for her purse, and then to the kitchen to make sure Whiskers had plenty of food and water.

When her cell phone rang, she was surprised to see Kyle's number.

"Hello?"

"Stephanie, it's Kyle." His voice sounded strained.

"Is something wrong?"

"Yes. I mean no. I, uh. I learned something today about your father. I think I know who killed him."

"What? Who was it?"

"I can't tell you on the phone. Someone may be listening. Meet me at the old factory in an hour. I'll bring the information."

"The old factory? Why there? It's deserted and creepy."

"We can't risk meeting where someone will see us. Listen carefully. The front gate is locked, so you'll need to go in the back entrance. Park on the old Greer Road and walk."

"Kyle, this is weird. Why can't we meet somewhere else? If you're worried about someone seeing us, I'll meet you in Brewster. Or for that matter, come to the house."

"If you want to know, meet me there. Don't tell anyone."

"But wouldn't it be better if I told Matt. He could—"

"No! There are some people you can't trust. Wolves in sheep's clothing. Don't forget it was a dark pickup that ran you off the road that night."

"What are you saying?"

"Just be careful. Don't tell anyone. This might be your only chance to learn the truth."

"Kyle, you're scaring me."

"That's not my intention. If I didn't think it was important to you, I wouldn't have called."

"Okay. I'll come."

"Don't be late."

Chapter Thirty-Three

Carlos Gonzales had mixed emotions after his visit with Joe Rivers. He was satisfied that Joe wasn't involved in the murders of Robert Harris and Madelyn Denton, but disappointed Joe allowed someone to hinder the investigation. It didn't matter if the person was a prominent member of the community who always tried to throw his weight around.

With additional resources, Joe had the potential to solve the case years ago. Could have found the real killer and brought him to justice.

Carlos's phone rang and he pressed the button to allow the sound to come through his car's speakers.

"This is Matt. I'm on my way from Dallas but got tied up in traffic. I should be there within the hour. Did you talk to Joe?"

"Just came from his place. I was right—he did suspect something. He wanted to call in an outside team to assist with the investigation, but someone convinced him it wasn't necessary. In fact, this person hinted he could lose his job if he didn't wrap up the investigation promptly."

"You're kidding me."

"Wish I was. You're not going to believe who the person was."

***

Carlos decided to stop in Brewster at a favorite steak house for dinner. Maria was away for the evening, and the idea of cooking didn't appeal to him. There wasn't much more he could do tonight. No reason to hurry back to Driscoll Lake. A leisurely meal was just what he needed after the type of day he'd experienced.

He ordered a steak, baked potato, and salad and was almost through with his meal when Vince Green called.

"I didn't have to wait for the cruise line. The passenger goes by the name of Jorge Cantaro. He was traveling with a woman by the name of Angelica Rossi. We tracked him to a village in Italy."

"Is he who we think he is?"

"Not confirmed yet, but I'd be willing to bet money. Carries a Brazilian passport. What's more, Rossi became suspicious after he acted strangely on the cruise. She suspected he was hiding from someone. She talked with her brother, who contacted the national police, who in turn called me. Rossi told them Cantaro left Monday on a flight to the US. He flew out of Rome to Atlanta, and from there he caught a connecting flight to Dallas. If our suspicions are correct, he could be in Driscoll Lake. I'm on my way there now."

"He's taking a big chance on coming back here, so you can bet it's not a social call. I'm in Brewster but will leave right away. Meet you at police headquarters in half an hour."

Carlos stood up, threw some bills on the table, and rushed from the restaurant.

***

Kyle sat in the press box at all home games, but Christine always met him at the concession stand during halftime. They would have a snack and enjoy the half-time show together. There was a time when Emily joined them. Now she was older and preferred to sit with friends.

Just before the second quarter ended, Christine left her seat and made her way to the concession stand to wait for Kyle. Ten minutes into halftime, he still hadn't shown up, so she reached into her purse for her cell phone.

It wasn't there.

Emily walked up with a group of friends. "Hey, Mom. Where's Dad?"

Christine shrugged. "I don't know. He was supposed to meet me here ten minutes ago. Maybe he got tied up."

When the announcer walked by during his break, Christine called out to him. "Bud, is Kyle still in the press box?"

"No. Haven't seen him tonight."

"That's strange. He was supposed to be here."

"Sorry. He never showed up."

"Okay, thanks."

"Did you call him?" Emily asked.

"I can't seem to find my cell. Let me borrow yours."

"Sure." Emily pulled the phone out of her pocket and handed it to her mother. "He's on speed dial two."

"Thanks. Who's on speed dial one?"

"You, of course." Emily grinned.

Christine pressed the number. The phone rang several times before going to voice mail. "Hi, this is Kyle. I'm not able to take your call."

She waited for the greeting to end. "Hi honey, I'm here at the game. Looking for you. I've misplaced my cell, so I'm calling from Emily's. Call me." She looked at Emily. "I'm going to try his office."

No answer.

Something was wrong. Kyle always attended the games. Always answered his messages. He would have called her if something came up.

Except I don't have my phone.

She didn't want to alarm Emily. "Honey, I'm going to go to the car and see if I left my phone there. Go on with your friends. I asked your father to call me at your number, so do you mind if I hang onto it for a while?"

"No problem. See you later, Mom."

Christine hurried from the stadium, thankful she parked close to the entrance. She unlocked the doors, searched the floorboards and between the seats, to no avail.

She mentally traced her steps. She talked to Kyle just before she went inside the convenience store.

That's it. I bumped into that man. Guess I didn't pick it up.

She dialed the store and asked if someone found a phone. No one had.

Christine went to the ticket office. "Can I come in and use the computer? I can't reach Kyle. He didn't show up for the game, and he's not answering his phone. Want to see if I can track it."

"No problem." The woman unlocked the door.

Christine signed into Kyle's account and clicked on the find my phone icon. According to tracking, he was on Greer Road.

She frowned. *That's strange. Why would Kyle be at the old factory?*

***

Judge Curtis Lawrence sat in his reserved seat on the fifty-yard line of Panther Stadium, trying to concentrate on the game. The home team was ahead by twenty points late in the second quarter. Everyone on the home side was in high spirits.

Everyone that is, except him. He couldn't shake the feeling of uneasiness. He found himself constantly looking for anyone acting in a suspicious manner. His personal cell phone rang, startling him. He didn't often receive calls. The number was for family and a few close friends. When a call came, it was usually his son. Kyle wouldn't be calling now. He would be in the press box.

He pulled the phone from his pocket and looked at the caller ID. The call came from a blocked number. Probably one of those robot calls, selling the latest dream vacation or some other scam.

He put the phone back in his pocket without answering. When it rang again a few seconds later, again showing a blocked number, he decided to answer.

"This is Nigel. Don't ask how I got your personal number—I have ways."

A cold sweat broke out on his forehead. "What do you want?"

"I'm calling of my own accord. I wasn't forthright with my last call. I've learned the real identity of the person I've known as Jorge. He flew to Dallas a few days ago."

"He's in Texas? Why?"

"I have reason to believe your son is in danger."

"My son? Why?"

"The newspaper article. His attempts to help Stephanie Harris. I believe Jorge will kill anyone that stands in his way. If I were you, I'd watch my own back."

"Uh, yeah. Sure. So why did you call to warn me?"

"I'm a private investigator, not a killer. I don't want any association with one." The line clicked dead.

The judge swallowed hard, took a deep breath, and put the phone back in his pocket. He had to warn Kyle. They didn't see eye to eye on most things, but he never intended to endanger his son's life.

He got up from his seat and made his way toward the concession stand. Kyle always met Christine there at halftime. As long as he was at the stadium, the judge felt he was relatively safe. He'd have to think of something to do before the game ended.

Christine was near the ticket office, holding a cell phone, and pacing back and forth. When he got closer, he saw tears in her eyes.

"Is something wrong?" he asked.

"Judge. I'm glad you're here. Kyle never showed up for the game. He's not answering his calls, but I tracked his phone. The GPS indicates he's at the old factory."

"The old Cameron place?"

"Yes, but there must be some mistake. He wouldn't have any reason to—"

The Judge didn't wait for her to complete the sentence. He rushed from the stadium. Kyle's life was in danger.

He got in his car and reached beneath the seat for his pistol.

It was missing.

***

Matt didn't arrive at the stadium until halftime. He spent more than two hours stuck in six lanes of traffic due to an unfortunate accident involving an eighteen-wheeler. It took a long time to remove debris from the freeway.

He phoned Stephanie twice after he finally left Dallas, but she didn't answer. He wasn't too concerned. She was probably at the game. The noise from the crowd would make it difficult to hear a phone ring.

When he got to their seats, she wasn't there. He figured she'd gone to the concession stand, so he checked his phone to make certain she hadn't called. When halftime ended, and she didn't appear, he started to worry.

He dialed her cell phone and then Helen's number. No answer.

Matt tapped the shoulder of the person sitting in front of him. "Excuse me, did you happen to notice if a young woman was sitting here?"

"Haven't seen anyone. The seats have been vacant all evening."

"Okay, thanks." Something was wrong. He got up from his seat and walked to the ticket booth.

"Stephanie Harris was supposed to meet me at the game. Have you seen her?"

"No. I looked for her, but she never showed up."

"Are you sure? Maybe someone else saw her."

The woman shook her head. "Sorry. I've been here all evening."

"Okay, thanks."

Matt phoned the police dispatcher. "Sandra, this is Matt. Have there been any reports of accidents?"

"Nothing, it's been quiet. Why do you ask?"

"Stephanie Harris was supposed to meet me at the game. She didn't show. I haven't been able to reach her by phone."

"Want me to send an officer to her house?"

"Yes, and have them be on the lookout for any signs of an accident along the way. Tell them to look closely in the area near Taney Creek. She'll be driving my mother's car — a red Altima."

"Sure thing, chief. You're the second person tonight to express concern over an accident."

"Oh yeah?"

"A doctor from Brewster called. He hasn't been able to reach Rachel Jackson. Said it was unusual for her not to answer. He wondered if she might have had a wreck or something."

Matt rubbed the back of his neck. Something didn't add up. Both Stephanie and Rachel not answering calls? It could be coincidence, but his gut instinct told him otherwise.

His phone rang. "Stephanie, where are you?"

"It's Carlos. I'm on my way to the station to meet Agent Vince Green from the FBI. We feel sure we know who killed Robert Denton and Madelyn Harris and took the money. He could be in Driscoll Lake as we speak."

"I'll be right there."

When Matt whirled around, he bumped into Christine Lawrence. "Sorry, Christine."

"Matt. Glad you're here. I haven't able to reach Kyle all evening. He didn't show up for the game. I tracked his phone. The GPS showed his location was the old Cameron Manufacturing place. Do you think you could send an officer by to check—"

Matt didn't give her a chance to finish. He ran from the stadium. Stephanie, Rachel, and Kyle all missing.

It couldn't be a coincidence. Something was terribly wrong.

Chapter Thirty-Four

Stephanie parked behind the factory and got out of the car. An eerie silence surrounded her. The road was dark and deserted and the derelict condition of the old factory building gave it an ominous look.

Vines grew along the walls of the old red brick building that once housed the offices. Many of the windows were broken, the others covered in a thick layer of dirt and cobwebs.

"There's an opening in the fence near an old boxcar," Kyle had said. "Go through there and meet me in the office building."

She found the opening and slipped inside the fence. Even the abandoned boxcar, with one of its doors opened, had a frightening look. Stephanie was thankful she'd brought a flashlight. She gripped it a little harder and walked to the loading dock. Some of the factory doors were missing. The smell of mold and decay was almost stifling. Although the night was warm, she shivered.

The factory was empty. The open door leading to the offices caused Stephanie to believe Kyle had already arrived. It was deadly quiet. She strained her ears for the slightest sound.

"Hello? Kyle, are you here?"

Silence. Like the calm before the storm. The stillness before a tornado unleashes its fury. She wanted to leave but felt strangely drawn to her father's old office—the place where he died.

She hesitated a moment before opening the door and going inside. Pale moonlight streamed through the dirty windows. Kyle stood in the center of the room where her father's desk once sat. His expression was blank—almost as if he was unaware of her presence.

Like a moth drawn to a flame, she rushed toward the spot. The remnant of a dark stain was visible on the bare floor.

Is this my father's blood? Stephanie knew the answer and turned to look at another stain near the door. Madelyn died there.

She turned back to Kyle. "I came here for answers. What did you have to tell me?"

He stood motionless and silent.

"You said you knew something." She snapped her fingers in front of his face. "Kyle, talk to me!"

He jerked his head and looked at her, almost as if he saw her for the first time. "I'm sorry. I shouldn't have had you come, but he threatened to harm Christine and Emily."

"Who said it? Kyle, tell me!"

"I don't know for sure, but I think it's—"

The sound of footsteps came from the hallway.

"We need to get out of here, now." Stephanie rushed toward a window. She tried to raise it, but it wouldn't open. "Kyle," she whispered, "Help me!"

Kyle remained standing in the center of the room—as if transfixed by the sound in the hallway.

"Kyle!"

"It's too late." The voice came from outside the door.

Stephanie turned. Rachel Jackson stood in the doorway, her face ashen. A man stood behind her with a gun in his hand. His face was unfamiliar, but there was something about his voice.

"Get in there with your friends." He pushed Rachel to the center of the room and pointed to Stephanie. "You. Move away from the window."

Stephanie turned and stood beside Rachel and Kyle.

The man came into the room. Stephanie had a sickening feeling in the pit of her stomach. *His looks are different, but the way he walks. I've seen that limp before.*

For the first time in twenty years, she found herself staring into the face of Phillip Denton.

"Well, now," he said. "This is good. You're all here. The place where it all began."

***

Stephanie clenched her fists, nails digging into her palms. It took everything within her not to reach out and wrap her hands around Denton's neck. She'd never been prone to violence, but if it weren't for the fact he had a gun, she would choke the life out of him.

"You. You're the one who killed my father."

"I had to."

"Why? He never did anything to you."

"I needed a scapegoat. Someone to blame for the theft. Someone who had access to company funds. I had no other choice."

His smug expression served to escalate Stephanie's anger.

"I should have known you took the money."

"Karen Fulbright did her job well. She knew how to manipulate the books, forge the checks, and keep separate records. All I had to do was to give her extra money on the side and promise her the lifestyle she wanted."

"But she died."

"Yes. After Karen had finished the job, I made certain she'd never talk."

"So you killed her and made it look like an accident."

"I wasn't in this alone." He turned to Stephanie. "Didn't you consider the possibility your accident wasn't a coincidence?"

"You mean the same person—?"

"I make a mistake in not eliminating him, but I'll do that tonight—after I've finished with the three of you. You see, when someone is no longer useful to me, it's time for them to go. I don't leave any loose ends."

"So that's why you killed my mother?" Rachel said. "Because she was no longer 'useful' to you."

"Killing Madelyn wasn't part of my original plan." He shook his head. Tsk tsk tsk. "The woman had no head for business. If she hadn't been stupid enough to give me control of the company—"

Rachel lunged at him, but Kyle grabbed her by the arm.

Phillip waved the gun. "A little violent, I see."

"What do you expect? You bring out the worst in people."

"That's been said of me. If your mother hadn't come to the office that night, she'd still be alive. I'll never forget the look on her face when she walked into this room and saw Robert slumped over his desk. The realization she would be the next one to die." He chuckled.

"You're despicable," Rachel said. "A sick, evil man."

"I may be, but at least I'm a rich one."

"You had control of the company with a top salary, a home, nice car, and the respect of the community."

"It wasn't enough. Your grandfather made sure that trust fund was more secure than Fort Knox. I wouldn't have seen a penny of it, and I wanted it all. It's better that your mother died. She would never have believed Robert took the money. The FBI would have caught up with me."

"What makes you think they won't catch you now?" Rachel asked.

"When I leave here, I'll never have to return. I always cover my tracks. By the time someone discovers your bodies, I'll be well away from this place."

Kyle finally found his voice. "What have you done to Christine and Emily?"

"They're safe at the football game. I never intended to harm them. If you hadn't raised suspicion with the newspaper story, I wouldn't have to kill you. Now another young girl will go through life without a father. A wife without her husband."

Kyle started to charge at him, but Phillip raised the gun. "Stop, or I'll kill you now. Stephanie will be the first to die, just like her father. Rachel comes next. You'll have a few seconds to live with the guilt of knowing it's your fault. Wonder who'll write the newspaper article about history repeating itself?"

***

Judge Curtis Lawrence turned off his headlights as he turned onto Greer Road. He parked the car a safe distance from the factory. If his suspicions were correct, he needed to be quiet and slip in unnoticed. He was certain Phillip Denton took the Beretta. Phillip knew he always kept a gun in his car.

He should have stopped at his house for another one, but there wasn't enough time. It may already be too late.

He popped the trunk, grabbed a tire iron, and started walking toward the building.

The Judge had only walked a short distance when he saw a red Altima parked at the side of the road. It looked like the one Nell Bradford drove. Stephanie was probably using it, which meant she was inside the building with Kyle.

He entered through the back and made his way toward the abandoned boxcar. The light of the waxing moon wasn't in his favor. Sweeping clouds temporarily hid the moonlight, and he quickly walked to the loading dock. A faint light came from the old office building.

He stopped—certain he heard footsteps on the gravel. After listening for a few seconds, there was only silence. He quietly made his way inside the factory and toward the office building.

***

Stephanie looked Phillip in the eye and defied him to shoot. "What's stopping you? If you're going to kill us, might as well get it over with."

Rachel gasped, but Stephanie knew what she was doing. She'd studied the profiles of several killers during her research. Often, they got their highs on prolonging the moment. Some seemed to savor the essence of fear in their victims.

She wouldn't give Philip the satisfaction of knowing she was afraid, even though she was trembling inside.

"Don't try that routine with me. I know what you're doing, but I'm not a character in one of your novels. You'll never outsmart me."

"That's not what I'm trying to do."

"Sure it isn't. Wonder what the headlines will say? Famous novelist writes her own death scene? And that talk show host will almost certainly tell the audience about your death."

"Talk show host?"

"I know all about your interview. A declaration of your father's innocence on national television. You're as much to blame as Kyle. You just had to come back here and start asking questions. Too bad. If you'd stayed in Denver, you could have lived."

"Phillip, let Stephanie and Rachel go," Kyle said. "Haven't you killed enough? Just get out of town and don't come back. No amount of money you stole is worth any more lives."

"Shut up! You must think I'm stupid. Stephanie would go straight to her lover. I wouldn't make it to the state line before Matt Bradford had the sheriff, the FBI, and Texas Rangers down on me."

"I won't say anything."

"He'd be able to coax the truth from you. I know how close the two of you have become. He even stayed at your place while you were recovering from your little 'accident.' You don't fool me. And now, it's time you die." He raised the gun and took aim.

"No!" Kyle jumped in front of Stephanie.

"Denton, stop!" Curtis Lawrence rushed into the room and swung a tire iron.

Phillip whirled around as the gun went off.

Kyle collapsed on the floor.

Rachel screamed.

Stephanie stood transfixed at the scene before her. Curtis Lawrence grabbed Phillip from behind. Both men struggled for the gun, and the tire iron fell to the floor. The gun discharged a second time. Phillip fell, a pool of blood coming from his chest.

It was over.

Stephanie, Rachel, and Judge Lawrence rushed to Kyle's side. Rachel felt his pulse. "He's alive, but his pulse is weak. He caught a bullet in the abdomen. Somebody call 9-1-1." Rachel took off her lab coat and pressed it to the wound.

Curtis Lawrence reached into his pocket for this phone. His hands shook.

"Here," Stephanie said, taking the phone from him. "Let me."

"Son," Curtis said. He knelt beside Kyle and took his hand. "It will be all right. Rachel's here. She's a doctor. She'll know what to do."

"Dad."

"Don't try to speak. Save your strength."

Rachel looked at Stephanie and shook her head. "It isn't good." She mouthed the words.

Curtis Lawrence looked at Rachel. "Don't just sit there. Do something!"

"I'm afraid there isn't much more I can do. I'm doing my best to stop the bleeding, but he's losing a lot of blood. The bullet must have hit an artery."

The Judge's voice was almost a whisper. "Kyle, I'm sorry for all I've done. I never treated you right, but please believe I love you, and I'm very proud of the man you've become."

Kyle's voice was barely above a whisper. "Thanks, Dad." He turned to look at Rachel and Stephanie. "I'm sorry. It's all... my... fault. I left... note... explaining..." He struggled to take a breath. "Tell Christine and Emily... I... love..." Kyle closed his eyes.

Rachel felt for the carotid artery. "There's no pulse. I'm going to try CPR." She began chest compressions. "Come on, Kyle. Breathe!"

There was no response. Blood soaked Rachel's lab coat.

"He's gone," she said.

The Judge hung his head and wept.

Both Stephanie and Rachel looked at the body of Phillip Denton lying on the floor near the doorway. Rachel walked toward him, bent down, and felt for a pulse.

She shook her head. "Nothing."

Stephanie became aware of the smell of smoke. She walked toward the window and looked in the direction of the factory.

"The building is on fire. We've got to get out of here."

Chapter Thirty-Five

Matt raced through the streets of Driscoll Lake. He had to get to the factory before it was too late. Stephanie was in danger.

"Please God," he prayed. "Let me get there on time."

He reached the entrance and slammed on his brakes. He was surprised to see a pickup truck parked nearby. Brian Nichols stood at the open gate.

Matt jumped out of his truck. "Brian, what are you doing here?"

"I own the place, remember?"

"Were you inside the building? Have you seen anyone or anything?"

"No, why?"

"I think Stephanie, Rachel, and Kyle are inside. Their lives could be in danger."

"What?"

The sound of a gunshot rang out from the direction of the factory. Matt took off in a run with Brian right behind him. They were half way there when they heard another shot.

When they were almost to the building, Brian ran ahead to an open door. Matt stopped him before he ran inside.

"Wait. We don't know who's in there. If you go charging in, they might shoot again. Keep quiet and follow me."

Brian stepped aside and allowed Matt to enter first. They saw flames at the back of the building. The fire had already started to spread.

"Call 9-1-1," Matt said. "I'm going in."

"Matt, wait! It's too dangerous."

He ignored Brian's words and ran into the burning building.

***

"Judge, come on. We need to leave." Rachel shook his shoulder. The smell of smoke filled the air.

Curtis Lawrence remained bent over Kyle, weeping.

"Judge, there's a fire. We need to leave."

He stood up and looked down at Kyle's body. "What about my son? I can't just leave him."

"There's nothing we can do for him now," Rachel said. "If you stay, you could also die."

"Doesn't matter. I don't have anything to live for."

"Yes, you do. You have a granddaughter. Come on. Let's go while we can still make it outside."

The Judge followed Rachel and Stephanie into the hallway.

"It looks okay here," Stephanie said, "but the fire could spread fast. Maybe there's a way out in front."

They hurried down the hall toward the factory. Stephanie put her hand on the connecting door. "It's hot— we can't go that way. Quick, let's try the outside entrance." She led them to what was once the reception area.

"Let me," Judge Lawrence said. He pushed against the door. "It's bolted from the outside. Let's try the window." They ran to the nearest one and attempted to pry it open.

"These old wooden windows have been shut so long. It would be almost impossible to open them." Rachel said. "Wait. I'll be right back."

She ran from the room and down the hall to where the bodies of Kyle and Phillip lay. She stepped over Phillip, grabbed the tire iron, and ran back where Stephanie and Judge Lawrence waited. He took the iron from her and swung it at the windowpane.

***

Brian hung up from the emergency call and ran back toward the door. The heat grew more intense. Flames shot into the air toward the back of the building.

"Matt," he called out. "Get out of there now."

Matt didn't answer. Brian looked around for a source of water. If he could wet his shirt and hold it over his mouth and nose, he might stand a chance against the smoke. Sirens wailed in the distance, but he couldn't wait. Matt was inside and if he was right, so were Rachel, Stephanie, and Kyle.

Brian thought the gunshot came from the office building. He ran in that direction when he heard glass breaking.

Rachel, Stephanie, and Judge Lawrence stood by the broken window.

"Rachel! Hurry, the fire's moving fast." Brian held out his arms while the judge helped lower her to the ground. Stephanie climbed out next and then Judge Lawrence.

"Is anyone else inside?" He asked. "We heard gunshots."

Rachel shook her head. "Kyle and Phillip Denton are dead."

"Phillip Denton?"

"Yes. All these years, he was alive. He killed Kyle. What are you doing here?"

"Matt and I saw the flames and—"

"Matt? Where is he?" Stephanie said.

"He's inside the factory looking for you."

"Brian, you have to do something. He'll die in there."

He turned and ran toward the open door of the factory just as Matt staggered outside.

"I couldn't make it," Matt said between spasms of coughing. "Got... to... try again."

"They're safe. They got out through a window."

Stephanie ran to Matt and threw her arms around him. Tears streamed down her face.

"Are you okay?"

Matt gasped for breath but nodded.

"It's over, Matt. Phillip Denton killed my father and Madelyn. Dad was innocent."

"I'm glad you—" Matt stumbled and fell to the ground.

Rachel ran to his side. "Smoke inhalation. He needs oxygen. We need to get him to the hospital."

***

Matt opened his eyes and touched the oxygen tube in his nose. He tried to take a deep breath. It still hurt, but at least the racking cough had subsided.

Stephanie sat in the corner, eyes closed, her head leaned back against the chair cushion. He watched her sleep. She was alive. She was here. He said a silent prayer of thanks.

She opened her eyes and looked at him.

"Hey, there. How do you feel?"

His voice was barely above a whisper. "I'm okay. Hope this hoarseness doesn't last long."

"Rachel was here about an hour ago. She said your voice should be back to normal in a couple of days."

"That's good." Matt looked around the room. "This seems familiar."

"Yeah, but this time you're the patient, and I'm going to take care of you."

Matt tried to sit up. "I need to get out of here. I have things to do."

"Not yet. You need to take it easy a couple of days. Carlos has everything under control. He said he'd call you tomorrow and fill you in on everything."

"But—"

"No arguing."

He laid his head on the pillow. "Yes, ma'am."

"Brian stopped by earlier. He said you ran into the building, knowing it was on fire. Why?"

He took her hand. "Because I thought you were inside. I lost Tara. I couldn't bear to lose you too."

Chapter Thirty-Six

Stephanie and Matt sat on the porch and watched the sunset over the lake.

"I can't believe it's over," she said. "I wish Aunt Helen was still alive to know."

"Did you talk to your mom?"

"Yes. She wasn't happy to learn how close Phillip came to killing me but was relieved to know about Dad. We had a long talk. She confessed she felt like me—not wanting to believe Dad was guilty, but trusting the investigation's findings." Stephanie paused for a few minutes. "I can't understand why Kyle didn't say anything."

"Fear. He was only a teenager. Living with a domineering father like Curtis Lawrence. Kyle thought his father killed Phillip as well as your father and Madelyn. The Judge was the one who pushed Phillip's car in Otis's pond. Kyle happened to witness the incident, but was too scared to talk."

"What about the body in the trunk?"

"My guess is it's Phillip's identical twin brother, Roger. That would explain the DNA match to the bloody clothing found years ago. Phillip broke off contact with his family years before he came to Driscoll Lake. Likely Roger found

Phillip and became suspicious, so Phillip killed him to ensure he wouldn't talk.

"Curtis Lawrence claims he wasn't involved in the murders—only that Phillip demanded he get rid of the car."

"How did he become involved?"

"There was a long-running feud between the Lawrence and Cameron families. It went back several generations over a property dispute. The Lawrence family claimed the property was rightfully theirs and Curtis wanted his hands on the piece of land."

"Pat Turner told me he tried to date Madelyn in high school. And Christine said he wanted Kyle to marry Rachel."

"Probably figured if one of them could marry a Cameron and produce an heir, they could come into money. When that didn't work, he wanted revenge. He denies involvement in the embezzlement. Claimed Denton only said he'd come up with a way to destroy the Cameron family for good."

"Did he know Phillip's whereabouts?"

"No—only that he was alive. Phillip always contacted him through a middleman. The Judge confessed to being the person who forced you off the road."

"Phillip insinuated the same person killed Karen Fulbright. So was The Judge responsible for her death?"

Matt shook his head. "He claims he wasn't. Also said he never intended to kill you, only scare you away. But when you didn't die, Phillip didn't trust anyone to take care of you, so that's why he came back. He wanted to make certain no one would talk. He tricked Kyle into thinking he had taken Christine and Emily and would kill them."

Stephanie shook her head. "Phillip was an evil man."

"By the way, we found the missing pages of Carol's journal. Kyle had them in his desk. She mentioned his father's name, so I'm sure that's the reason he took them."

"Why did he always try to protect The Judge?"

"Remember, his mother abandoned him. Curtis Lawrence is the only parent he knew until he was sixteen."

"I guess we'll never know how Kyle knew of the journal's existence."

"We do. He sent an email to Pat before he went to the factory that night. It explained everything. Helen must have read Carol's last journal shortly before her death. She was the one who approached Kyle about writing the first newspaper article with the stipulation he didn't tell anyone the request came from her."

"Why didn't she just talk to Carlos?"

"Like you, she probably didn't think the journal was enough to reopen the case. She hoped someone would come forward with information. She was already sick, so she told him where she hid the house key. When she went to the hospital, he found the journal and took it to his office. After he had learned you were searching for it, he returned it when you were away."

"Did Kyle want me to die?"

"No. In fact, he was the one who left you the notes—not as a threat, but as a warning. He wanted you to discover the truth without having to tell what he knew, but he realized it could place you in danger."

Stephanie shook her head. "So many people with hidden agendas—The Judge, Kyle, Phillip Denton."

"And all for different reasons."

"I would like to read the journal page sometime."

Matt reached into his pocket and pulled out an envelope. "I have it right here. Carlos brought it."

Stephanie took the piece of paper from the envelope.

...the cabin belongs to Curtis Lawrence. The middle of the night departure is a little strange, but I've often wondered if Curtis was involved in some shady dealings.

At least I know I'm not seeing Jeff's ghost or hallucinating. I'm glad I didn't say anything to the doctor—he could have insisted on stronger meds or placing me back in the hospital.

"No wonder she was afraid to say something. In her other entries, she questioned her own sanity. Phillip must have been the one she saw in South America. I wonder if he was responsible for the plane crash that killed her."

"We'll never know. Denton was a ruthless and cold-hearted killer, so it wouldn't surprise me if he somehow tampered with the plane."

"Did he start the fire?"

"Rachel said he never left her alone, so there's no way he could have done it. The investigation is still ongoing."

"At least the building wasn't a total loss. And I'm glad they were able to remove Kyle's body. Have you talked with Christine?"

Matt shook his head. "Mom went to see her as soon as she got back to town. Needless to say, Christine is shocked over the whole thing. Emily is taking it hard."

"I can understand that. I was once there."

"Yes, you were. But it's all over now." Matt pulled her into his arms and kissed her.

***

For the second time in a month, Stephanie entered the sanctuary of Driscoll Lake Community Church. She sat beside Matt, Rachel, and Brian. Each of them wanted to show their support for Christine and to pay their last respects to Kyle.

Stephanie harbored no ill feelings toward him. No matter how misguided his judgment had been, he took a bullet meant for her. When the family members entered the church, she was surprised to see Judge Lawrence with them. He sat between two men whom she didn't know.

"I'm surprised he was allowed to come," she whispered to Matt.

"The two men are FBI agents. Rest assured he's not going anywhere for a long time."

***

The clear October sky held a hint of autumn—the intense heat of the long hot summer seemed to have passed. Stephanie stood beside Matt, Rachel, and Brian and listened to the minister's words.

Judge Lawrence wept openly. A woman dressed in a long, flowery dress sat next to Christine but showed no emotion. Stephanie assumed she was Kyle's mother. Next to her was a man with long, gray hair pulled back in a ponytail.

Christine dabbed tears from her eyes throughout the short graveside service. Emily had a blank expression on her face. Stephanie knew from personal experience Emily would need a lot of help to get through this.

When the service ended, Stephanie stood in line to pay respects to the family. She reached Christine and embraced her. "I'm so sorry for your loss."

"Kyle's actions could have got you killed. If I had known—"

Stephanie shook her head. "You couldn't have. Don't blame yourself. Everything is in the past as far as I'm concerned."

"Thank you."

Matt took her hand as they walked from the gravesite with Rachel and Brian. The FBI agents led Curtis Lawrence away.

Rachel shook her head. "I never suspected he might be involved."

"Hard to say who was greedier—The Judge or Phillip."

"At least Curtis Lawrence had a conscience toward the end. If it hadn't been for him, we might not be alive."

"True." Stephanie watched Christine and Emily climb into a black limousine. "I hope Christine will be okay."

"It will take time," Matt said.

"Some people are already asking why Kyle kept quiet all those years. I'm concerned about Emily," Rachel said.

Stephanie nodded her head in agreement. "Yeah. I know what it's like for everyone to think your father is a criminal."

"It's all over now," Rachel said. "I'm sorry I blamed your father."

"Like I told Christine, the past behind us. Let's look to the future."

The two women embraced.

Matt and Brian stood back, allowing them to have their moment. When Stephanie looked toward Matt, he walked up and put his arm around her. Brian waited with his hands in his pockets, as if unsure how to approach Rachel.

She motioned to him. "I guess we'd best be going."

The four of them made their way to Rachel's SUV.

"What are your plans now, Stephanie?" Brian asked

"I'm leaving for Denver this week. I have to take care of some things there, but I've decided to keep the house on the lake."

"So you'll be coming back?" Rachel asked.

"Yes," Stephanie said. She looked into Matt's eyes and smiled. "After all, this is home."

A Note From the Author

Unseen Motives began as a simple idea when I was still a "want to be" writer. I envisioned a character standing near the shores of a lake one night when she sees something unusual on the opposite side.

Years later, I began to develop the story of a young woman who returns to her hometown twenty years after her father's apparent suicide. Although the book is a work of fiction, I did incorporate some actual events into the story. The drought and heat wave of 2011 were real, and someone did find a part of the space shuttle Columbia eight years after the disaster. Driscoll Lake is based loosely on my hometown, but the characters are fictitious.

I originally planned this book as a stand-alone novel, but as I started writing, many of the characters began to take on a life of their own. Less than half way through the first draft, I realized the town of Driscoll Lake had other secrets to reveal. Not to mention there is still the question of who started the fire at the factory. *Unknown Reasons* is the second book of the Driscoll Lake trilogy. Look for it in 2017.

I hope you enjoyed reading *Unseen Motives*. Would you consider leaving an honest review on Amazon or Goodreads?

Until next time,

Joan

Acknowledgements

With appreciation...

To Beverly – Many years ago, when I only dreamed of becoming a writer, you urged me to write a book. I never forgot your words of encouragement.

To my friend, Sarah – It's been a long time since I read a snippet of the factory scene to you. Your words, "I want to hear more," help give me momentum to continue.

To Adam of Writer's Detective – Thank you for answering my questions about detectives and police investigations.

To my writer's group, Sandi, Brett, John Mark, Sandy, Laura, Annette, Patti, Ken, Rachelle, and Tj – Some of you were there for the initial rough draft, while others came near the end. Throughout the process, your feedback and support have been invaluable.

To my beta readers – Michele, Laura, Nancy, Staci, and Rhodema –Your input has helped this to become a better, stronger story.

To the staff of AIW Press – Much appreciation for your help and for publishing this book.

To John – last, but certainly not least. Husband, friend, confidant, encourager. I couldn't do this without your love and support.

Other Works

Driscoll Lake Series

Unseen Motives

Unknown Reasons

Unclear Purposes (Coming Fall 2018)

Novellas

The Stranger

Anthologies

Unshod

Macabre Sanctuary

Bright Lights and Candle Glow

Quantum Wanderlust

About the Author

Joan Hall likes to create character-driven fiction with strong, determined female leads and male characters that are sometimes a bit mysterious. Her favorite genre is mystery and suspense—often with a touch of romance.

When she's not writing, Joan likes to take nature walks, explore old cemeteries, and visit America's National Parks and historical sites. She and her husband live in Texas with their two cats, Tucker and Little Bit.

You can connect with Joan at http://joanhall.net or on the following social media sties:

www.ingramcontent.com/pod-product-compliance
Lightning Source LLC
Chambersburg PA
CBHW061320170626
46817CB00001B/249